ECHO BAY

Other Books by Richard Barre

The Innocents
Bearing Secrets
The Ghosts of Morning
Blackheart Highway
Burning Moon
The Star
Bethany

ECHO BAY

A NOVEL

Richard Barre

CAPRA PRESS
MEMORABLE BOOKS SINCE 1969
SANTA BARBARA

Copyright © 2004 by Richard Barre
All rights reserved
Printed in the United States of America

A Robert Bason Book
Published by Capra Press
815 De La Vina Street
Santa Barbara, CA 93101
www.caprapress.com

Jacket and book design by Frank Goad

LIBRARY OF CONGRESS CATALOGING-IN-PUBLICATION DATA

Barre, Richard.
Echo Bay : a novel of suspense / by Richard Barre.
p. cm.
"A Robert Bason book"—T.p. verso
ISBN 1-59266-042-8 (hardcover)
ISBN 1-59266-043-6 (hardcover numbered)
SBN 1-59266-044-4 (hardcover lettered)
1. Tahoe, Lake (Calif. and Nev.)—Fiction.
2. Drowning victims—Family relationships—Fiction.
3. Steamboats—Fiction.
4. Shipwrecks—Fiction.
5. Salvage—Fiction.
I. Title.
PS3552.A73253E28 2004
813'.54—dc22
2003021070

Edition: 10 9 8 7 6 5 4 3 2 1

First Edition: May 2004

For Susan…always

I am half inclined to think we are all ghosts…we are so miserably afraid of the light, all of us.

Whenever I take up a newspaper and read it, I fancy I see ghosts creeping between the lines.

—HENRIK IBSEN

Thanks to all who kept this writer's head above water: Susan for her patience and critical eye, Shelly Lowenkopf for his guidance and enthusiasm, Robert Bason for his empathy and support, Frank Goad for his talent and good humor, Harry Sims for his invaluable feedback, E.B. Scott for his magnificent *The Saga of Lake Tahoe, Volumes I* and *II,* Jim Bell for his historic Lake Tahoe photographs and fine book *Tahoe's Gilded Age*, the wonderfully helpful Gatekeeper's Museum on Tahoe's only outlet, and the Santa Barbara Library for being there.

ECHO BAY

Lake Tahoe, 1940

It is an act of mercy…
Isn't it?

Her name is *Constance*. In her day, she is a shimmering water-borne phantom: breathtaking one moment, lost in her element the next. Even now she is like nothing the lake has ever seen. Men and women still turn to stare at her regal lines, her upswept knife-edged bow. With their children they have waved and cheered. Only now, they cannot save her.

No one can save her.

She lasts four hours past midnight, as though awaiting the curtain that will grant her the end she deserves. Slowly, defiantly, she has closed on Echo Bay when the storm hits, rain in driving sheets, thunder in percussive sets, Stateline's bright diamonds to the south all but vanished with her. And, near enough to hit with a deck gun, the darker Nevada side where her odyssey began, forty-four years before:

Home.

Echo Bay.

1896.

Star-spangled pennants and straw hats and a brass band and champagne and a profile so white the celebrants must shade their eyes as her hundred-and-sixty-nine feet leave the ways.

William McKinley soon will be sworn in; the Spanish-American war lies ahead. The gay nineties are at full rip, an era that knows and appreciates a lady for what she is.

Hardly this darkened hulk, the crew aboard the tow agree in silence. Shameful how she's been brought to this, they brood; and with the Tamarack himself watching: Cyrus Chandler Holmes, indistinctly separated from the night, the occasional red of his cigar and waft of smoke the only indication he is present at all.

Yet in a way it is fitting. The Tamarack, after all, made *Constance* what she was and would become. Loved her, if you will. He, if anyone, has the right to feel her torment and release her from it, stop the ravages that time and man have wrought.

Hasn't he?

The rain comes harder now, sluicing off the tow's blunt wheelhouse and driving the crew below. They crowd the ports to keep *Constance* in sight, to see her as she is not. No longer a bride, she is a pain-wracked dowager embarrassed by the stains that have bled into her dress, bewildered that no one has come forth to tend her except in this slipshod fashion. A thoroughbred led away on a crude leash.

Halfway out, it is as if she understands.

Her pride, the way she meets the rising chop, the bearing that would always be hers – each conveys acceptance. She seems to embrace the water that holds dear its secrets and its dead, the water that has entered to know her as it never could before.

The crew light cigarettes; they drink from flasks they'd known they'd need, ask again if only by their inability to meet each other's eyes.

It is an act of mercy…

Isn't it?

Squaw Valley, 1984, Men's National Final

He is alone on the mountain. Alone and not alone.

Activity he has shut out swirls behind him; a start gate harbors him, if only for the moment he will leave it. From far off he hears a disembodied voice: the Coloradoan's time, forty seconds off *his* first run, an eternity in the downhill. But his first time is not enough.

Not for him.

Not now.

Take no chances, they've told him. Especially under the conditions that cost the Coloradoan: flat light with ice, shave-off piling up in the turns, the temperature falling, more treacherous with each run. Just finish and it's Sarajevo.

They do not understand:

Who it is for and why.

He feels the tap on his shoulder, sets his goggles, seals them. The world is amber now; he draws breath to focus and calm: mind out front, legs strong enough to hold the turns and absorb the shock, no compromise.

The timer is activated.

He coils, hears the matching count, the last human sound until it is over. Drummed in since age seven: If you can hear the crowd, you might as well be in it, watching.

Five…four…three…two…one:

He explodes.

The light is bad, the ice worse, but he puts them from his mind; they are *his* light, *his* ice. From first tuck the speed is there, for this is what he has prepared for more years than not. He *is* the course, the descent, the burn, the need.

The gates bend to him, shudder in his wake.

Hip in, lead shoulder forward, carving, carving…

The pounding is ferocious; scraping obliterates all other sound. Halfway down, roaring from a chute and into a turn, he is peripherally conscious of a sign held by a team member. It is the round amber of a traffic light, their prearranged code: *"Slow down. You don't need it."*

His mind frames a name.

Like a current, it surges into his performance: Ice or no ice, light or no light, he is ahead of the run that put him in first, alternately on and over the edge of control. As it should be.

The name comes again.

This time, however, it is from a crack in a vault, a sprung door. This time he sees the face to which it belongs: contorted, gasping his name, and he is *there,* hearing its voice again…

Begging him: *Let go…*

A millisecond, but enough.

He is too deep into a gate; an edge catches. At once his balance is a memory. He is airborne, one ski gone, the ice an onrushing semi.

God oh God–

He hits at freeway speed: slams, wheels, bucks, bounces –
directly at the safety netting between him and the scattering
crowd. At which point his remaining ski digs in and shatters, he
ricochets along the netting's frozen length, and there is only the
furnace roar of his own pain.

1

New Mexico, Present

N O ONE SAW HER GO UNDER.

Not her brothers, who'd abandoned their fishing poles for a Tarzan romp in the vines, an illicit *cerveza,* and a turn-green rum soaked crook. Not her old man, who by their count had popped his third Tecate by the time the old Mercury drew up in the mid-morning heat, clouds of dust heading for his throat, sun on a water-bounce for his cap-shaded squint.

Rosalinda Quesada Luna, age nine.

La Florera, her family called her.

Flower girl.

Elizabeth's age, Shawn Rainey kept thinking, trying to drown the thought with peach brandy, his knee stabbing him now in earnest. Which would make *La Florera* two years younger than Nathan, Nate on his way to middle school in a year. Years gone to bloody where, Shawn added, shifting his weight to little effect. Bending to rub the knee, he had a flash of when he'd landed on it: flat light, snow flurries, blurred faces hunched deep into their parkas. Suddenly flying for real, the mountain exploding white, pain that became his universe even as the course monitors swarmed him once he'd finally come to a stop, their voices under his own ice-crusted moan.

Jesus, he's alive?

Had to be doing close to eighty.

Shawn straightened, arched his vertebrae, felt them crack. This made his second hour after parking the pitted Sable bought from the guy he'd replaced, adrenaline giving way to the washed-out faces waiting now in silence, somebody murmuring a rosary down the way, other side of the sheriff's deputies hunched over a chart.

She's playing with us, they'd nodded to each other as the searchers first spread out. *Such a tease our girl has become* soon became *a prank that has gotten out of hand,* Rosalinda in for a switching when they finally would turn back a branch to discover her hiding place, find her dissolving in giggles. Which ground down to *Merciful God, please let us find her.*

Down to that.

Shawn knew from having filtered it through his piecemeal Spanish, *Florera's* Kmart sneakers, jeans, and T-shirt piled under a cottonwood while the old man stared out at the green murk, bathed now in the generator floods, a deputy named Ortiz going over it yet again with the brothers. The old man looked as if he'd opened his eyes to a nightmare world in which the colors and players all were wrong and he still was trying to blink them away though it had been hours since the sun delivered him to the darkness.

At one point a mud-spattered Caprice pulled up, teenager at the wheel, woman in front – the mother, it turned out – female relatives in back. But after wailing like a chorus, their cries sank under the weight of the heat and the lights, the smell of mud and despair. Like the rest of them now, they just stared, breathed and stared – as though the scene were made of poorly fired clay and to move was to shatter the last vestige of hope into the night.

In the glare the Mexicans looked as pale as Shawn did. Already he'd asked Ortiz the few questions the deputy would answer someone like him, nobody from the larger newspapers even giving it the time of day, though they could have picked it off the same scanner Shawn had. As his boss had laid it out, *sex is news* – sex, murder, fire – bring it on, the more the merrier. But simple death is like birth: The relatives read it, so we concede the space. You get the point here, Shawn?

Shawn did. All too well.

Depending on when they brought her up and worked over her, shook their heads and took her away followed by the relatives and onlookers, the pond would gradually return to the crickets and bottom feeders, the coons and night birds. *Girl Drowns* would sum it up: four lines, well in, her name if the news pool's night editor was in the mood.

Shawn sipped from the half-pint in his pocket.

Why was he not now on the road, phoning it in? Was it the need to tell old man Luna it might have happened anyway, even if he had been alert? That what the man faced was only just beginning, how life could change in a heartbeat: words he'd wished someone had said to him when it mattered. But either the moment passed or it hadn't yet come, Shawn didn't know which, so he said nothing. That was the problem with life: It knew, you didn't.

The brandy had joined his pulse in lockstep. He could tell from the direction his thoughts were taking: fool's gold in random flecks. Gawkers – coarse big-bellied men and women, dirt-streaked kids – were statues in the light. Bugs spun, black snow. The tangle surrounding the pond was a wall of snakes appearing closer each time Shawn glanced up.

Thirty yards out, deputies in the skiff splashed the hooks again, dragged and splashed again, visibility impossible for divers. Apart from the occasional moan from a relative, conversation lay like trampled ground cover, the mother having slipped into the same vacant shock as the old man. Bubbles from the river-fed aquifer led to finger pointing and murmurs by those unfamiliar with how the pond sustained itself.

Or didn't, Shawn threw into the mix, an image not dissimilar from this one afloat beyond his reach. To dispel it, he looked down. Near where Ortiz was standing a string of fish, abandoned in the excitement, surfaced and rolled, driven by a gulping small-mouth bass. Somewhere between seven and nine-thirty, when Shawn finally left, his knee having had it with him, Darvocet popped so he could drive, he saw the bass had given up and stayed down.

Forty minutes later, Shawn stopped at Quincy's for the single beer that soon became three with Bushmills backs. He'd heard it on the way home, scanner: They'd found the flower girl. Wedged in a knot of submerged roots a stone's throw from where she'd gone in.

Shawn pictured it without much trouble, tangled hair and painted nails, the sodden pale form. He drained his glass, watched Art, Quincy's night-weekender, pour him another and set it up. And now it was *Florera's* living face Shawn saw in the draft, peering out from the yellowed sleeve in the old man's wallet opened up to show the deputies and, indirectly, Shawn before he'd lapsed into silence.

"Bad one, huh?" Art ventured: directionless, in case Shawn decided that was the way he liked it, nobody much in the bar on Sunday night, one couple in a back booth lost in each other.

"Nine years old," Shawn answered his beer. "Never made it out of the damn pond. Make sense of that."

Art stopped wiping the glass he was polishing and set it down. "You gonna be all right?"

"Ask the family that one."

"Not looking at them," Art said, "I'm looking at you. You ever think about professional distance?"

"Now and again. You ever think about hanging out a shingle?"

Art shrugged, hesitated, broke open the cash drawer, walked to the juke, fed in quarters. Emmylou came up, "I Still Miss Someone," Art setting the remaining quarters down beside Shawn's glass. "On the house," he said, head tilted in the direction of the pay phone.

Shawn looked at the quarters, at Art again.

"Go," the bartender added. "Probably catch 'em still up, you get to it and quit mooning. Elizabeth and Nathan, right? The next Brooks Robinson?"

"Clemente," Shawn said. "You always been this much of a pain in the ass?"

"So I'm told. Don't thank me or nothing."

"Thanks, Art."

"Just make the call."

Shawn slid the quarters off into one hand, left the stool, steadied as the room did. Once at the alcove, he dialed and waited, night air blowing in under the back door, air that minus the day's heat smelled of Rio Grande, dust, and cottonwoods with their feet in the water. He heard Emmylou hold a note no one else could then a voice that generally rattled around inside him long after whatever words had faded, even the hard ones, even just hello.

"It's me, Loren – Shawn."

In the pause, he saw her straighten, blonde hair angled against the receiver, saw her rub her neck when she heard who it was. *God – now what?*

"The kids still up?" he asked. "I'd like to say hello if they are."

Shorter pause. "You know better than that, Shawn."

"Meaning what? They're out?"

"Meaning San Francisco time, remember? Subtract two hours?"

"Vaguely." Trying to cover for his forgetting the time differential after too much booze. The fact was, he wasn't sure what time it was *here*. "Some secret as to where they are, Loren?"

Extended sigh. "Terry took them to a film."

A film.

Shawn could picture it: NR-17 or whatever bullshit Terry Dahl felt like, Loren at home at her laptop banging out plays nobody would read because she wouldn't let them. Pal Terry: *nobody-has-to-know-but-us, kids-have-to-know-what-their-friends-are-talking-about* Terry – doubtless taking a vote that ended three to nothing while ripping along in his Beemer. Shawn popped another Darvocet: a headache now to go with his knee, the beer and Irish having not nearly enough effect on either.

"Okay," he said. "Tell me when they're due, and I'll call back."

"Not a good idea, Shawn."

Not a good idea… How many times since they'd run away to Vegas then Frisco, neither one looking back, only forward? Loren Slater Rainey was as restive as he was then, if for different reasons, hers literary, that whole black-turtleneck rapt-attention scene, his the more miles from Lakewood the better.

Unfortunately, the distance mainly had applied to them, their wing-it and wedding-chapel underpinnings, something he might have seen coming if he'd only looked around now and then.

He took a breath. "Loren, if you don't mind, I would really like to talk to them."

"You're not supposed to call here. When is that going to sink in?"

"Thanks. I really needed that."

"As for your tone, go find a mirror. You can thank the one who did it to you."

Shawn flashed, saw his anger-management numbers veering off like Spitfires homing on a Fokke-Wolf, as much as hearing their engines in his head. "Loren, look, I'm asking. I don't know how else to put it."

"The question is why, when you know the answer?"

"My kids, too," he said thickly. "Remember?"

"Remember?" Up a notch. "Let's talk about where you're calling from, shall we? Rally 'round old Shawn while he buys another round and we all hate the bad ex-wife?"

"Loren, people go to bars. Hell, we went to bars. It's not how you say it is."

"Then what is it, your knee? Fate and how it robbed you? Poor Shawn, hard-luck Shawn: two tenths of a second versus a spot on the platform with "The Star Spangled Banner." You ever think about that, the why it happened part? About playing the game the way other people do?"

"Will you just listen? A girl Elizabeth's age drowned today. I covered it. I just wanted to talk to her...to them. Tell them–"

"What, Shawn? That you're not really like the last time they saw you in action?"

Shawn widened a scratch on the wall as Emmylou gave way

to Steve Earle, "Goodbye Is All We Have Left to Say."

Loren took it as an opening and plunged.

"Now *you* listen. Do you know how much I envy your way of making people feel for you, on and off like a faucet, what I'd give for that? *God!*" He heard her lighter's metallic snap, her long exhale. "All right, let me in on what you'd do if you were me, these kids you cared so much about you nearly put Terry in the hospital while they watched? Do you know what that does to a kid, the lessons it imparts? The fear?"

"My kids, too," he repeated, leaning to take weight off his knee, knowing this was going to end badly but short on fallback. As always, she was right – in microcosm. That was her gift, small-picture solid.

"I know," she was saying, "your kids, too. And now Nathan has trouble in school and Elizabeth cries in her sleep. While Terry, by the way and thanks for asking, still needs therapy for his hand." Exhale, another lighter snap. "I'm truly curious, Shawn. What would you do? Something I can use this time, because I would honest-to- God like to know."

A breeze off the river took voice under the back door – or was it the windows in the restroom? Either way it felt like something undead had found his neck and run a finger over it before pulling back with its cape around itself.

"Here's one for you, Loren," he said before lowering the receiver into its cradle. "I would, too."

2

THE TRAILER WAS DENTED AND DOUBLEWIDE; cheap digs that could move, Shawn had figured, even though it was up on blocks. He opened an eye to sun dissecting the bed, TV mumbling on the bureau across the room. Public access, a hiphopper named Mr. Beanie was doing his thing in a studio barely large enough for him and the host, a kid not much older than Nathan dressed in baggie pants, the requisite three inches of underwear showing.

Shawn fumbled for the remote, remembered throwing it at the screen the night before and missing. He stumbled over and killed the set manually, in the process stubbing his toe, which screwed the pain back into his knee. Inside of thirty minutes he'd popped six ibuprofen – low on Darvocet and not quite needing it yet – started the coffee machine, and was leaning off the edge of the bed, wondering if the place had been this trashed before he'd come home from calling Loren, when his cell phone rang.

It was the shift editor telling Shawn that he liked Shawn's take on the drowning story…that if it were up to him they'd use it, all of it, but budget cuts had prompted a review of the whole news operation, check back in a month or three and sorry about that. Throwing in that he always felt Shawn was too good for the job, nothing he hadn't said before.

"So you did, Ray," Shawn said after a pause.

"Fucking new economy, almost makes you miss the nineties. Stay in touch, now, you hear?"

"Yeah, I hear. Don't sweat it, Ray. Appreciate the thought."

He tossed the phone in a drawer and shut it, moved to the living room with scrambled eggs he'd gone two rounds with the day before, salsa from a past take-out tamale dinner. Through the half-closed blinds, sun flared off the swimming pool across the drive, several kids already making noise, when he heard steps and a rap against the siding.

"Mr. Rainey? You in there?" Female hand shading worn eyes peering in: which meant Dorothea, the Anglo half of the managing Zepedas, the Mexican half likely in town getting garden supplies, Liquid Plumber, or loaded.

"Mr. Rainey, telephone for you. Person-to-person on our line. Mr. Rainey?" Dorothea sounding impressed, Shawn already thinking odd; anyone he wanted to reach him used his cell phone number. In fact, he'd never even bothered to connect a landline. Which meant what, collection agency? It was possible, but he doubted it; where he lived was not widely held knowledge.

Frustrated in light of such an obviously important call, Dorothea gave it a final try. *"Mister RAINEY?"*

Shawn hollered that he was coming, found his sandals, opened the door as she was descending his steps. He followed her across the pink crushed lava rock and scalloped concrete borders into her pink-and-white trailer: pink-shaded lamp with white ruffles, pink Princess phone on the small maple table, low-backed pink-and-white-seated chair that hit him square in the kidneys.

He picked up the phone and listened, trying to identify sounds from the other end, but all that came through was a presence. For a cold moment he thought it might be Cort again, although he knew that couldn't be. It couldn't be Cort again for the simple reason that this time he was sober.

"Rainey," he finally said.

"What, I catch you in bed or something?"

Shit, Shawn thought, instantly recognizing the voice, *shit, shit, shit.*

Anytime Terry Dahl called it had to do with the kids – that or some ultimatum Loren wanted delivered by male. Which meant Loren could float above it all, part of the same strategy that Shawn had walked into ten months ago: his metaphorical Yugo meeting their metaphorical Peterbilt head-on. Blood alley. San Francisco.

Sunday, it had been, Golden Gate Park, the Conservatory, where he'd gone to drop off the kids after a weekend, his turn for custody. And there it came again in full reverb echo, the come-on he'd swallowed hook line and sinker: Terry's voice saying that even though Shawn had been returning the kids at the agreed-upon times and places, he – Terry – had incontrovertible evidence that Shawn's environment was unstable and unsuitable. Dangerously unfit.

Looking back, it had been so obvious to anyone without a flash point, Terry trotting out the usual suspects: drugs and alcohol, the women who frequented Shawn's place, the examples *that* set. This as Loren eased the kids over to the fern pond, where they made wishes and aimed pennies while she angled glances back at him, Shawn too stunned to feel anything but stomach drop, a cop on your tail when you think you've done nothing wrong, but aren't that sure.

"That's a crock and you know it, Terry." Scanning the database for anything remotely compromising, nothing yet. "I'd laugh if it weren't so pathetic."

"Not a helpful attitude, Shawn. Under the circumstances."

Drop in temperature. "What circumstances?"

"Right on, *hombre*, a man should confront his shortcomings. Sheila Ainsworth – cherry little brunette with a rack like gangbusters. Ringing any bells?"

Ice storm. Full-on Weather Channel alert.

"Well now, that's more like it. Bells *are* ringing for me and my gal." Terry smiling as if Shawn's reaction hurt him more than Shawn.

Sheila Ainsworth. He recalled her, a pretty girl coming on to him at the Buena Vista Cafe's farewell party, him still gut-shot over Loren, the kids, Terry, their screwed-up arrangement, by then Terry in the house Shawn had bought for them. He and Sheila had been hot and heavy for a month before Sheila quit phoning, the whole thing suddenly making sense now, Terry still smiling as if it hurt.

"All's fair, Shawn, don't tell me otherwise," Terry said. "Besides, videotapes don't lie."

"And bullshit is bullshit. You get that?"

"You think keeping your voice down here might be a good idea?" Glancing at the kids and Loren. "You think this is my idea of fun?"

"Only based on what I know of you."

"Uncalled for, Speed."

"There's the truth for you. Always in the way."

Shawn caught Loren's eye before she broke off, handed the kids more pennies from a bright new roll. Locked and loaded.

"Bottom line is we've already filed, Shawn. If it were just Nathan, I'd be less inclined. But Elizabeth's eight now and she needs–"

"I'm her father, dipshit, I'm aware of her age." At which point the flash went off: "And what kind of garbage have you been feeding her? Answer me."

The pained smile went to smirk. "Grow up, Speed, it's called going to court; mature people do it to settle their differences." Nonetheless giving ground to Shawn's advance, Elizabeth and Nate hearing and glancing over, Loren's confidence starting to show cracks.

"I asked you what you've been telling my daughter." Ignoring the envelope Terry had withdrawn from his coat and was attempting to hand him.

"You want to back off here, Sport? Not make it worse?"

Houston, we have ignition.

Shawn said, "Whatever it is, it's not going to work. *You hear that, Loren?*" Turning to Lizzy, then, Nate almost as wide-eyed as she was. "Sweetheart, whatever they told you about me isn't true, I swear it. Not even close."

Elizabeth's eyes were high beams that pierced. "Dad, they told me to look for them. They said they'd be under things in your closet. They said I'd be helping you. Do you believe me that I was trying to help?"

And there it was, the full extent: tapes that Sheila had made of them at her place, surprising him with them afterward. Tapes she'd obviously hidden at his place instead of erasing, as she'd sworn she had.

Tears were forming; Shawn knelt to his daughter, wiped them

away. She was so perfectly cast from her mother, delicate features and inner light, but with *his* green eyes, a lighter version of the chili-powder hair he'd seen in pictures of himself at that age. He drew a breath, steadied.

"Lizzy, we talked about this, remember? I'd never do anything to make you cry. I'm your dad. I love you."

"Might have been wise to give that some prior thought," Terry tossed in. "You being such an aware parent and all."

Shawn felt Terry's envelope brush his hand. He saw Loren's look, saw the three of them again at the offices of Rainey/Dahl, media strategist Loren being drawn to Terry's orbit like a wayward moon. As through a detached lens, a fog of alcohol and grass, Shawn saw the split again, saw himself forced from his own partnership because his assets, unlike Terry's, were market-value facade: winter-jock contacts followed by a wider pool of jock acquaintances.

All of this Shawn saw before he uncoiled and, despite his knee, the height and weight disadvantage Terry held over him, knocked Terry ass-over into the fern pool and colored the water with him before a security guard and an off-duty cop pulled him off his ex-partner, ex-mentor, ex-confidant.

New Mexico time…

Shit squared…

"How'd you get this number, Terry?" Shawn said into Dorothea Zepeda's pink Princess phone.

"Truth or Consequences isn't the moon, Shawn, though it's close." Like a timing chain spitting out teeth. "Lucky for you, I'm also in a forgiving mood. At least in your case."

"That's supposed to put me at ease?"

"The idea, anyway. Stand to lose anything if I explain it to you?"

Shawn had the sense a rattler was closing on his exposed foot, the feeling actually strong enough to make him look down.

"You have the balls to ask?"

"Pay attention here or wish you had: pink trailer, scabby gravel, cactus in pots? Woman looks like she rode with Sonny Barger at Altamont?"

Shawn felt the eggs and salsa rooster-tail acid.

"You're a gambling man, check it out," Terry added as if he were standing alongside, about to crawl into Shawn's head, his specialty. "Good looking dude getting out of a white rental and coming up the walk, cell phone to his ear – he look familiar?"

3

THEY SAT IN FRAYED-WEB FOLDING CHAIRS behind Shawn's trailer, Shawn in shorts, faded tee, and knee brace, Terry looking dressed for a media presentation in suit and shined boots, tinted glasses, Mexican Christmas beer he'd found in the back of the fridge dangling from one hand.

Gas stations and fast-food outlets stuck out across the highway; traffic fired north to Albuquerque, south to Las Cruces and Ciudad Juarez, the Black Range rising up in the distance.

"Interesting," Terry was saying to the surrounding fissured asphalt, plastic petunias and metal shade extenders, *palo verde* trees and distant peaks, the crushed lava rock. "More water than I would have expected, all things considered."

Shawn let it go, sipped his reheated drive-in coffee.

Terry shook the gold chain bracelet out from under his sleeve, where it caught the light. "Hard to wash the small town out of the boy, right? All those small-town values."

"I can think of worse things."

"Don't take it wrong. I always admired that about you."

"Sure you did," Shawn said, choosing to minimize, curious despite the throb in his temples, the crosshairs with Terry sighted in that kept appearing. "How's the hand?"

"You did it a favor. Knee acting up again?"

"Not much."

"Yeah, I can tell." Terry said with a glance at the brace. "And the newspaper business?"

"Same as the asshole business, I suppose. Which judging by that suit appears to be as good as ever."

Terry broke another grin that sank of its own weight. "No need to be rude, Speed. That business fed you, if memory serves."

Shawn thought about responding, instead looked off at the mountains. Trucks rumbled by on 25.

"Hey," Terry said. "Time out. I'm the guy who refused to press charges, remember? Me with the face and the broken hand."

Shawn flashed on *Too little, too late,* countered with, "So what'd you do, charge off on the red eye when you heard how I'd called up Loren and harassed her?" Attempting to compartmentalize the image of the cop and security guard hauling him off Terry as a crowd swelled around the fern pool, Loren white-faced and the kids looking stunned. The subsequent court order.

Terry swigged the last of his beer, clinked the empty down. "Nothing so dramatic, I'm afraid. Six-ten to Las Cruces, rental car from there. Not a bad drive, you're fond of desert."

"I rather assumed you'd made it. The question was more along the lines of why."

Terry creaked around to look at the trailer. "Got any more *cerveza* in there? I seem to have gone dry."

"If there is, it's by some oversight."

"Get you one?"

"Not for what it might cost me."

The grin broke. "Taken as a compliment."

Shawn watched him step into the trailer, marveling at the way Terry could push buttons in people and still come off as the great conciliator. It was what made him so good at flacking – that and a well-honed self-deprecation that charmed people. He remembered a time after they'd first hooked up, Exec-of-the-Year Terry winking down at him from the dais, saying in effect, *Play the hand I deal and this is you, trust me.* Followed later by, *It's not how good you are, it's knowing who buried the bodies.* Proving it often enough to drive the point home.

And yet, Terry looked older than the fourteen months it had been, Shawn recalling a rumor he'd heard that all was not golden inside Terry's Golden Gate. But that was the PR business, your basic bucket with holes in it you tried to keep filled. Besides, when Shawn threw himself up for comparison, Terry was Ozymandius in a summer weight.

"Like old times," Terry said when he'd banged outside with his beer and creaked the chair frame, freed the pants fabric as he crossed an ankle over. "You and me."

"And your selective memory," Shawn tossed back.

"We had our innings, you have to admit." Tilting the longneck and lowering it, another grin dawning. "The time you pulled the cosmetics maker's fat out of the–"

"Terry? Before I lie down with a bottle of ibuprofen, why are you here?"

"Old Speed, two seconds ahead with snow piling up in the turns, and he's still pressing."

Shawn leaned forward, took the weight off his knee preparatory to getting up, maybe knocking Terry over. "Don't forget to say goodbye to Dorothea. She keeps track."

"Whoa, simmer down. You want it straight, you got it." Pause for effect. "A client came to me with a job that has your name all over it. Big money, a piece of the action, the whole nine yards." Creaking back in the chair.

Shawn said nothing. Just stared at him.

"Don't give me that Shawn Rainey good-time rock-and-roll, look around you," Terry said, raising a hand to indicate pretty much everything in view. "Still want me to take a hike? Or are you so thrilled here in Bumwad with What's-Her-Face over there you don't even want to hear it?"

Shawn got it, all right, what he'd seen so often at contract time: Terry Dahl, full-tilt visionary on fire with whatever-it-was – Jimmy Swaggart in a business suit. *Walk with me and come out whole.*

"Stuff it, Terry. I've caught the act before."

The barb stuck not at all; Terry smiled. "Growing up where you did – Tahoe, I mean – you recall the *Constance*?"

Shawn just looked at him.

"Queen of the Lake, that *Constance*? I don't mean in person, I mean old photos of her. Course you do. I can see it on you."

"You want to run that by me again?"

"If I may take that for surprise, join the rest of the lake. But sixty years down she's still a cover girl up there. Travel guides, books, those old photos – nobody doesn't like Sara Lee. Except that all this time she was beyond reach in five-hundred-plus feet of ice water, technology was catching up. And this client – *my* client, mind you – sees it as the first step." Glancing around as if he might be overheard.

"Are you out of your mind?"

"One word, pal: Disney. The smart one."

"Disney…right."

Terry's eyes previewed a grin. "The man had an eye, you'll admit. All I'm saying here."

Pause. "Disclaimer, Terry: Don't mistake what I'm about to say as interest because it's not. We clear on that?"

"You see me going anywhere?"

Longer pause. "First step toward what?"

The grin broke big. "You ready for this? Resorts, casinos, the goodwill after they bring up the old girl and restore her – give her back to anyone who's seen her however and said to himself, 'Damn, check *that* out.' We're talking pride, Shawn, historical societies in heat. Hell, the line of people waving money will stretch around the lake, and that's just the VIPs."

It was so absurd that for a while Shawn could think of nothing to say. Finally he said, "You came all this way to tell *me* that?"

Terry blew a breath; his eyes scanned the mountains. "Big deal, it means you'll have to go back there, so what? We tested it. Lakewood loves you, even after all this time."

"You did what?"

"Polled you, and skip the con, this is me. I mean Speed Rainey, *that* happy horseshit. Hell, to those people you walk on water. It's only me who knows you like this."

Shawn was conscious of his grip on the thin aluminum arms, of heat welling again. "You really want to go there, Terry? Because if you do–"

"Fuck that, I'm doing you a favor. No idea why, looking at you now. Guilt, maybe, at the way things turned out."

"Guilt…right. I might be more impressed if you'd ever felt some. That or anything else."

Shrug, a conspiratorial wink. "Straight up, I need you. So far

RICHARD BARRE

43

it's solid, but these people need to know you're involved. National Downhill champ, French and Austrian champ, Sarajevo champ, you hadn't fucked up the trials. Are you reading this – what your spearheading means up there?"

"I'm reading it," Shawn said, the boil spilling over, hissing in the flames. "You've fucking promised me to them, haven't you?"

"Let's just say they aren't the kind to sit on their hands."

It took effort. "No kidding. Which must mean hurting you would be the upshot if I refuse."

Terry's smug look vanished. "Bad thought, sport – more along the lines of who you'll be hurting besides me. In addition to your-self, of course."

Been there, done that – in spades. "Before you take a permanent hike, Terry, you want to explain that?"

Terry reached into his suit coat and held out an envelope.

Shawn saw fourteen months ago, Terry's grin bordering on shit eating, and heard, "Friend of mine works for the cop lab, has access to one of those programs that adds years to missing kids? Have a look and tell me what you think. Because once my lawyers get through, that's what Elizabeth and Nate will look like when you're allowed near them again."

Snap: high heat, searing metal, bitter burn. Shawn was up and out of his chair, then he wasn't; he was cocooned by pain and clutching his knee, Terry having driven a boot into it, Shawn barely hearing through gasps that were his, *"You had your free shot, Speed. This time the meter's running."*

Shawn's knee was wrapped in ice and up on the couch when he heard the knock, saw Dorothea Zepeda through the Plexiglas, light behind her fading on the hills.

"It's open," he said.

"Your knee hurting again?" Poking her head inside.

"Just a slip."

"There's Epsom salts at my place, if you want."

"No thanks, Dorothea."

She looked skeptical, but it passed, no match for the news she bore, saying, "That friend of yours is a peach. Came back with flowers and champagne, said you was celebrating and wanted me to celebrate, too. It's a shame all men aren't that considerate, one Mexican in particular."

He let it go, heard Terry again, bending over him: *"Reality check, Speed. You recall the movie, real-estate guy to his sales people, 'First prize is a set of steak knives, second prize is you're fired?' That's you and me here. Piss it away in Bumwad, Shawn, or win the knives."*

"Terry? Get fucked."

"Oh, I don't think so. You don't care about the money, well and good. But you have a problem and I'm the one who can make it go away. Court order, legal standoff, penny-ante bullshit – all gone – Nate and Liz back in your life. Life back in your life."

Liz... Shawn felt something shoved into his pocket, saw Terry's boots backing off, and heard, *"Room number's on the card, I leave Las Cruces at nine. One-time offer: I don't hear from you by then, our next contact will be through Jerry Lizardi. You remember him?"*

Shawn did: thousand an hour and eight-thousand-dollar suits. Big press, big spectacle, big wins. He managed a nod, Terry adding, *"Be smart for once. This is your Get Out of Jail card. Don't blow it."*

"Wasting your time, asshole. I like it here."

"Truth or Consequences, my man. Ever wonder why I kept you around when I could have had Loren right then, period, end of story?

You kept my hands clean, dug the dirt out, nails all nice and buffed. In a word, you're a fixer, the best I've seen 'cause I made you. So go fix it."

"So, then…you're okay?" Dorothea's question floating in on him.

"Fine, Dorothea. Just the knee."

"Dark in here," she added. "You want a light on before I go?"

"No – thank you. Maybe the phone there on the re-charger, though. And that bottle of pills."

4

LOREN WAS CALLING FROM ACROSS THE STREAM, waving to him because he couldn't hear her. Shawn knew that time was out of joint because the old van he and Joe Don McCandless and Tam Engleman and Jake Sharpe and Sonny Hardin used to haul their gear up to Alpine and Boreal – places they could afford to ski then – was parked there, the sliding door open and somebody shadowed inside.

Cort, maybe, that Black-Irish grin of his.

Or their mother.

Watching him.

He knew it was a dream because Loren was naked and she was stepping into the stream, her eyes fixed on his, and he couldn't remember her naked and she hated the water. Now the water was rising around him, aroused yet feeling Cort's eyes or whoever's boring into him.

The water reached his knees yet he couldn't go forward, only back as Loren strode deeper into the stream, which was now a river raging toward a waterfall he couldn't see but could hear.

Mist billowed from its unseen base and her blonde hair lay on the water, which had enveloped all but her head, those eyes that never left his. Then Loren was moving with the current, fast toward the waterfall, him limping after her, telling her she had to hold on – that as soon as he fixed the van and drove them to the chairlift, he'd be back for her. At least as long as there wasn't good snow, in which case he'd pick her up later in the lake.

But then Cort's voice was coming from the van, telling him, *Let go, Shawn. You know you could have, if you'd wanted to.*

Shawn woke drenched in sweat, the words as real as if Cort were in the room. He took a deep breath, limped to the bathroom, washed his face and more ibuprofen down, then limped back, too much trouble to undress. Besides, he knew he wouldn't sleep, that the little he'd gotten was the result of the Darvocet and the beer, stale now in his mouth.

For a while he watched an old movie: Cagney as a producer of musicals who somehow winds up at West Point directing a cadet talent show, gradually drifting from it. Now, more than Cort's voice, Loren stayed, the ache where she'd been and was no more. Trying to bring her dream body into focus, Shawn realized he barely recalled their time together, the feel of her skin. That was months before the thing with Terry had grown like kudzu vine, eighteen before she sued for divorce.

Shawn checked back in on Cagney, prancing now with Virginia Mayo and the cadets led by Gordon McRae, everybody young and agile and beautiful, and he turned it off, his knee throbbing again.

What was Terry up to? Terry, who back then had seen something in him nobody else had; Shawn pitching him one day, riding a *Chronicle* grunt-job into an interview with Henri Dufresne, one of Terry's pro skiing clients. Terry *had* seen something, all right. Shawn proved it with the people he'd brought in, spenders who grew the agency, leading to a partnership role. Until such time as Loren became the one Terry serviced.

Ten months of lies, razor-edged looks, and hard time later, he and Loren split, custody to her with visitation, Shawn drunk at a motel that finally got as tired of him as he had of himself. Rock bottom – or so he'd thought – he got his act together, enough at least to bargain in family court, not his day for the kids that red-water Sunday but eager to show he'd adapted.

Adapted...

After being cuffed in front of them and led away, Terry's last-minute dropping of assault charges and the restraining order that followed, Shawn had drifted to small-town jobs close enough to drive back, tempt fate, watch Lizzy on her way to Brownies, Nathan to baseball practice. Loren's spotting the car led to no uncertain terms: out-of-state or jail. So when Shawn got wind of a news-pool job in New Mexico – Truth or Consequences, in a rat bite of irony – he'd taken it.

He'd tried, like crazy he had. Four months had eaten a hole in him not even booze and pills could fill; going on nine, it was the size of Tahoe. Then came Rosalinda Quesada Luna, his call to Loren, Terry showing up, all of that. Yet something showed up with Terry that had not been there in the dark days before.

Hope, his kids back. Him back.

All he had to do was *go* back – back to where it had started. Everything that over the years had grown as steep and treacherous as KT-22 in flat light, thick with ice and ruts, ball-breaker chutes, wind-exposed rock that took it all and more in nothing flat.

He reached for the remote and punched the TV back on again, froth featuring Gene Kelly and Debbie Reynolds he turned up loud.

5

SHAWN STRAIGHTENED HIS SEAT and leaned into the descent, felt the letters of introduction Terry had sent along with business cards, fact and contact sheets, travel itinerary, odds and ends. As his ears popped, he ran Terry's briefing through again.

"Basically, the deal's in its infancy. The poll you lit up showed the pros and cons split, but the locals, when they have it laid out for them, back *Constance* sixty-forty. Strongest tilt against is the granddaughter of the man who built her – big-time lumber and transportation money. Old growth went to prop up half of Nevada, at least the half that counted then, the mother lode half. Comstock Silver Mines."

"Holmes, Seneca DeWitt," Shawn had said. "His son was Cyrus Chandler Holmes."

"And score one for our side."

Shawn heard horns from Terry's end; Terry was phoning from his car. "The school I went to is named after him."

"It was a joke, Shawn, lighten up. The name you may not

know is Catherine Mulvhill. Woman's a certified *pistola*, still lives in granddad's house on Echo Bay. All by herself, she's ninety percent of the nays, meaning she's your target, even though Nevada law states that any vehicle abandoned fifty years or better on state land is considered state property. The rest are the usual leave-it-be-or-I'll-rend-my-garment types, anything-you're-for-we're-against. Ones that think it's a shrine, even though nobody died."

"Somebody have to die for it to qualify, Terry?"

There was a pause, another horn. "In case you're not just blowing smoke, *Constance* is a symbol for a way of life most people yearn for, at the very least are curious about. Who cares if it ever existed? People have made it what it is and that's what we're going to give them. And don't tell me you don't itch for a peek at the old girl or that your old man didn't have a picture of her someplace."

Shawn took a breath. "How are my kids, Terry?"

"So I get a little spouty, sue me. Things work out, Loren and I might even bring them up to the lake, do some water skiing. Sound like a plan?"

He pictured it, said nothing because he couldn't. Through beach towels wrapped around after they'd clambered back into the boat, he felt their damp warmth and shivery exuberance, smelled their banana-scented sunblock, and heard, *See me cross that wake, Dad? You see that?*

Terry asked if he was still there.

"I'm here. There anything else?"

"Yeah. Make a statement with your wheels, a Jag or Caddy or something. And buy a couple of suits if your old ones don't fit."

Shawn thought of some Goodwill customers who'd gotten lucky after the split. "When did they ever fit, Terry?"

"Cut to present, boy, beaucoup futures on the line." Shawn heard him curse before saying, "Sorry, world's full of assholes. Got you in at the Marcourt up there – see Bob Lamont, number-two man. He's on board, knows everybody important to us."

Shawn thought about it. "Bad idea."

Pause. "So deal. I'm listening."

"Little things play big to some people. Why give them a target?"

"Too cozy with the gaming interests, not enough with the locals…"

"You always had the gift, Terry."

Pause. "All right, your call. Meet Bob, though. He has some things for you, and he speaks for a group we need."

"Like they need us…"

"Damn – some teacher you had. Oh, and check in with Mal Kadich up there; he'll run you through the dive op. Pretty impressive what they're attempting. Deepest dive undertaken at that elevation, let alone salvage and restoration."

"Yeah, I'll do that."

"And see Neville Autry at the Chamber of Commerce. They know a good thing when they sniff it. Already planning the dock they're going to build us, who they have to grease."

Shawn remembered the name from Boy Scout days, Neville Autry an accountant whose uniform didn't fit very well, son Neal a kid nobody liked because his dad always gave him the cush chores.

"Need I say there's a lot riding here?" Terry continued. "Put simply, donations have dried up with this Mulvhill dame. She's that big."

"Sorry. I don't get it."

"You'd have to be her, sport: site's sacred, never meant by her grandfather to be anything else, intended for deep water, honor the memory, blah-blah. Bringing it up, even sending divers down, is tantamount to grave robbing. Like that."

Shawn said nothing.

"Spearhead, remember? The others add up to spit; the key is the Mulvhill woman. Appearances to polish up your star, put the pressure on, tilt the balance, and presto – she's aboard and we all live happily ever after."

Something there in the delivery, unspoken. *Leverage?* "What's the matter, Terry? Worried about getting your money's worth?"

"From you? Hardly. Not when you consider what redhead's school picture I'm looking at right now."

Shawn fought it, but lost. "I swear to God, Terry. You and me for good when this is over."

Chuckle blew out into laughter. "Spoken like a man who's in for the duration. Just don't forget to sleep with one eye open and remember who leads in this dance." Clicking off.

As Shawn did the same, he turned his image of the man into one of both his thumbs pressed deep into Terry's windpipe.

With the credit card Terry sent, Shawn rented a blend-in gray Cherokee, no Jag or Caddy statements. He left the side street, took the elevated freeway toward town. Despite how much it had grown since he'd been there, the malls and the big boxes, the loopy casino architecture, Reno always reminded him of the home spreads you found off piney foothill roads: broken washing machines and rusting pickups, rabbit hutches and old transmissions. Gambling had raised the ante, but like Vegas to him it still smacked of Dogpatch with dealers, trucker hats and green eyeshades, relentless sun and motel tans – that incongruity.

Yet, under the circumstances, how different was he?

Not much, he guessed.

After visiting an outlet shop – heavy on the blazer/polo/chino/oxford route he knew played better up the hill – Shawn found himself sweating despite the SUV's air-conditioning. Apart from *why* he was going back, so far he'd managed to put off that he actually *was*. But as he left behind the hundred-degree heat and burnt-rock valley, the show-and-slot signs, and wound into the grade, he had an overpowering desire to pull off and turn around.

Not yet, he told himself.

Not *this* yet.

Pines started appearing on the dun-colored slopes, cotton-woods and willows on the riverbanks and gravel bars. Rock faces twisted in and out of slash canyons. He killed the a/c, let down a window and smelled water. A flume like the one that had transported logs to the valley sawmills back when the Comstock was devouring Tahoe's old growth played tag with the highway. Below him the Truckee ran green and rapids-white while the double-lane widened and fell away off the buttressed fringe. Then 80 leveled out and he saw the exit for Truckee and took it. With the brick facades of railroad old town, the heat returned, eighty-six on a bank sign. He toyed with the idea of cutting over and entering Lakewood from the Squaw Valley side, opted instead to keep going, up and over the summit, approach it from along the lake. Ease the transition.

He pulled off at the summit, set the brake, let the dust roll by him, tasted it in the 7000-foot air along with the smell of forest. At the base of the slope ending at North Lake, Tahoe stretched on its twenty-two-by-twelve-mile axis toward South Shore. Even at this distance, Harrah's and Harvey's and Caesar's and whoever else by now had convinced the powers that tall was better reflected back at him. And, in between, the most impossible water he'd seen before or since, a shifting palette of emerald sliding over into blue and, finally, indigo where the real depths, the 1600s, began.

Outcrops came to points; bays – Carnelian, Agate, Hurricane, Echo – matched with sweeps of their own. This late in August, Mount Tallac – California side, southwest – showed no snow, just evergreen attempting the climb. Out of sight lurked the smaller lakes of Crystal and Fallen Leaf, gems he knew from fishing picnics and training hikes.

Scenes played: He and Cort learning to swim, mom casting a watchful eye while the old man drank Pabst. Summers later, showing off to Robin Vasquez, holding his breath until she screamed. For a moment, Shawn wondered what happened to her, let the scene shift to night, he and Robin staring up at the moon from the back of Liam's pickup, the one the old man used to ferry Shawn up Mount Rose when he'd begun to show promise. Shawn's own wheels, then, the VW van closing in on last-gasp even before he'd saved the money to buy it. Blatting around, blitzed enough on Mickey's Bigmouth and Carlo Rossi to break off road reflectors until Cort-pal and new deputy Arn Tennell pinched Shawn and company outside Carnelian Bay: one DUI, five underages, one destruction of county property, one muffler violation. One long night, mother crying and the old man swearing he'd earn back the fine, every damn cent.

More flashbacks: road-crewing the summer of his junior and senior years to scrape up payback and satisfy the court; road sealer trashing his Redwings, but him getting harder and all-out faster. He and Cort water-skiing, six-packs to the brother who stayed up longest, Robin running them from her dad's hot new

Mirage. Shawn refusing – absolutely refusing – to go down until Cort upended, usually when Shawn could barely stand the rest of the day his legs were so shot.

He and Cort that last afternoon…

Unable to see Lakewood for the mountains but already feeling its weight, Shawn got back into the Cherokee, bought time by heading left on North Lake, around to the Marcourt.

6

Bob Lamont was about what Shawn expected: tan and suave, slicked hair and a suit that looked Italian. Shawn had used the hotel men's room to change into khakis, white polo, and blazer, was in the bar nursing a draft and feeling like someone even *he* didn't recognize, when the man approached, hand thrust out.

Appropriate, Shawn thought.

"Shawn? Robert Lamont – Bob. Great to have you on board. You know they still play your wipeout on Wide World of Sports? KT-22, right?"

Shawn nodded, already deciding it would be a short visit.

"Unreal," Lamont added. "Always gets a gasp."

"Too bad there aren't royalties."

"What? Oh, yeah. Seriously, how you doing? Heard you'd had a run of luck, not all double-zeros."

Casino sounds filtered in, electronic slots and poker, the music of something for nothing and nothing for something. Air vents whispered, fed by the big a/c units. The bar smelled faintly of maraschino cherries and smoke they hadn't been able to leach from the carpeting.

"Seriously, Bob?" he said to the question. "You'd be bored stiff."

"Neither me nor the media around here, as you'll find out." His face clouded. "How long's it been since then, anyway?"

"Long enough," Shawn answered. "Eighty-four."

"Right. I still can't believe you–"

"Terry said you had some things for me?"

"Never mind me, I'm just the help. You must be anxious to get going, at least as much as we are and that's huge. Hang fire a second while I get them."

He left and Shawn exchanged glances with the bartender, a thirtyish woman with streaked hair and shadowed eyes, black vest and string tie over a white blouse, *K.T.* on her nametag. As she racked a highball glass, reached for another, she said, "Are you really Shawn Rainey?"

"I sometimes wonder."

"Sorry. Guess I expected ten feet tall. From the talk, I mean."

"Got *him* fooled, anyway." Tilting his head toward Bob Lamont's exit point.

She cracked a smile. "That wouldn't be too hard."

"I was afraid you'd say that."

The smile broadened. "Get you another draft?"

"Depends. How much you got back there?"

"I see. *That* kind of day."

"Fun and sun. Sun and fun."

She'd brought the draft and was back at work when she asked, "You're honest-to-God going to raise the *Constance*?"

He took a moment reconnecting. "That's the plan."

Shake of the head, then, "God, I'd love to ride in her from the pictures I've seen. Feel like I was somebody from back then, the hats and veils and long coats. Is there really a chance?"

And there it was, his fulcrum to lever her up, see the water part at her passing. "Better than that from what I know of it."

"Hey, if you need any help…"

Bob Lamont entered, trailed by a kid in hotel uniform carrying a banker's box. "Here you be," he said, waving the kid off. "Terry said you had a laptop and modem?"

"That's right."

"Check the website, if you haven't already. There's a disk inside with the address. File has a list of groups we could use your help with ASAP. But I heard you won't be staying with us?"

"Strategic decision. Nothing personal."

"You're missing a bet. Everything you need's right here."

"Exactly how I'd spend my time, but thanks."

As he left with the box, Shawn thought he caught the bartender smiling, even though she was looking down at her hands wedging limes.

Shawn drove west – Brockway, Kings Beach, Agate – everything reminding him of something. The spot where he and Robin rafted out to a night-moored cruiser, drank beer and smoked pot, tipped over on the way in, pulling up to her house soaked and unable to halt the giggles. Cedar Flat where he and Joe Don McCandless hauled shakes for a builder named Frank Love who'd ultimately stiffed them for the work, Joe-D convincing Shawn to keep watch while he released the brake on Love's new pickup, sending it down a slope and through a retaining wall, Joe-D pumped and whooping as it hit the water.

To his amazement Love actually sent them their wages, Joe-D

telling him *that* was how you did it, you hit back harder, Shawn calling Joe-D a headcase who might have gotten them killed for all he knew. Joe-D laughing that a guy like Frank Love had bigger things than a couple of high-school sophomores to fuck around with, *that* he knew for a fact.

Then there was Rubicon, far off down the lake and lost against the Jeffries and Ponderosas and shadowed undergrowth.

Rubicon, where it had finally come to a head with Cort.

Even though it wasn't yet sunset, drivers had their lights on, camper shells and RVs, sport-utes towing boats. The cooling air held pine pitch and dust, grasses and seeping creek beds. Shawn passed streets he knew too well, the buildings housing the sheriff, finally Lakewood looking as if little had changed beyond curb-to-curb paving and new names on the signs. The Holmes Bank mall was still there, the drug store he'd worked nights to earn lift money, the service station his father owned at which gas-jockey Cort proved as popular as tourist-magnet Fanny Bridge across the lake outlet that became the Truckee.

Horns made him realize he'd slowed to a crawl, deep breaths before veering down-lake to an unobtrusive grouping of cabins. Promising the innkeeper a C-note to keep his stay quiet, he unpacked, thumbed through the bankers-box files: backup articles on the *Constance* launch, past and upcoming lake events circled in red, photos of people, a list of their boats and places. And headlines: TEAM TO PROBE TAHOE'S *TITANIC*; PLAN TO RAISE AND RESTORE *CONSTANCE* OUTLINED; SUPPORT/OPPOSITION FOR CONNIE PROJECT.

He spent an hour with the website, enough to get a feel for the dive project's magnitude and intricacy, let alone the salvage. A hundred million, Terry had floated past him; when matched with the task, it no longer seemed extravagant. It also gave him a sense of the boulder he had to roll around the lake's seventy-three-mile perimeter to bring it off.

Committing himself to an uninterrupted tomorrow, Shawn walked to the other spot he'd contemplated, an old-Tahoe-style lodge that served drinks and food. By now the clouds were glowing coals, moments later ash. Water lapped at the stones beneath the deck and boats hove in, all engine gurgle and laughter. Then it was dark, bright pinpoints denoting communities around the lake's periphery. Quite simply, it was stunning. Yet for Shawn the mountains and the lake, the tiara-like lights, might as well have been an anchor.

An anchor...

After an hour screwing up his courage, he got in the Cherokee and headed back toward Lakewood, stopping for a twelve-pack and some Grenadiers at a liquor store. About a mile out, he found the turn.

The house was modest, unrepentant, the last of its kind on a street of upgrades and split-level makeovers, the only yard without decorative boulders and terraces, aspen and red dogwood groupings. Lights shone behind the drapes as Shawn cruised it and circled back slowly, forever-seeming before he was able to step out with the twelver and knock softly.

Light flooded, ghost-rimming the figure that answered without speaking.

"It's me, Pop," Shawn said. "This a bad time?"

They listened to the Giants game from Arizona, a late-inning tie, Shawn on the couch he remembered their getting when he was twelve. His father still had grease under his fingernails, still wore his gray hair in a brush-cut, though the military line had given way to a sun-speckled forehead. Liam Rainey accepted the beer but said no to the Grenadiers, Shawn figuring doctor's orders from the jaw-set. And for the first time his father looked diminished to him in his work shirt, the gray cotton pants that seemed to float on him.

One thing had not changed: Though Liam's glasses had thickened and tiered, he was still sharp-eyed, the irises cold and deep as lake water.

Feeling them on him and already looking for a way out, Shawn scanned the living room. Everything looked the same as when he'd left, a year after the docs had done what they could for his knee, told him the rest was up to him. It crossed his mind that if he got up and went to his room, he'd find his old rehab weights, the stretch bands and pulleys he cursed. Tacks from the ski posters he'd ripped down as soon as he could get at them.

He forced his mind back to the living room. Despite the clutter his mother always preferred – Hummel figures, knick-knacks, the scenics she used to paint and hang as though open space betrayed an empty mind – the living room was immaculate, dusted and nothing out of place. Except for him.

Liam Rainey ran his palms along the arms of his chair. "Giants have a shot this year," he said.

"Guess I've lost track," Shawn responded.

"Too bad. Baseball grounds a man."

As if to re-form a lost consensus, they listened as Bonds drew a walk and the right fielder singled.

"Long time no see," his father finally said.

Shawn nodded. "Too long."

"You here for money?"

"No," Shawn said, recalling the abruptness – blunt as the ballpeins his father used to hammer out dents. "Thanks."

"Not as though I have any to give. You doing okay?"

"Ups and downs," Shawn said as the next man popped out, Bonds holding at third. "You?"

"Same as ever."

A forceout drove in Bonds, no reaction from his father. Then, "You been up to see your mother yet?"

The question. Shawn shook his head. "Just got in."

"Son, whatever there was between you and her–" Cutting it short. "I know she'd like it. You know where to find her?"

"You wrote me." Then, because not saying it seemed worse, "Shall I call you when I go?"

"Why not just say when?"

"Tomorrow?"

"Promised I'd have Bill Palmer's mower ready for him." The Giants' half ending with the one run, D-backs coming up, bottom of the tenth. "You staying someplace?"

"Sunnyside," Shawn answered, thinking, *Don't do it, don't make me–*

"You like it there, fine. But it's just me here, and I won't bite. Hell, I'm usually in bed by now."

How to say it? "When the dust settles, maybe. Right now I have no idea where I'll be or when." Lame, even to him: someone who, ever since he'd borne the brunt, had sworn not to use words like the old man did, as bludgeons.

"Not asking you to pal around, just save your money. Hell, you can't use it, I can."

"Pop, I'll think about it. I will."

Arizona's cleanup hitter drove in the leadoff single with a homer to right to win it. Liam Rainey leaned over and turned the set off.

"Same old same-old," he said, settling back. "Loren and the kids doing okay?"

Shawn felt a pang, followed by guilt for not having written to explain it to his father. "We're not together anymore, Pop. I'm not sure I told you."

"Yeah. Must have slipped your mind." He sipped beer. "Not to be rude, but why *are* you here?"

Leaving out Elizabeth and Nate, Shawn told him: money to raise the *Constance* and restore her; launching then into pride and prosperity for the lake towns, in particular ex-railhead Lakewood she'd once called home. Practice for later on.

His father was silent. Then, "Heard something to that effect, though not in detail. Never seem to get the details until after you've signed the check." He coughed, coughed again. "Plus, people usually tell a person that, they have themselves in mind. This prosperity you're talking about include you?"

It brought a flush, Shawn feeling like he was back in third grade and hating it, Joe-D McCandless filching Marlboros from his dad's pack. Even at that age Joe-D the kind who'd eat light bulbs and tell Shawn they tasted like Rice Crispies. *No shit: here, have one.*

"Pop, it's a job like any other. Compensation goes with it."

"No need to get defensive. You run up against the other side yet, the Catherine Mulvhills? Like there's more than one."

"We expect to convince people, Pop, not ram it down their throats. It has to benefit everybody."

"That'll be the day."

"Look, I'm telling you–"

"I'm not deaf, either, Shawn. Nor as broken down as I look."

Shawn expelled breath. "I didn't mean it like that."

"No? How did you mean it?"

"Just that we need this to work." Pause. "*I* need it to work."

His father looked at him as if seeing something he hadn't before. "Well, you've done your job; consider me told," he said. "Also that you know the way out so I can go to bed."

Shawn was out before he knew it, headlights probing a street that looked only forbidding now, eyes peering from behind the facades: judging him, shaking their heads. Just before he hit the highway and his turn, he thought he saw Cort emerge from a tangle of berry vines and young cedars, try to tell him something Shawn couldn't make out. But it turned out to be just an overgrown road sign.

7

THURSDAY MORNING HE WAS UP AT SUNRISE, walking the bike path along the lake. With a mist holding, the air was spectral pearl, the sun laying down a bright path – as if all Shawn had to do was step onto it, what he sought as close as that. Boats close-moored seemed suspended, the air and water as one. Then the mist was gone, the path diffused into shards of mirror. Squinting, he could see himself out there water-skiing. Distance swimming in response to a dare he couldn't make it to this or that buoy. Racing the old Catalina 24 somebody had grown tired of paying slip fees for and sold cheap to Cort, who'd renamed it *Blackbird*. The perfect cover, he'd called it, ratty enough that other sailors took it for granted until the gun sounded and Cort off-keyed "Bye-Bye Blackbird" from the stern.

Shawn felt the walk in his knee and headed back to shower and change; on a whim, he checked e-mail and saw:

Dad,

Don't tell mom I used her e-mail without permission, she gets mad. I miss you. Elizabeth does, too. Can't you come back? We want to live with you. Dad, they don't like you very much. They're always talking about you.

Nathan.

P.S. If you get this, don't answer because she'll know and I'll get in trouble.

Fighting throat-clutch, he sat with his photographs: Nathan in his Little League uniform, Elizabeth grinning from a diving board, one of both at a ball game. He reread the birthday cards and thank-you notes the mail had forwarded to his many addresses – *Love you, Dad, when are you coming home? Isn't this a neat stamp?* He let the shower beat on him until the hot ran out. He nursed coffee at the restaurant across the highway and when that didn't work, bought the local weekly and set it next to his breakfast.

Damnit to hell...

The paper, when it came in focus, was filled with *Constance* stories: TAHOE'S *TITANIC* TO SAIL, BACKERS SAY; *CONSTANCE* FEVER SWEEPS LAKE; DIVE TEAM TRAINS FOR CONNIE. Photos were from the perspective of the dive, its source the man Terry mentioned, Mal Kadich. He was shown against a bow-on shot of *Constance*, circa 1920, the photo taken inside the office Terry rented to distribute information. Also mentioned was the independent survey dive the year before, on which Kadich's salvage projections were based.

Shawn made a note of the editor's name so he could check in, broaden the man's perspective beyond logistics. In a related article, he reread how *Constance* had been towed from her Lakewood berth and scuttled: August 29, 1940, despite pleas from those who'd become aware of Holmes's plan to spare her further indignity after the mail contracts had lapsed and roads had rendered her obsolete.

Rusting and un-maintained.

Open to further vandalism.

Turning the page, he caught a letter from Catherine Mulvhill. Incensed in tone, it noted the steamship's long history and defended her father's actions, his desire for an appropriate resting place for his favorite, Catherine confident that wiser heads would prevail. Unstated but implicit: *When encouraged by certain parties to invest in this desecration.*

Shawn recalled his file on the woman: late seventies in age; strong ecological stands; scholarships, charities, historic preservations. Though reclusive, Catherine was a more-than-willing adversary – as those who crossed her found out. Product of C.C. Holmes, heir to Seneca's lumber dynasty, and wife Eunice Dexter Holmes, Catherine had been married briefly to Landon Mulvhill, a lawyer who worked for C. C. and died shortly after their marriage.

She had never remarried.

Shawn refolded the paper, asked for more coffee and a north-shore phone book but found no listing for Robin Vasquez. Not surprising: After this long and as striking as she'd been, she had to have married – that or fled as he had, without a backward glance. He wondered if she'd been more successful than he had in that regard. He hoped so.

In the classifieds he found an ad for McCandless Lumber, a cross listing for McCandless Door and Hardware. *Not bad if that's you, Joe-D,* he thought. *Or, if it's still your old man working it, he should have at least a phone number. Who knows, you might even have–*

"Sir...?"

He hadn't noticed the waitress, asking if he wanted anything else before handing him the bill. When she'd left with his card he flashed on what he'd promised the old man last night, Liam knowing him as well as he knew himself and obviously liking the knowledge no better than he ever had. Shawn signed the slip, took himself out to the Cherokee and without stopping at his cabin headed back toward town.

She was off the access road, up the hill beyond the nine-hole golf course: short walk in, view of the lake and town, the national forest behind, the day rare even for Tahoe.

Marybeth Beatrice Rainey.

Born September 12, 1934.

Died April 7, 1987.

No other inscription. As if whoever had put it there could think of nothing else to say.

Devoted Wife and Mother?

Beloved of Liam?

A Life of Denial and Dedication?

Nothing but stone, Shawn replaying all of it until he found refuge on a retaining wall, the inscription, the view, all a blur. *I'm sorry, I'm sorry, I'm sorry,* until he could no longer form the words. Thinking there was still plenty of room to chisel in *Dead of wounds caused by son Shawn Andrew Rainey following the events of October 14, 1983.*

Shawn let a radio talk show he'd punched on and the photo of Nate and Lizzy he'd mounted in a dash frame ease him down the hill. The space Terry had rented was among a waterside grouping of shops and offices; Shawn entered to a table spread with fact sheets, a woman named Suzanne Padget – tanned, coiffed, fifty-ish – who told him she was delighted at his involvement, Shawn figuring her as the wife of an early donor. In answer to his question, Mal Kadich more than likely was on his boat, *Deep VI.*

She gave him directions and a phone message from Bob Lamont about a VIP reception Saturday evening at the Marcourt: five o'clock, guest of honor. Shawn left her his cell phone number, promised to post his itinerary and check in regularly.

Deep VI was a wide-beamed fly-bridge that would have looked more at home in a marina with other forty footers. Instead it was tied up at a private dock lined with Woodie restorations – Chris-Crafts, Garwoods, a Century with the engine hatch open – boats that sold for four figures in the nineteen-thirties, six now when you could find them. The man working on the Century directed Shawn around the gangway, and in answer to his hail, Mal Kadich stepped out, looking like his photo: outdoor face and forearms, anchor tattoo on one; dive watch left wrist, gold bracelet right; khaki shirt over jeans.

"Sorry, no interviews today," he said. "About to shove off."

"Shawn Rainey, Mal. Terry might have mentioned me?"

"Hell, why didn't you say so? Step aboard."

After showing him around the boat, the gear they were using to train – night dives to simulate conditions, dual tanks suspended in cage-like apparatus, assorted esoterica – Mal said, "Easy to see why Terry's high on you. Women will eat you with a spoon."

Shawn's initial reaction was to be put off, but he went with it.

"Be a first," he answered.

"Never shit a shitter, son. You got time to motor out where I'm headed – to the site?"

The question took him by surprise. "Better another time."

"I say something wrong? You look a little peaked."

"Altitude," Shawn covered. "Forgot the effect it can have."

"Get used to it. Forty minutes, bring you up to speed. Something to lay on your public."

"Thanks, I'll drive it," he said. "Meet you there."

But by then Mal had started the engines and was gesturing at Shawn to release the lines. For a moment as he did it, Shawn thought of bailing, how that would look: strange at best, compromising at worst. And Mal Kadich did not look like the kind to keep it buttoned; every time they wound up near each other, he'd have to endure the look Mal was giving him now. "Long as there's a head aboard," he shouted over the rumble.

"Two, if it comes to it," Mal shouted back. "But a flash like you? Has to beat hell out of a downhill run."

Mal went inside, took the helm, piloted them out; thinking that being in the cabin might distract him, Shawn went in and stood by.

Mal eyed him and said, "You aware that's the same dock our girl was towed from to put her down?"

"Vaguely."

"That's right, you were raised up here, weren't you. Makes you feel something, I imagine."

Shawn felt the cold, Cort's hand again, the strength of it at first. He took his eyes off the water and leaned into a banquette.

"Hey, you okay?"

"Yeah." Swallowing.

After a look, Mal said, "Then you know what we're attempting. Basically it's to load air into her ballasts, loop straps attached to a crane setup once we've dislodged her. Use her buoyancy to reel her into a floating dock."

Shawn gave a nod. "The website went into it, but that's a lot easier to grasp. You really think she'll lift off?"

"Betting on it, son. A good portion of what I own."

Mal reached over and released a drop-lid, pulled out a pack

of photo enlargements. Though the lighting was spotty, the images were clear: stern shot with her name across it, Shawn feeling a thrill despite his churn. Bow and anchor ports, both flanks looking up from where they were lodged. Porcelain commode and sink, deck and interiors awaiting the next stream of passengers, Shawn mentioning how intact she looked after sixty years under water.

Mal said, "Cold as a bitch down there, bio-organism activity is close to zip. As you can see, she's more or less upright on a shelf, five-sixty stern, five-twenty bow. Nobody's salvaged a boat that deep this high, though. Hell, up to last year, nobody'd even ventured the dive."

"So what's made it possible?"

"New gear, new ideas about gasses incorporated into software. Ingenuity in the face of incentive."

Shawn let the engine throb take him. They were well out by now, the shoreline vague in the haze that had formed with noonday: water and white light, glare, the dim ragged saw of mountain rim. It had been a day similar to this one, clear at first, then turning. As if, despite the brightness, he and Cort had sailed off the edge of the world into something neither had seen coming.

Which, of course, they had.

Mal slacked the engines; by degrees the haze was replaced by an indentation in the shoreline. About two miles at its widest, a mile between inner points, Echo Bay was as Shawn recalled: blue water sliding into green, massive boulders, wood structures tucked in around a large open space.

He tried picturing it as log chutes, sawdust cones blowing sparks, lumber wagons, bustling docks; later on, a sleek white ship debarking and boarding men and women. He couldn't, it was too placid. Through tall pines and cedar, he could see a house of significant proportions – rock, beam, slate – and knew instinctively what it was. Still, he asked about it.

"Stonehouse," Mal told him. "Your basic Holmes mansion."

"Catherine Mulvhill," Shawn said.

"Likely watching us through her scope."

"You've seen her?"

Nod. "Through the big window. Hell, I've seen her out there on the point with a video camera on a tripod. Not like she's slinking around."

Shawn reached binoculars off a hook, stared back through deep shade at lawn leading up to stone porch, arched windows reflecting the shadows and the lake: Alpine Gothic. "Ever met her?"

"Heard her speak one time, and she is something. But then I wouldn't want to spoil it for you."

Shawn brought the glasses down. Regarding him, Mal said, "Never mind her and all that, wait while I run a scan of our girl. You got any pulse at all, that should do it, sure as H-two-oh."

It was like looking at the ultrasound of a baby awaiting delivery, a heartbeat all that was missing. There was the profile he'd seen in every old picture of her since he was a kid – as if it were a face he knew from memory, not needing the whole to recognize it, just a glimpse. He had the feeling he should be able to reach over the side and touch her, that close was she in distance and time.

Mal said, "So near and yet so far, right?"

Shawn heard but didn't see him. Instead he saw his father's blue eyes, his mother's even features matched with an insouciant shrug and a smile that swept whatever and whomever like a lighthouse beacon.

For a time, at least.

No running from that.

"Yeah," he said to Mal starting the engines. "So near and yet so far."

8

Four o'clock, Shawn in the Cherokee, Mal and *Constance* well back of him: From the road the lake seemed as placid as earlier, an illusion, he knew. If anything was change incarnate, it was that old dowager, blue heaven one minute, all slate wrath the next.

Better than you have taken me for granted and paid.

Don't believe it? Try me and see. But I play for keeps.

He'd used the cell phone to call ahead to see at which of the two locations he'd find Joe Don McCandless, heard from the clerk Hardware and Door, Nevada side. As he drove, he punched up Bob Lamont's number and left a message: He'd be at Saturday's reception, was looking forward to it, guest of honor, blah-blah-blah. Hearing himself lie was like old times with Terry, nobody better at it than Terry was, though there were times when Shawn felt they were becoming interchangeable parts, a more than disquieting appraisal. He forced his shoulders down with a long breath and drove, let his mental notes flow past like the trees along the fringe...

Bob Lamont: innocuous from a distance, potential pain in the ass. Side note: Pick and choose; don't let the man start calling shots.

Suzanne Padget: so good, so far. Connected, but to whom? Useful…?

Mal Kadich: glory and fortune hunter, but key. From appearances, in it for the duration.

Constance Project: in light of the odds, when pigs flew, but a ticket to his kids. Side note: Use it, see it, don't get caught up in it.

Shawn Rainey: frank assessment, damaged goods – already showing cracks. Slim possibility of spackle.

McCandless Door and Hardware was a medium-size box, a failed market reborn as such. Customers and employees in blue tops bustled among the tools and home-improvement fixtures – brass, pewter, ceramic – nice things, plus departments for kitchen and bath design. The door section reminded Shawn of a funhouse maze it was that well stocked. He asked a blue-top where he could find Mr. McCandless the younger.

"In back," she told him. "If you'll wait, I'll get somebody to–"

"Thanks," he said. "I'll find it."

"Sir, you're not allowed to–"

"It's a surprise." Raising a finger to his lips.

He was through double doors and into stacks when he heard a familiar voice from an office: loud, a phone conversation – if you could call something that one-way a conversation. He waited till the phone was slammed down, gave it a moment, then stuck his head around the jamb. The man at the computer, keyboarding with less-than-agile fingers, still looked hard, linebacker shoulders wedging a nipped-in waist. But today's wedge was less pronounced than Shawn remembered, the hair less sun-bleached and more widow-peaked.

"*Shit,*" the man said as if his fingers had betrayed him and he were about to fire them.

"Literally or figuratively."

Joe Don McCandless spun in his chair, ready, it seemed, to blow up the blocking guard and drive his running back clear to Reno.

Shawn put up his hands in mock surrender. "*No más. No tengo el balón.*"

"*Son of a bitch,*" Joe Don McCandless said.

"I've been called worse," Shawn said.

They sat in the outdoor-furniture section, containered pines forming a screen from the parking lot. They talked about how well nobody-calls-me-Joe-D-anymore was doing, Shawn saying he'd seen it firsthand in the aisles. About how Joe Don's old man looked in on the two stores but that Joe-D was the man now, bullshit and all.

"And I do mean bullshit. You think I got this pale water skiing?" he said. "Four Winns cuddy cabin last birthday, and I'm fucking never out in it."

"Tough times," Shawn answered, drawing the swipe he expected, the laugh lines crinkling deeper but less wild. Rivers that had settled into their beds, though still-lurking rapids kept the banks honest.

The grin faded. "Forty in thirteen months. You believe that?"

"Matter of fact, yeah," Shawn said.

"Just not very often, right?"

An employee led a husband and wife over to check out their set, Joe Don getting up to greet them, grin that it was the best-warmed seat in the house. Then he led Shawn out to a red Ram crew-cab and drove them to the Marcourt bar, Shawn looking around for K.T. the bartender but not spotting her.

"Sad about your mom," Joe Don said after they'd ordered.

"Yeah," Shawn answered. "Thanks."

"Your old man okay?"

"Lost some weight and hair, but he's still at it. Sounded the same, anyway." Leaving it at that, nothing more warranted.

"You and what's-her-name still together, the one you left town with?"

"Loren." He shook his head. "Split three years ago."

"Bummer. Kids?"

Shawn told him, wishing he'd thought to bring the dash photo. Joe Don pulled out his wallet, flashed two boys posed outdoors in a meadow: great smiles, all Joe-D.

"Conner's on the left, after my dad. The other one's Shawn."

Shawn scanned to determine if he was serious, concluded he was.

"Damn, Joe Don. What to say...?"

"Don't say anything, just know." His draft with a shot of Maker's Mark arrived, Shawn having declined. Joe Don split the shot, shuddered and chased it. "I thought you'd cashed out up here, the stuff with your brother..."

Shawn sipped his beer.

"So why *are* you here, and don't tell me it's your old bud. Buds call each other once in a while."

"No argument from me. You deserve better."

"I should hope, or I'd have to beat the crap out of you." Followed by, "Look, I know you. If you're here, there's a reason."

Leaving out Elizabeth and Nate, Terry's chokehold on him, *Constance* his way back to the light, Shawn explained it, or tried to. He waited for reaction: laugh...whistle...*something*.

Joe Don waved two fingers at the bartender – Eddie, from his tag – then shook his head and grinned. "Speed, Speed. You been reading my mail?"

"Meaning what – bogus or real?"

The Joe-D smile broke from the grin. "How's six figures real, six more now that I know you're aboard?"

Eddie brought the drinks; Joe Don waved Shawn off, handed Eddie a MasterCard, watched him leave with it. "Put it this way. You have any idea the economic potential here, the high rollers and A-list acts, the marriage trade, businesses like mine on the trickle-down end? Not to mention the symbol she represents to us rednecks."

"I'm getting there. I think."

"Take it from one who's in place. *Constance* is pot of gold spelled backward. You wait."

Already tired of the money end and thinking it was going to be a long haul to daylight, Shawn asked if Joe Don ever heard from Robin Vasquez and got back, "Hear me about *Constance, Shawn*. The kind of money that's up here now, you won't believe. And I don't mean old money, the stone-and-timber crowd. I mean the whizzes that saw what was coming and stuck it into real estate. Thing now is to buy lakeside, leave one wall and put up the dream house, with no argument from guys like me they're making rich." He tossed off the remaining shot. "They're the ones you want, ground-floor types looking for the next big thing. One-up on the old-lake crowd."

"So noted," Shawn said. "And the other side?"

"Fuck 'em. Let it smell like progress, they're ready to bleed. *They should all suck bottom. Right, Eddie?*"

Nod from the bartender at the raised voice. "Yes, sir, Mr. McCandless."

"Hear that? Eddie knows." Catching the meaning, then, as Shawn let it slide: "*Shit,* my big mouth. About sucking bottom, I didn't–"

"Forget it, none taken. You were telling me about Robin?"

The smile returned. "You really *don't* know, do you?"

"Know what?"

"All in time, my man." Pitching the shot glass to Eddie, who caught it one-handed as if it weren't the first time. "For now, steaks on Mac Hardware, meet the little woman. No arguments."

Joe Don led back too fast, Shawn easing up, not wanting to start off with a ticket. As he did, he became aware of a pair of lights slowing; nudge of the pedal, the lights kept pace. Slowing again, they did the same. Beers up, high enough from Joe-D, Shawn had to laugh – day two and already paranoid. Still, he kept an eye out before the restaurant appeared lakeside, Joe Don already squealing into the lot.

Shawn followed, watched the lights sweep past, tried to ID the car, which looked the way they all did now, Accord knock-offs.

Joe Don was grinning by the entrance, let the host escort them into a private dining room where a woman waited, a half-full champagne flute in front of her. Café-au-lait skin; gold bracelet, necklace and earrings aglow in the mini-spots; sleeveless top over flowing pants of the same color: lavender, Shawn guessed as dark eyes tried to see into him. Not exactly what he expected.

"Damn, Hon," Joe Don said too loudly. "It's just Shawn."

The woman extended a hand. "Hello Shawn," she said. "Welcome back."

From the corner of his eye, Shawn saw Joe-D looking as if he might bust a gut. "Good to see you, too, Robin," he finally said.

8

J OE DON GULPED SCOTCH. "Shawn's going to pull it out for us, aren't you, Speed. Robin's in real estate, she knows the score."

She eyed him. "Nobody likes a patronizer, Joe Don."

"Who, me?" A wink at Shawn. "Not when I'm right and you know it. Right, Shawn?"

He said nothing. Dinner had been a coaster ride of old times, glances, veiled references, Shawn attempting to steer the talk as Joe Don got louder and drunker. To looks from Robin, he'd kept at it: what it was like seeing Robin with his old pal, on and on. As to why he was here, Shawn repeated for Robin what he'd told Joe Don. At least it gave him a chance to look at her without feeling as if he had to break it off out of guilt.

Lord, she was beautiful, even more than he remembered: first taste of strawberries after years of failed crops. Blink and it was summer, he was back in her pickup, Robin having spotted him walking, her boyfriend Cort's younger brother. Offering a lift, she'd talked about skiing, who his challenger might be that year, her hand brushing his before finding it as if lost. In the room that used to be Cort's and now was his, they'd drunk sherry purchased with her fake ID, tasted the sweetness on each other, Shawn well past setting edges to slow it down. Cort, then, lost-in-thought distracted, bursting in to tell him some bit of news, Robin not moving to cover herself as Shawn had. Rather using the sight of herself to set in stone Shawn's lake-cold sense of betrayal. Cort's grin and fuck-it shrug his and his brother's epitaph to each other.

"Real estate," Shawn said now because it seemed called for.

Robin glanced at him. "Don't believe everything you hear."

"Tell him the name of your company."

"Our company. And I'm sure that Shawn—"

"Target," Joe Don put in, "as in target of opportunity. Want to try and guess the logo?"

"No idea," Shawn said. "A bull's-eye?"

"My man, Speed, in tune with the universe…"

"Joe Don never misses an opportunity to remind people the idea was his."

"Investment properties, but Robin's the one kicking butt. Regular nose for it, right Hon?"

"Funny, Joe Don. Keep it up."

"Congratulations," Shawn said to her.

"Thanks, but would you offer congratulations to a guy?"

"Why not?"

Joe Don winked. *Your action, pal, don't look at me.* "Boys room," he interrupted. "You two lovebirds keep it going till I get back?"

Shawn regarded his glass.

Robin said, "Joe Don, you are seriously pissing me off."

"*Moi?*" Winking again.

"Why didn't you say something?" she said, when he'd gone.

Shawn shrugged, saw Cort doing it and segued to a neck stretch. "Glad to see him, I suppose. I will if it keeps up."

"Two things, *amor: cuando puercos vuelen* and Joe Don McCandless is not big on subtleties. Or have you forgotten?"

"Not even if I could."

"You're also thinking you need him for what you're after, aren't you?"

Was he? "I doubt it's as grand as that."

"Sounds like you. Keeping your options open."

"You were never just an option, Robin, if that's what you meant."

"Which means what, Shawn? That I'm back in your plans?"

He turned the snifter in his hands. "Planning and I aren't often seen together. Tell me about Target."

"Not now, but a nice dodge."

"It's a specialty of mine – the going gets tough, the fast get going. Only I'm not fast anymore."

She looked at him. "That mean I could catch you if I wanted?"

"I'm no catch, Robin. Least of all yours."

"Then why do I feel as if I might have a shot?"

"Beats me. Gas pains?"

She smiled, went serious. "Joe Don doesn't mean it, you know. He tell you he was in the Army in '91? Burning oil and burning Arabs?"

"No. And I didn't know."

"How could you? He doesn't talk about it, at least not to me. But he has his moments."

Not quite sure why, he said, "I'm sorry."

Shrug. "For some reason, he still likes you. Doesn't mean he's not overcompensating tonight."

"There's a laugh, the way my life is now."

"And how is that?"

He sipped his brandy, its taste now only harsh. "Maybe I'll tell you sometime. Spoil another dinner."

"There's that word again – *maybe*. You know, for the longest time I hated you for leaving the way you did. Now I can see it was just you being you."

"And what would I have said, Robin? That meant anything to either of us."

"Poor Shawn, so puzzled by it all. You ever think it might be time to stop carrying your brother around?"

Welcome back, Shawn. So nice to see you, Shawn.

"Robin, if we don't stop this, there's going to be nothing left for Joe-D to come back to."

"Who says there is, anyway? Oops, overly direct me again."

"That part I do remember."

"Do you?" Searching his face the way she had before she'd kissed him the first time. "Then here's another: Be careful around him. You're showing up at a not-so-ideal time." She was deciding how much to add when Joe Don ambled in, drink in hand.

"Sorry to be so long, but the bar was packed." Reclaiming his chair. Then, with a closer look, "Damn, what'd you two say to each other? Talk about me..."

They'd seen Robin off in her Volvo wagon, were on the road back to Shawn's Cherokee, when Joe Don said, "You and the queen bee of the lake, *mano a mano*. You remember her at all?"

Shawn glanced over, caught the grin and the reference. "Catherine Mulvhill. Should I?"

"Try for once."

"There's a coffee place ahead. One for the road, on me."

"What for? Hell, I sweat that much booze." Holding his hand out steady to prove it. "Come on, think: *Catherine Mulvhill. Ski team.*"

Shawn put the two together, began to shake his head, stopped as it clicked: Holmes High, her family's name. The team before the big sponsors sought him out individually.

"Tell me you're kidding."

Joe Don whooped. "Woman likely bought your boots and not just them. She's still doing it, biggest donor up here, has been for decades." Headlights lit his face, slid off, left it in shadow. "And three guesses what else. Know who's working for her now – chief fuckhead or whatever?"

Still processing the ski-team connection, Shawn shook his head.

"That asshole builder we went two falls with, ran his pickup in the lake? Guy you got so wide-eyed about."

Muscles and vague tattoos, slick-backed hair: "You are joking…"

"Bad-boy Frank Love, I shit you not." The grin broke big. "Dude came into the store once and saw me, now he sends in his gardener. Welcome to the good times, huh?"

"More like a time warp."

"I can see where you'd say that." Road hum filled in for conversation, then Joe Don said, "She is something, isn't she? You ever in your wildest dreams picture Robin and me together?"

Shawn let the words form. "There's a lot I don't see coming, Joe-D. Or maybe you guessed."

"Bullshit. She talk about us at all?"

"Only that you were something yourself."

The grin twisted. "Pass on that one, Speed. Just don't go pushing your luck."

"If I run into some, you'll be the first to know."

Joe Don slowed, pulled into the Door and Hardware parking lot. Wanting only bed, his photo of Lizzy and Nate, whatever grounding he had left amid the coming storm, Shawn thanked him, adding, "Like we hadn't missed a beat."

"Yeah, well, now you're up here, don't be such a damn stranger."

"I won't." Knowing it wasn't true, old friendship no guarantor of new, but that he had to say something, white lies for all occasions.

He reached for the door. Joe Don stopped him with a hand, the McCandless neon sign bathing his face in red.

"New subject, bud. This thing with *Constance*? It's important to the business, important to me. Whatever needs doing, things you can't or won't do, I'm there. You get the drift?"

"I do, Joe-D. Thanks." Shawn reading Robin's *showing up at a not-so-ideal time* as financial, the man cash-strapped. So who in hell wasn't – him? There was one.

"Last tag," Joe Don said, the amiable bozo act now red flint. "Between us? Don't fuck it up."

9

FRIDAY MORNING SHAWN WAS RETURNING FROM BREAKFAST and a walk, the air blue crystal, the surface blue glass. From behind a boat a wet-suited skier waved back at him, even Shawn's knee getting with the program, that kind of feeling to the day.

Then Terry called.

"Hey," he led off. "How you doing up there?"

Shawn walked the cell phone around the cabin, hoping to lose the connection. No luck. "Getting my feet wet," he said.

"Salvation's in the full immersion, Speed. Where'd you end up staying, anyway, your old man's?"

"Sorry. Mine to know, yours to wonder."

There was a pause. "For now. Bob Lamont said you impressed him, said you seemed a straight-up guy. Of course, I let it ride."

Bingo on Lamont: Small or big, it got back to Terry.

Shawn played it that way, gave Terry details of what he already knew, concluding with, "Lamont has a thing planned for Saturday, a reception for me. I should know more from that, some of the players."

"Bob's involved, it'll be done right. You met Mal Kadich yet?"

Score one for Mal; he hadn't reported in.

"He took me out to the site," Shawn said. "Ran an image sounding for me."

"And…?"

"Strange how something you've only seen pictures of is right down there. I didn't think it would affect me that way, but it did."

"It's waiting for us. Don't forget that part."

"How could I possibly?"

"There's my spearhead. You have a crack at the old lady yet?"

"No, and for a reason," Shawn told him. "Heard about her, though."

"I'm sure of that."

"My point is, I don't want to force it, make her think she's the reason I'm here and get dug in."

The laugh was short and sharp. "I hate to be the one to break it, sport, but Catherine Mulvhill is most assuredly aware of you. If not at this second, damn sure the next."

Stonehouse, the Holmes mansion, Mal's binoculars: sun-mirrored windows staring back across light chop, the chill that had settled in him.

"You know that for a fact?"

"I know her M.O. Though hopefully not better than you will."

"I guess we'll find out."

"That we shall," he said. "Break a leg Saturday, or whatever you tell a hotshot skier."

"That would be acting, Terry."

"And few better at it than you. However, to help you remember, I want you to take a listen to something."

There was a pause, then Elizabeth and Nate, likely one of

those chip-recorders. Nate first: "I can't wait to come see you, Dad. Terry and Mom say we might go water skiing with you. Way cool. Late." Eleven going on twenty. Then Lizzy: "Dad, I miss you. I got a new tooth. Did we do something to make you mad? Did I do something?"

Shawn took seconds to unclench; at least they hadn't found out about Nate's e-mail and come down on him. He said, "Terry, you'd screw a nun out of her rosary beads, and God help her if there's gold in her teeth. Be glad you aren't here right now."

"Shawn, I am shocked, shocked at your language." Laughter followed by ice:

"You think I'm a bastard now, try crossing me."

Shawn left at nine forty-five to see Sheldon Spring, the newspaper editor he'd called about an interview. Not far out he again had the impression he'd picked up a tail, this time at the wye. But the car went past as he turned into the sheriff's entry before making a loop back. He set aside the feeling and focused in, explained his mission to the editor in broad terms; what *Constance* back would do for the lake, the pride, the history and revenue that entities from private to municipal, up to state levels, would share.

It went well enough, old skills coming back. Still, a good portion was spent rehashing his ski career, particularly its ending. His anticipation of the questions made him no more comfortable, either. Human interest, Sheldon Spring asserted, putting a face on it, promising the paper would try to provide a photographer for Saturday's event. "Tell me something," he asked Shawn at the door. "Off the record, if you like."

"Depends on what it is," Shawn answered.

"What do you get out of this? Personally, I mean."

Damned if he did, damned if he didn't. "Money-wise, a piece down the line if it goes well."

"And if it doesn't?"

"Because it deserves to, Mr. Spring, it will."

"Sheldon. Money-wise, you said. There something other than money at stake here?"

Shawn smiled to buy time. Side note: *Sharpen the act, more of same lining up for a run at him.* "Be there Saturday," he said.

Second-guessing himself along those lines but calculating the damage at nil, Shawn dropped in on Suzanne Padget, requested that she send flowers along with a note: *Overdue thanks to someone who helped a kid go faster and farther than he dreamed possible.* Signing it, *Shawn "not so fast anymore" Rainey. P.S. May I thank you in person?*

"And you're sending these to whom?" Suzanne Padget asked as if she hadn't heard him the first time. Incredulous.

"You're thinking red flag to a bull?"

"It occurred to me. But I'm sure you know what you're doing."

"There's always a first. If you can, make it wildflowers."

He was heading east to see Mal, further cultivate a potential ally, when he noticed another car tailing him, this time no doubt about the kind. Spotting gravel, he swung off to allow room for the Crown Vic, which sat behind him as the dust rolled through. The occupant got out, read Shawn's plate number into his radio, adjusted his Sam Browne, and stepped around to the passenger side.

Apart from the facial lines and thinning hair, Arn Tennell looked as ascetic as the time he'd stopped Shawn and crew up by Carnelian and held them overnight. That hands-on-the-wheel-or-your-ass-is-mine look.

"Last thing I expected to see up here," he said. "Even though the guy at the liquor store swore it was you."

"Good to see you, too. How you doing, Arn?"

"Small town, I suppose it was just a matter of time."

"You make sheriff yet?

"Next in line, if it's any of your business."

"Nice to hear persistence pays."

Arn hooked his thumbs in the belt. "Amazing your old man didn't run you off, save me the trouble."

"Hasn't gotten to it yet."

"Smart guy, always the mouth. Want to hand me your driver's license and get out of the car, hands on the roof?"

"Arn, I know you don't like me, but is this really necessary?"

The cop broke a smile on life support. "Not going to have trouble with you, am I? Because I have to say I'd welcome it."

Big surprise crossed Shawn's mind. Reaching into his wallet, he handed Arn his New Mexico license, got out and put his hands on the roof, passing drivers on North Lake craning for a look. A breeze had sprung up and was sending clouds in from the hot Reno side, waves against the rocks below them, Shawn thinking thunderstorm if it held.

Arn looked up from Shawn's license. "New Mexico, huh? Nice there…far away. When you going back?"

"As soon as possible."

"Sorry, wrong answer. Right answer is today. You want to come around and get this, please?" Holding out the license.

It wasn't until just before it happened, after he was out of sight of the road, that Shawn realized his mistake. By then he was hands-and-knees down, sorting through fire for air that wouldn't come.

Squatting beside him, Arn said, "You should be more careful, take care of that knee, or what's left of it. While you're at it, give thought to people who recall how you killed your brother and got away with it. All so your mom could drink herself to death."

"Due respect, Arn? Get fucked."

The smile again. "You know, sir, I believe I see the problem now. Indeed, I do."

Anticipating the kick to his head, Shawn deflected it with a rolling forearm and, before Arn had his baton out, managed to scramble around to his feet within view of the traffic. Arn stood frozen. At length he sheathed the baton, got back into his car, rolled down his window, and leaned out.

"Here's the deal, shitbird," he said. "A kid I thought of as a brother died at your hands. I take that personally. Clear enough for you?"

Shawn nodded. "As can be."

"Then I'll see you around. Count on it."

10

SHAWN LAY GAZING UP AT THE CEILING. Outside in the dark, the hiss of cars defined the drizzle that had begun about the time he'd limped in, that was now rain against the cabin.

Something heavy struck a pothole, dopplered in volume before fading past, and Shawn heard again the thump of waves against a sailboat hull, the creak of the boom coming around, whump of air as the mainsail snapped taut:

The fuck you think you are to tell me anything?

Echoes: *Anything...anything...*

Then:

You're nothing but a thief yourself.

Yourself...yourself...

Wheels turned off through a puddle, the splash bringing to mind another object striking water:

Let go, Shawn...

Let go...let go...

Light from the store just down had become a noir slash, his

room revealing only shapes: corner chair and floor lamp, bureau and wood-frame mirror, glow coming from the window beside the commode-half he could see. He took a deep breath, felt it where Arn had suckered him, Arn proficient enough to know how much force to land. Fortunately he'd taken the drop on his good knee. Still, he hurt and had reduced the day to checking messages: requests for appearances and a phone interview. That had led to a reheated burrito and a store pint, *Constance* files until he could no longer concentrate, early lights-out.

Shawn capped the brandy, set it aside. The slash above him defocused into 1983 newspaper headlines; he fixed on them and saw:

LOCAL MAN LOST. LAKE SEARCH UNSUCCESSFUL

BROTHER SHAWN QUESTIONED: TENSIONS ALLEGED

DA: NO CHARGES. SHAWN, FAMILY IN SECLUSION

MOURNERS PACK SERVICE. SHAWN: LOOKED UP TO CORT

Then:

SHADOWED SHAWN DEDICATES OLYMPIC BID TO BROTHER

Finally:

DISASTER: RAINEY HURT IN BRUTAL WIPEOUT. BID ENDS

He killed the slash with lamplight, put on a jacket, and went outside. Rain spun in the lights. Farther along the air was a damp cloth. Headlights glared, passed, ran with house floods, bled off the pavement and the lake. Over the Nevada-side mountains, lightning flashed. Moments later, thunder answered.

Shawn crossed a dark fringe of rocks to the lake. The water felt cold as he ran it back and forth through his fingers. Cold as the snow and ice that had produced it. Cold as an October lake squall.

Let go, Shawn.

Let GO...

Shawn left his hand in until it was almost numb. Then he picked up a rock and chucked it as far as he could into the goddamned rain and the goddamned lake and the goddamned night.

11

J OE DON AND ROBIN WERE THE FIRST FACES SHAWN SAW AFTER parking in the upper lot, Robin looking less like a mother of two than a runway model. She was in a blue strapless something, white-lace shawl, high heels. Joe Don wore a Sears-looking light-gray suit, white shirt, clip-on tie: the rhino at a gazelle reception. The evening felt scrubbed after the rain: clean scent of the cedar and pine the hotel was built around, lake behaving for the boaters still out, benign white clouds turning pink.

"What?" Shawn said to them. "You don't have anything better lined up?"

Robin flashed a smile; Joe Don said, "North Shore Chamber, Dude. Me and Neville Autry and Neal the dickhead, remember them? We're like *that,* you believe it?" From his breath, several up already.

"Shawn and everyone else now," Robin said.

"Whatever floats," Shawn said.

"I can think of other things that float."

"I'm sure you can, Joe Don," Robin said. "Ice, for instance."

His smile was all sweetness. "Pardon my ignorance. Was that, like, a putdown?"

"Must we start so early?"

"I keep telling you. Early gets it done."

"I'll remember that trying to get you up tomorrow."

They crossed a drive, started toward the Marcourt's patio entrance: clumps of balloons and a pedestal sign, the mid and lower lots filling with Lincolns, M-Classes, Yukons, Beemer SUVs. Joe Don said, "Might see Tam Engleman tonight. Sonny Hardin if he can get the old lady to stay home."

"I figured they'd be long gone by now," Shawn answered.

"Were and came back like some other prodigal we know – right, Hon?" Draping her in a gray arm, Robin twisting from him. "Don't see them much. Tam's consulting on something, don't ask me what."

"Water quality," Robin finished for him.

"Right, like there's a shortage. Sonny owns a motel up Incline, comes in once in a while to buy toilet parts. That long hair of his? Fell out from worry – four kids. Guy could pass as a doorknob."

Shawn grinned at the description. Pony-tailed Sonny had been the most panicked getting stopped by Arn that night, actually eating the roach they had going around with the beers, upchucking it on the holding-tank floor. Two guys stuck in with them scrambled for it in the urk, one putting it into a pocket before squaring off at the other, at Shawn and company, at the cage itself.

"What about Jake?" Shawn asked him when it faded.

Joe Don went sober. "Didn't make it back. Ragheads, man, don't get me started."

Blackness so akin to last night's he could taste it rolled through Shawn. He saw Jake vapor-trailing him down Siberia, losing ground but determined to catch up. Jake's smile, his way of cracking jokes that no one else got; that, or the timing so off it hardly mattered.

He joined the line of attendees, some recognizing him from his Olympic trials photo on the sign, then they were on the already-crowded patio, white-gloved waiters bearing trays of wine glasses and hors d'oeuvres. Easels displayed glue-lam enlargements of *Constance* around the lake, heyday shots to race the pulse. Outdoor heaters glowed, a combo played renditions of pop favorites; mini lights twinkled in the younger plantings, the vine maples and red dogwood. Across and on a raised section, Shawn spotted a bar and what he hoped was a familiar face, though it was bent to her work.

"You believe this?" Bob Lamont said at his elbow. "Tell me you haven't still got what they want."

"And that would be...?"

"To be around a winner. Tell me you can't feel it."

Bob, do yourself a favor and don't say anything more, because if you do...

"Glad you're pleased, Bob."

"Pleased, my butt. Got you down for a few remarks, okay? For now, I got some people I want you to meet."

"Here for you, Bob."

Forty minutes later, he'd met and swapped optimisms with 1) the head of the Casino Employees Association, 2) his ash-blonde opposite, a tilt to her head as if receiving signals from Las Vegas, 3) Chamber heads Neville Autry and son Neal reminiscing about their Scout days, Shawn's skiing records: *Anything we can do,* 4) Food and Beverage Association heads: *Way to go, counting on you,* 5) Lodging Association reps, women in gabardine who talked in staccato bursts, 6) PR types fairly jumping out of their slip-ons with ideas: *Holler when you'd like a presentation,* 7) home-owner reps pumped with their authority, 8) sockless entrepreneurs with boating tans and yacht-club polos, diamond watches and hungry eyes, 9) open-faced women in *Voyage 2006* T-shirts, *Constance* steaming dead-on from their chests.

Eager guests approached with glossies for signature – him shooting out of a starting gate – Shawn wondering about their lives. And *himself*? No mystery there. See Terry Dahl say jump, see Shawn Rainey ask how high. Dipping into his blazer pocket, he squeezed the dash photo of Elizabeth and Nate he'd remembered to detach. Before a woman in a sari could reach him, he'd reached the bar.

"Hey, there…"

"Mr. Downhill," the bartender said, straightening up. "Or should I say, Mr. In-Demand."

"Shawn works, and I once knew a hill named KT."

"Sounds like the start of a limerick."

"If I were that clever. You any relation?"

She smiled. "Doubt it, mine's more Katie than K.T. Kristen Tamara, last name Ware. And aren't you glad you asked."

"*Ware…*as in *be*ware?"

"All depends." She refilled a man's wineglass and, as the man moved off, said, "Should you be wasting your time on the help?"

"I'm applying for a job. Any openings back there?"

"And leave your public?"

"Me they can do without. It's you they can't."

She brushed back a wisp. "Now wouldn't a certain employer love that?" Nodding toward the pole microphone where Bob Lamont was calling for attention.

His intro went on for what seemed like eternity: National

Downhill champ two years running; giant-slalom runner-up one of those years, fourth the next, eight hundredths separating first from fourth; seconds from winning the '84 Olympic trials in record time – Shawn thinking another galaxy, another him. Endorsements, commentary when he wasn't competing, kids around the lake and the country pretending to be him.

When he finally stepped up, a photographer he assumed was from the paper aiming and flashing, he opened with, "Anybody know who Bob's talking about?" Unassuming and unrehearsed. "Lot of faces out there – old friends, new friends from tonight. I'm no speaker, but I'll tell you this – being back is way beyond what I expected."

"For God's sake, don't ask him what he means or we'll be here all night." Joe Don to laughs.

Shawn waited, smiling, then, "Lucky for me I'm not here to reminisce. Rather, to see if we can take hold of the future, so the kids of the kids of the kids can experience what the generations who did held in their hearts. That is, to sail on Tahoe's first and true queen."

Loud applause.

"*What I mean to say is join us.* If we can dream it, we can make it happen. But only with your help."

Sustained applause, more flashes, people making way for a slim woman in a denim dress, her waist-jacket embroidered with wildflowers. Even as he spoke, Shawn kept thinking that if it *was* her, was Catherine Mulvhill, then *Thank you for small favors.* Assuming she'd gotten the flowers.

Light shone on her silver beads and earrings, lodgepole posture leading to short gray hair, bright probing eyes. Eyes that already, it seemed to him, were past his blazer and shirt and counting his vertebrae. He could see Robin and Joe Don, Joe-D's eyes rolling in the woman's direction, a boxing fan anticipating the blood for which he'd paid. Shawn said, "To those who question the honor and respect we intend for *Constance,* I will tell you now, I was one of you."

Finished with his vertebrae, the eyes were inventorying his ribs as a player might scale a xylophone.

"That is, until I looked into a cause that deserves it. So that tonight I can in good conscience—" squeezing the metal dash frame until he felt it crack "—ask your help in doing what we propose to do well and right."

The cheers hardly overwhelmed her, Shawn guessing her off smile said more about her than anyone could have told him. *Not a bad hand,* it said, *but oh my, can this be trump in mine?*

He disengaged, let his eyes travel the faces. "There is a table here to make that happen, fact sheets for those of you on the fence. And contact your elected officials – it works. Meantime, thanks for putting up, I hope in more ways than one."

Crescendo, Shawn scanning to see the people he'd met nodding, Lamont with thumbs up, the combo hitting an up-tempo rendition of the Olympic anthem. Hand extended, smiling, Shawn stepped down to her.

The hand that accepted his was firm and dry and slightly calloused. It was not an indoor hand, and she withdrew it, he noticed, before the photographer could react. He said, "It has to be who I think it is. Catherine Mulvhill?"

"Last time I checked. And it looks as if the night is yours, Mr. Rainey." Calm, even, live-it-while-you-can, followed by, "See? Already I feel as if I know you."

Read own, or was it just him? "That would be my pleasure."

"You're better than I was hoping, but I'm not here to start anything, just see what I'm up against."

"Thank you. I think."

"You're welcome. And the person I gave the flowers to seemed pleased."

A group had formed, Shawn envisioning them ready to raise their programs should blood end the round. "And the message with them?"

"That I kept. Not that you should attach meaning to it. I didn't."

He eyed the crowd: no sign of Joe Don, Robin hanging back a row, others he'd met having faded to the donation table. Side note re them: *Practice name-memory drills, get in the game.* He said, "If I may, what would you say to a quiet word. Just Shawn Rainey and Catherine Mulvhill?"

"It's Mrs. Mulvhill to my thorns, as you seem intent on becoming. And no, I don't believe your words will alter anything."

"If I just listened?"

It surprised her, but only momentarily. "I suppose that's only fair – on the grounds that hope is where you find it. Let me tell Frank."

"Frank Love that would be?" An exploratory jab to let her know he'd done his footwork.

"That's right, Frank mentioned that he knew you – one summer, I believe. Ten minutes? By the lake?"

As she was taken by the crowd, Shawn wondered if that meant in ten minutes time or that which she'd allotted him.

Shawn leaned on the rail lining steps to a crescent of beach: stones mostly, boulders and trees to either side. Party sounds came from up the slope. Tahoe's length spread south; angled across from him, Rubicon Point, Shawn thinking not just Cort's

Rubicon, but his own. To the west, the sun had left apricot clouds to flare as crimson.

He heard her steps behind him, her voice.

"Tell me, Mr. Rainey, have you traveled much?"

"Some," he said as she joined him. "Not a lot."

"I have. This place is like no other."

"So it is." Small waves marched in. "Did you really come here to see what you were up against?"

She smiled. "How does the saying go? 'Your friends close, your enemies closer.'"

"Mrs. Mulvhill, I am not the enemy. You may think I am, but I'm not."

"Your hand," she said, looking closer, "it's bleeding."

He found and held a handkerchief to it. "Caught it on a sharp edge."

She pulled out a pack of cigarillos and offered him one, lit them with a worn silver lighter, let her smoke curl around her. "Mr. Rainey, most people tonight are simply myopics driven by self-interest. That I understand: avarice I can outlogic or out-spend. Then there's you. With a couple of exceptions, you're a blank since you abandoned us. Which has me curious, depending on how far you're prepared to take this."

"In other words, the key to my heart."

She shifted to face him. "Let us say you are for real, in part because you're seen as one of *them*. I am not one of *them*. I am, however, this lake's moral compass, a status bought and paid for in whatever arena you wish to name. Environment, education, sponsorships, planning..."

Pausing for reaction. When none came, she resumed.

"I am neither a tree hugger nor racked by guilt at what my

family did before they turned from logging. I am not someone you can exploit as out of touch. I touch schools and libraries and fire departments, law enforcement agencies, charities. Coming up on eighty I don't care what people think, not that I ever much did. Nor do I care how my words are perceived. I give money away and still I'm in the neighborhood of a half-billion dollars. Most important, I will not allow *Constance* to become less than legend. Do you understand that?"

Shawn nodded. "I do now."

"Then this will be the last conversation required on the subject."

"It's possible."

She exhaled. "It's also possible that you're patronizing me, a course of action I would hardly recommend."

"Not at all." Wondering how he'd come to be smoking a cigarillo. "I just wanted to see what I was up against."

"And?"

"Everything they said and more."

"Except dissuading, I take it."

"I didn't say that."

"No games, please," she said. "Not dissuading based on what?"

Shawn considered his answer, no point in being oblique. "*Them,* as you put it. Or if not them specifically, anyone excited at the possibility of her. All the old photos in all the businesses and all the homes, the dream within reach. Can you not see that?"

She angled smoke to the side. "Mr. Rainey, children get excited by rabbits at Easter. A week later, they're on to something equally frivolous while the creatures wind up neglected and pathetic. I will not, on my life, permit that."

"Wonderfully wrought," he said. And to her look, "Believe me, I know. I dealt in PR for years."

And now? No mirrors for you tonight.

"Interesting admission, Mr. Rainey, but one of which I'm aware."

The car shadowing him suddenly became more real. "What you're saying is, it takes one to know one. With all due–"

"Respect, I know." Waving it off. "You also seem too smart for all this. Then again there's that slut, hope."

He let it pass.

In a bit, she said, "So unnecessary. Such a waste of time."

"Then end it," he said. "If you can't give it your blessing, at least let it go forward. Good people are involved."

"People like you, that would mean."

"Try me. Expect something of me."

"It may come as a shock, Mr. Rainey," she said, wetting her fingers and extinguishing the live end of the cigarillo before returning it to the pack. "But I already do."

It began a lull that held until they started back. Walking the path, he said, "Not to change the subject, but I meant what I said in the note. About being grateful."

"That's disarming, but I was at Big Mountain the year you won the Nationals. From what I saw, you found a way on your own."

One of the nicer things said about him – recently for certain. He was mulling it when the railing above them split like a shot and a man – salt-and-pepper crew cut, black leather coat – tumbled backward down the slope to shouts.

Shawn had time to see Joe Don McCandless in the gap, rubbing his right hand, then the man slid heavily to a stop. White-faced and bleeding, he was older than that shake-hauling summer and heavier, but any doubt about who it was vanished when Shawn helped Frank Love to his feet and the flash went off in his and Catherine Mulvhill's face.

12

SHAWN SIPPED COFFEE-SHOP COFFEE, between sips looking over at Joe Don and Robin doing the same, Joe Don's little finger in a cast anchored at the wrist the med-center people had put on.

"Don't give me that look," Joe Don said to him. "You'd have done the same thing."

"Maybe if he'd had as much to drink," Robin put in.

"Frank Love is horseshit, always has been." Clip tie gone, coat jacket showing a tear at the shoulder seam. "He also swung first."

"The way you baited him, who wouldn't?"

"Damnit, Robin. He had it coming."

"And you surely gave it to him."

"Fuck me. Whose side are you on?"

"Sanity? Civility? Or is that too much to ask?"

Joe Don broke out a grin. "Pretty nice crossover, though. Right, Shawn?"

Shawn was about to say he was looking forward to reading

about it in the newspaper, particularly to the photo work, when Robin said, "And so useful in your play for support."

"Put a sock in it, Robin."

"You going to belt *me* now?"

Shawn glanced up; people were looking over their booths. "Am I wrong or was the idea to cool down, not torch the place?"

"Well fuck you, too," Robin said, getting to her feet. "You can drive him home and put him to bed."

"Yeah?" Joe Don shouted after her. "Who do you figure paid for that bed and that house – you?"

"Every day for ten years and still paying."

The whole room was watching now, the night manager beginning to slide their way, a worried look on his face. Shawn waved him off, threw in apologetic, grabbed Joe Don's forearm as Joe Don was rising to spill the heat with Robin into the parking lot.

"Goddamnit, Joe Don, no more."

"Okay, okay, I'm cool – life in the fast lane." Pulling free his arm with a glare at the faces that said, *The fuck you looking at?*

The faces turned away, though the night manager continued with glances. "What?" Joe Don said, sitting down to face Shawn. "I'm supposed to just roll over and take it?"

"How about enough damage for one night?"

"Pisses me off, what can I tell you?"

"In case that was left unclear."

Joe Don drew breath, broke a grin. "That bad, huh?"

"Ever think it might be time to ease up on the firewater?"

"Back two days and already in my liquor cabinet. Sure, why not?"

"Good." Flashing on *himself,* the little booze he'd put away since Catherine Mulvhill, the frame-cut on his hand, again on her line, *Interesting admission, but one of which I'm aware.*

"Can we talk about something else?"

"I don't know why you'd want that."

"She knew things, Joe-D. I think she has a tail on me, somebody to cover and dig up. Which means she could have somebody on you as well."

Joe Don rubbed a spot above the cast. "Sucker's starting to smart. You want a pain pill?"

"No." Watching him palm one from his prescription bottle and wash it down. "Are you hearing me?"

"Yeah. But if it's that dipshit Love, we got nothing to worry about."

"You're lucky he didn't press charges."

"How many times…the guy swung first."

"Bottom line is who he has in his corner. But even without her, guys like that don't let it slide. I just think it would be prudent to–"

"What, cover my back?" Joe Don stretched, smiled. "Old Speed, worried about his homie. All of which tells me one thing."

"You going to let me in on it?"

Joe Don fished out a twenty, slid it under his cup. "Yeah. *Sometimes Love don't feel like it should.*"

Despite himself, the Mellencamp lyric and song, the recurring image of the Queen Bee as she steadied Frank Love up the steps, saying, "If this is how smart you are, save us all the trouble," Shawn had to laugh. Which started Joe Don, the two of them laughing all the way up to Joe Don's hillside split-level. They were still laughing as Joe Don got out in front of his darkened house and went inside.

Shawn was getting ready for bed when his cell phone rang.

"Rainey."

"Bob Lamont, sorry to ring so late. Thought you'd like to know that despite the disruption–"

"Bob, I talked to him. He's more than willing to pay the damages. He's just happy no charges were–"

"Slow down, you ready for this? We collected one-point-five *mil* tonight, with pledges for twice that. Highest per capita yet. Not even close."

And when did that happen? With luck it was when the crowd saw him take on Catherine Mulvhill – no VIPs, no lawyers, no committees – and come out whole. The perception that after everything they weren't stalled but might actually be rolling.

"Did you hear what I said?" Lamont asked again.

"I assume you're pleased."

"Pleased, hell. Those people I introduced you to? Every one wants you to come talk to their membership, shake the tree at leaf level. You seeing how this works?"

More than you know, Bob. "Tell me, how much do you know about Catherine Mulvhill? Her real interest in this?"

"No gloating, huh? Boiled down, not much more than what I've heard and read. That a problem?"

"After talking with her, yeah."

"Aside from misguided and contrary, she's well-regarded and reeks of old money. What'd she say that spooked you?"

"Anytime someone determined to hand you your head knows more about you than you do about her, what's that tell you?"

"I'll see what I can do," Lamont said. "Meantime, nice work tonight. You got us off the dime."

"If it's all the same, I'll wait for the paper."

He'd only just hung up when the phone rang again. He was contemplating throwing it out the window, figured it as something

Joe Don would do, instead picked it up to shut it up.

"Yeah."

"Haven't lost your touch, have you?" Terry Dahl said. "And am I the smartest fuck around, or what?"

"It's been a long day, Terry. What do you want?"

"We scored and you did good. That said, this friend of yours who had the dustup with the Mulvhill woman's man – he close enough for you to tell him to fuck off?"

Meaning Lamont had called Terry before he called him: further confirmation. "My friend agrees he was out of line and will settle up. He regrets the incident."

"Butt him out, Shawn, we don't need the headache. What worked tonight was the spontaneity and a house of hand-picked supporters. But there is no future there. Repeat—"

"Point made, Terry. I'm aware of it."

"That so? You also aware that we're talking eight and eleven years old here?"

He rubbed his temples. "Try every second."

"Eyes on the prize, Shawn, no impediments. You need to see things like that coming."

"The way I saw you coming – like that?"

"Speaking of which, how are you and Suzanne Padget getting on? She something else or what?"

Jury still out on the woman. "So far."

"She's also divorced and got a whopping settlement, including the house. Take her to lunch, buy her a Stoly, and see what happens. Better yet, buy her two."

"Loren help you with the hire?"

"Bob Lamont, actually, and the Stolys were his suggestion, so don't go getting ideas. She's there because she knows absolutely everyone. Anything else to report?"

"Yeah, I'm going to bed."

"Say again?"

"You want top-of-the-head, I was thinking it might be good to open up a dive to the public. Have a day with exhibits and media coverage. Strike a spark."

There was a pause. "Not bad. Clear it with Mal, but I agree in principle."

"Principle, Terry?"

He ignored it. "Suzanne can help there. Hey, I almost forgot. We're coming up tomorrow, all of us. That is, if you're up to it."

Shawn fought the feelings, experienced enough to know that nothing with Terry was ever a done deal, or if it was, it was done *to* you. "Where?" he said.

"That's right, your big secret. Okay, you tell *me* where. Someplace without a fern pool."

Shawn considered, finally seeing no reason the meeting shouldn't be close. "Sunnyside, the deck," he said. "You know it?"

"Back of my hand. Friend has his Formula tied up there, goes like a bat. Two o'clock? Oh, and Shawn – our deal, remember? Make a scene, try anything, it's over. Bye-bye Nate and Liz."

Shawn bit down, then said, "Terry, you know what? I don't think you could surprise me if you tried."

13

SUNDAY MORNING, SHAWN WALKED THE BIKE PATH, little left of the knee pain he'd brought with him. The day was clear, no traffic to speak of on 89; forest, shoreline, peaks, and canyons etched in sharp detail; Eagle Rock's 250-foot volcanic crag rising up. Too early yet for the boaters who later would buzz the bays, their skiers in tow.

He had breakfast across the road, drove through Lakewood to his old house, found no one home. Reviewing places his father might be, he settled on the Catholic church, where he spotted the pickup, waited there to meet Liam Rainey after eight o'clock mass.

"Morning, Pop," he said as Liam spotted him. "Thought I might catch you here."

"Safe enough bet."

Flashes: First Communion, Confirmation, altar boy, his mother with a kerchief over her head. Baptism, of course, the thought occurring that it must have been with lake water, the irony of that. He took off his windbreaker, draped it on the side of the truck bed.

"You look like somebody walked on your grave," his father said. "You feeling all right?"

The old man all the way: tight as a brush-back. "Not sleeping too well," Shawn answered.

"Been up to see your mother like we discussed?"

He nodded. "Beautiful spot."

"Had to pick it out for her." Tossing his old Rainey's Repair and Service jacket in through the pickup's open window. "We'd hoped to find the time when we were young, but we never did. At the end, she was in no shape. Mine's the plot next to hers."

"I saw it."

"Something you should think about. Not leave it till you can't and they just stick you anywhere."

Shawn toed the parking stripe between them. "I was wondering if you wanted to go for coffee, maybe a walk?"

"Thanks. Things to do."

"Pop, it's Sunday."

Liam Rainey cracked a knuckle. "Plus the Giants play in Philly, so the game's on early."

Shawn glanced at the cars leaving, new ones arriving, people getting out and heading toward the church. "Okay. Another time."

"Something on your mind?"

"Not really," he lied, noticing how easily it came, a snowball rolling down hill. In the light, Shawn could see white stubble where his father hadn't shaved, lines in his face making him look older than at the house.

"You eat before you came?"

"Wasn't hungry. Still not."

Shawn checked his watch.

"Game doesn't start for an hour," his father added, lowering the tailgate. "Sit."

Shawn did. "Truck's still running, I see."

"Once a mechanic, always a mechanic. The way it goes."

A car pulled in, the occupants nodding to Liam, curious looks at Shawn before turning for the path. His father waited until they were out of earshot, then, "Look, I'm abrupt, I know, comes from living alone. Or maybe I've always been. How about coffee back at the house, catch some of the game together."

The house. "Next time," Shawn said. "But thanks."

"Way I see it, we got here and now and not a lot else. As to whose fault that is..."

"I know, Pop. It's good seeing you."

"Is it the Mulvhill woman?"

Pause to recover. "You know much about her?"

"Live in a place this long, you know a little about a lot, none of it worth much." He bent to pluck a stem of grass, chew the end. "Thought you could charm her, is that it?"

Having learned what charm he *did* possess from the master, Shawn almost laughed: Blue-eyed, black-Irish Cort Rainey could charm lake trout from mud puddles, women from their church pews. In fact, he had no idea how he, Shawn – younger, fairer, shorter than his brother – had wound up with Robin Vasquez, hot as she'd been.

"It seemed a place to start," he said

His father made a sucking noise with his teeth. "Good luck there. But she's not the only one has a problem with raising *Constance.*"

He glanced at his father, Liam not glancing back. "That mean you're against it, too?"

"Live a while you find, more often than not, things are best left be."

"Pop, it's been researched. It is possible."

"Possible doesn't make it good or even right. You think you can feel what she's feeling?"

Shawn saw his kids and pushed off the truck, reached for his windbreaker.

Watching him, his father said, "Always was your way, to run off when it got tight. Why you liked skiing so much, we used to think."

"All the times you thought about it, you mean."

"Always had a mouth on you, too."

He blew a breath. "Look, I'm taking up your day. I'll call you."

"Son, two things. Everyone has a past, and say it now or wish you had."

"All right." *In for a penny, in for a pound,* the line he'd crossed already distant. "When she died…Mom. Did she…"

"What," his father said, "still blame you for Cort?" A soldier pondering the next step in a minefield. "I suppose that would be the obvious. Down deep I don't think she did. Look, I'm not sure what you mean…"

Up to here with wordplay, the dancing and dodging and inferring, he plain *said* it: "Think I killed her favorite son because I was jealous of him." *Yours, too, old man, it's in your face every time I look at it.*

"Shawn, for all I know, your mother blamed herself, that's why she drank. Or maybe she blamed me. All I know is, she had to put it somewhere."

Shawn looked out across the sweep of lake to where wind had raised a chop and *felt* it. "You know, Pop, I've never flat-out asked you what you thought about it. Well, now I'm asking."

"My Lord, kids your age are like a dog with a bone. You give any thought to what you might do with an answer?"

Try sixteen years. "I suppose."

"That's all you're going to say? I don't know what you're looking for that I can give you, only that it's years back when we were different people. And that's it. Shy of asking the dead, which we'll all be doing soon enough."

Shawn gathered up his windbreaker. "Well, thanks, Pop."

"Son, she loved you, God's truth. It's just that Cort left her without as much to give, who knows why? All I know is, it's beyond me."

He was about to scream, *What about you? You have any idea what it was like on the short end?* but realized his father had answered him. Love and its parcel went back to *his* father and mother, back to theirs, to Cain and Abel and Adam and Eve, so he just said, "Better get going, Pop, thanks for the time. I'll be in touch."

"Shawn?" Carefully closing the tailgate. "Don't go in the lake with that around your neck. One son's enough."

Shawn was nursing a beer, Sunnyside's deck crowded with day-trippers escaping the heat, when the four of them emerged and stood looking for him: Elizabeth and Nate, Loren and Terry. Elizabeth was now so pretty it nearly broke his heart, the hours and minutes that had brought her to it without him, while Nate still had enough little-boy charm to overwhelm the hands-in-pockets cool when he spotted Shawn's wave.

"*Dad...*" Both barreling into him, sunshine bouncing into his dark corners, driving to ground the sapping talk with his father. Pressing their faces to his, pulling back to take him in as he did them: sun-smell and freckles and peeling noses and new teeth and pure-them expressions that all the spin and filters in the world couldn't diminish.

By now all else had faded: others turning at the shout, servers bringing pitchers of beer to the tables under the umbrellas, boats leaving and returning to the marina; Loren, elegant in navy pants, white sandals, and cream top; Terry in a V-neck pullover that exposed the chain at his throat, sleeves shoved up to expose his gold Rolex.

"*Dad, you should see the batting cage Terry got me. It's got a pitching machine and everything. And Elizabeth got a stereo and–*"

"I can tell it," she rushed. "You should hear it play the CDs he got *me*."

Shawn bit down hard and said, "I hope you kids thanked him."

"I did." Nate.

"Me, too." Elizabeth.

"Hey, easy on your old man," Terry said pulling out a chair for Loren and taking one himself. "He has to last awhile."

As the kids ignored him, so did Shawn.

"Hello, Loren," he said to her.

"Hello, Shawn. You're looking well."

"Some kind of day here," Terry said to no one.

"Good trip up?" Elizabeth touching his lips as he spoke, his nipping at her finger bringing a giggle.

"Fog leaving the City, couldn't see the water from the bridge," Terry went on; then to Loren, "You get us some chardonnay, Hon? Shawn, whatever he's drinking?"

Loren nodded. Terry regarded him.

"So what'd you think of the eight-by-tens? Heard you signed a ton at the reception."

"All I can say is you must have gotten a good rate."

"Damn straight and more on the way. *Constance* facts on the back, this time, with frequently asked questions."

"Damn straight," Nate echoed.

Shawn waited for Loren to say something; when she didn't, he said, "Language, please."

"Aw, Dad. No big."

"Around me, it is."

"Anyway," Terry said, "Suzanne should have the rest by now."

"Hard to think I had to wait."

Terry smiled, sat up as Nate was starting to tell Shawn about a game in which he got three hits, Elizabeth with color commentary. "Nate, my man," he interrupted. "You ready to check out the boat?"

"Terry, he just sat down," Loren said.

"Hon, if we don't get on it, we'll be here all afternoon instead of out there."

Nate looked at Shawn: *What do I do?*

"Go ahead," he said, "You, too, if you want, Lizzy."

She bent to his ear and whispered, "*Elizabeth*, Dad, remember? Lizzy's a baby name. I'm almost nine."

"Sorry, I forgot." Whispering back. "And it's okay if you want to go with your brother."

"Thanks." Still in the whisper. "But don't leave, okay? I want to tell you about my Irish dancing and my swimming medal."

"It's a date. *Elizabeth*."

The giggle again, followed by a kiss, then she was heading after Nate to the dock. Terry was up and following when he turned and said, "Nate's coach says he'll bat cleanup if he keeps at it and Lizzy's the envy of her friends. In case you think I'm trying to buy them, Shawn."

"How could I, Terry, when you already bought me?"

"No need for your thanks." Grinning.

Goddamnit, Shawn thought when Terry was out of sight: bait taken, suckerfish landed and flopping in the well, Loren eyeing him and saying "That was uncalled for with Terry. And for your information, I do not appreciate your not letting me know of Nathan's e-mailing you. I told him the position he was putting us in. All of us, Shawn."

Sent Mail: She'd had to have known. Damn.

"Long way to make a point," he said.

"Is that why you think we're here?"

"I know you and I know Terry. That answer enough?"

She lit a cigarette, flagged a waiter and ordered the chardonnay, Shawn thinking she'd never looked more stunning. For a moment neither spoke, just glanced about. Finally his eyes came back to her.

"They look good, Loren. You, too."

She stubbed out the cigarette. "Shawn, I want you to understand something. This whole thing about *Constance* and you – it was not my idea."

"One thing I always liked about you was that you were never a good liar. Even when you were balling him."

"Unless you want to end this here, don't talk to me like that."

"End what, exactly?"

"The first I knew was when he called me on his way to New Mexico. You can believe that or not."

Their drinks came, the server opening the wine, Loren waving her hand to go ahead and pour. In two pulls, hers was gone.

Shawn sipped his beer.

"So, how is it being back?" she asked, breeze lifting blonde hair she ran a hand through. "Anybody around from when we were?"

Shawn went through it: his father, Joe Don and Robin, what Tam and Sonny were up to, Jake buying it in the Gulf, a rundown without anecdotes. She tapped her nails on the table. Then, as if having built to it, "Shawn, you remember when we ran off – the look on my dad's face when we got in your van?"

He saw sincere and returned the favor: "How could I forget?"

"You ever feel like the doors that closed, you closed on yourself?"

"Something specific you want to say here, Loren?"

"He's a good provider, you have to understand that. They lack for nothing."

"Meaning you don't."

"Meaning *they* don't, Shawn."

"Except the things that matter."

"You don't know that, and I refuse to argue the point." Draining the glass and pouring herself another. "All the same, watch yourself with him. He gets what he wants."

"Tell me about it."

"I mean it, Shawn."

"You think I like seeing how much they've grown? Who they're getting to be?"

"Then you should never have done what you did to him."

"It was a setup. You know damn well it was."

"I told you, I won't be talked to that way."

He took a long breath, ballooned it out. "Loren, I hope you sleep better than I do."

"So do I, Shawn."

The kids were back, then, out of breath, Terry his sunglasses pushed up, sitting heavily. "Surprise, the boat's ready." In effect,

Shame about it, but there you go.

"Come on, Dad." Nate. "It's really cool."

"Please, Dad." Elizabeth.

Terry gestured to the waiter to hurry the bill; he tossed off the wine Loren had poured him, re-corked the bottle, picked up the glasses in his other hand. "Sorry kids, but your dad has work to do. Don't you, Shawn. Besides, there isn't room for all of us."

"Dad, I'll sit in your lap." Elizabeth.

"Dad, I'll stay here while you go out." Nate.

"No, you won't," Loren told him. "Your dad wouldn't want that. Would you, Shawn?"

"No. But thanks for the offer."

"Then we're burning daylight. I'll call later, unless it's something that can't wait." Terry's look saying, *And if what's in your eyes means you'd like to start it up, here's the prize, the ones you'd do it to because Loren and I are one on this, don't think for a second we aren't.* Subtle as a freeway billboard.

Quick fierce hugs. "Have fun and mind your mom. Don't do anything I wouldn't."

"Dad, when will we see you again?" Elizabeth's big eyes welling.

"Soon, sweetheart, I love you. You too, Nate," to his son's scuffed Jordans and *gotcha* wave.

Loren said something to Elizabeth, took her down the steps, Nate turning to mouth a *Sorry, Dad.* Shawn walked his beer to the rail. Through burn and blur, he watched the turquoise-and-white Formula rumble from the dock, Elizabeth and Nate waving from its stern, dots becoming one as Terry opened it up and they rounded the point and were gone.

14

S HAWN WOKE UP WITH A BEER HEADACHE and the TV on, though the sound was off. He aired the headache with a tentative mile, stepping it up on the backstretch, then a Hi-Pro bar and coffee at the store. He was waiting outside at the coin machines when the delivery truck arrived with the Tahoe paper.

He bought one, scanned it, found the reception story but no compromising photo. No *Constance*-project spearhead Shawn Rainey dragging a dazed and bleeding Frank Love to his feet courtesy of *Constance*-project supporter Joe Don McCandless. He read the article, found it mostly accurate, no mention of the Love-McCandless dustup, lack of a corroborating photo the only plausible explanation.

Maybe…

Not that Catherine Mulvhill held back, her most memorable quote being, *As I made clear to Mr. Rainey, the tragedy of her loss is ongoing. But to perpetrate what he endorses would be equivalent to exhuming a loved one to apply lipstick.*

Shawn downed ibuprofen, dressed, and hit 89 east along the shore, *son-of-a-bitch* fighting admiration for her dominance of the medium, deciding the photo's nonappearance trumped all.

It was another great morning: water as if overlaid by plastic wrap, sun in the trees, Lakewood without traffic looking prosperous and alpine. He thought of his father getting up, easing out the stiffness, reading the same paper Shawn had before hitting the backlog of mowers and whatnot people brought him to fix and sharpen. Which brought back more memories: Cort at the station, able to put anything back on the road, Liam boasting, *Mother, wait till you hear what Cort did…* Shawn's increasing passion for skiing, his take on it the faster he went trying to impress them, the less their encouragement. As though seeing a path down which nothing good could come.

On a whim, he pulled in at a fitness place he'd seen, thinking why not, what could it hurt? Everything it should, he hoped, recalling the shape he'd been in, needed to be in to compete. How much was it different now, other than it was no longer a sport by which to prove himself?

Or was it?

After registering – morning workout without fail – he pulled in at Kings Beach, bought coffee and muffins to go. Thirty minutes later he was taking the Echo Bay turnoff toward the lake. He found the spot, the minimized and treed entrance, pulled up to the gate, pressed the intercom.

What had Mal called it? Stonehouse.

"State your business," a male voice responded. Vaguely familiar.

"Shawn Rainey to see Mrs. Mulvhill."

"That'll be the day."

"Not Frank Love…"

"And if it is?"

"If it is, I'm sorry about what happened the other night."

"Rainey, you were a punk then and you're a punk now. People are going to learn that. And the other night is something between your friend and me I look forward to squaring."

"In other words, making worse."

"So long, shithead."

"With the possibility I had a reason for coming that involved your employer's interests?"

Metallic silence. "Hello?"

"Keep your pants on, I'm checking."

Minutes later he met Shawn in a golf cart, his right eye still black, stitches fringing. He remoted the gate, drove them past old-growth pines, purple and white flowerbeds, rock walls, lawn that had no business being that green, to what looked like an abridged version of Yosemite's Ahwahnee Hotel: indigenous stone, wood beams, deep-set windows, slate roof. He stopped the cart, led Shawn through a stone lintel to a room overlooking the bay, left without a word. Shawn scanned the view, wondered if the wildflowers in a vase might be the ones he'd sent, finally concluding they were because he wanted them to be.

He scanned further: opposing walk-in hearths with split wood laid; Indian-print couch and chair groupings; iron floor lamps and wall fixtures; ticking grandfather clock; native baskets, some under glass. Rugs laid over buffed hardwood appeared too elegant to accept mere feet, so he avoided them as a housewoman, Chinese by her looks, relieved him of his burden: coffee and muffins waterside as soon as Mrs. finished her morning swim. She'd been alerted he was coming.

Shawn stepped through French doors to blue water, forest reaching almost to the crags. Downlake were The Maggies and Mount Tallac, the entrance to Emerald Bay and, of course,

Rubicon. Shaking it off, he followed the path leading past an arch-windowed boathouse with a cradled wood runabout – *Constance II, Echo Bay* – to a retaining wall cut by a gated staircase. The gate was open, so he went through to a slab patio, glass-topped iron table and scrolled chairs, one draped with a yellow towel, another with a terry robe. He spotted a bathing cap, arms synchronized to an easy crawl. In a bit they redirected toward a floating platform.

The swimmer paused there, glanced in the direction she'd come, around the lake, in at the house to settle on him. For a moment Catherine Mulvhill held eye contact. Then she started in.

He waited with the towel as she stepped out: blue one-piece, tanned arms and legs, face glowing with lake cold, a visage far younger than her years. She shook her short hair out.

"And what have we here, the Trojan horse?"

"If only." Handing her the towel. "You do this every morning?"

"The cold preserves everything else, it might as well preserve me." Slipping on the robe, the charm bracelet concealed under it, she slipped a flip-top pack and her silver lighter out of a pocket. "Cigarillo?" she asked.

"No, thanks. The other night did me for a while."

"My father smoked these." Lighting up. "The same brand, believe it or not."

The housekeeper, whom she addressed as Millicent, appeared to set down the coffee in a ceramic pot, the muffins on a ceramic platter with ivy leaves. Out on the point a grouping of birch trees caught the breeze and the light while a following sweep rippled the lake surface.

"You're bold, I'll give you that," Catherine Mulvhill said when Millicent had left.

"Not this morning." Pouring their coffees. "I came to thank you."

"I see. Should I be watching my silver?"

"For getting the photo killed. Needless to say I was expecting the worst."

Her eyes shifted to her cup, which she set down. "Are you always this presumptive of conspiracy?"

"Somehow it didn't seem like the paper. Any paper I know."

"Mr. Rainey, to save time I'll keep this simple. To have removed me not only would have looked absurd, but fraudulent and ripe for scrutiny. I can afford neither. It came down to the lesser of two evils."

"Interesting. On the other hand you could have run the risk."

Bite of muffin. "And what risk is that?"

"That my PR capital would be gone before yours."

"That is not a bet, it is a sure thing."

"Funny," Shawn said. "That's what your man said about getting back at my friend."

"Frank said that?" Frowning.

"Words to its effect."

"I'll speak to him," she said. "I suggest you do the same with the McCandless boy."

"Already have, for what it's worth."

She leaned back with her cigarillo, breeze taking the smoke before it reached him. "I saw you the other day, out there with your binoculars. What were you hoping to see?"

"The same as you, I imagine."

"You are here at my convenience, Mr. Rainey, if I need remind you. I asked you a question."

"Fair enough." Finishing his muffin. "Your life and how you live it. I admit to being curious."

"One sonar scan and a peek at the old lady and you're set.

Then again, not, because you're here."

"Mrs. Mulvhill, I didn't come to fight. Perhaps I should leave."

"In due course. And you'll know when you're in a fight with me. Just don't tell me you came here to thank me. I wasn't born yesterday."

"It happens to be true."

She smoked, gave him Bette Davis, the winter regent surrounded by lessers – all but two: change and time. "Mr. Rainey, you'd be advised not to keep underestimating me. You don't love it here, or here is where you'd have been. From that I assume you did not come galloping back out of a sense of duty when you heard of this idiot scheme to raise my ship." She took another muffin. "What did they offer you to take me on? Money?"

"Why? You plan to buy me, too?"

"Frankly, the thought had occurred, although I might need further proof you're worth it." Brushing crumbs from her robe. "At least to establish your value."

"Then I hope not to disappoint you."

The wind dropped a pinecone near them, its thud heavy on the flagstone path. She said, "So this *is* about money…"

Shawn saw Elizabeth and Nate waving at him from the speedboat, dots around the point. "Spoken like a person with a half-billion dollars," he said. "All due respect."

She smoked. "Mr. Rainey, you must have considered that your brother and what happened, all that nastiness, would find its way into this. Yet here you are."

"Probably because I had you figured for more, especially after our talk the other night."

"There you are. Mistake number one."

Shawn pushed back his chair and stood. "Then I'm glad to have it behind me. Mrs. Mulvhill, thank you for seeing me. I admit to hopes we might find common ground. Regardless and for whatever reason, thanks for what you did with the photo." He was walking away, almost to the next level, when he heard, "Mr. Rainey, I've changed my mind. I want you to view something with me. Up at the house."

"And give Frank Love something to stew about?"

"Frank won't bother you unless I say so."

"Don't tell me: the bleached bones of those who've opposed you."

"Stop being immature and learn something," she said. "Mainly, what and whom you're dealing with."

"Correct me if I'm wrong, but wasn't that just made clear?"

Catherine Mulvhill let out a breath, which seemed to deflate her slightly. "I didn't mean me," she said, crushing out her smoke. "I meant *her.*"

15

S HE TOLD HIM TO WAIT IN THE LIVING AREA WHILE SHE CHANGED.
On cue it seemed Millicent appeared, asked him if he
required anything and, when he said no, went out the way
she came. Which gave him an opportunity to scrutinize the
room, a not-unsuccessful fusion of Ralph Lauren and prewar
royal hunting lodge.

Chief among what he'd missed at first pass was the trio of oil
portraits against the inland wall, Shawn thinking the ghosts of
Stonehouse. There were three, spot-lit and heavy framed: Seneca
DeWitt Holmes (1814-1903), Lila Templeton Holmes (1832-
1915), and Cyrus Chandler Holmes (1866-1943). Father, mother,
son...grandfather, grandmother, father: ticks of the clock pendulum seeming like their heartbeats.

Seneca had the fiercest look, unkempt and disjointed, though
it might have been the artist's choice of poses. Instead of at some
distant horizon, he'd been directed to stare dead-on, so that his
eyes tracked the viewer. White-bearded, afloat in his bent-point
collar, he was reminiscent of Cotton Mather, that thunder-and-

lightning ministerial madness.

Lila was posed in a black dress with nipped-in waist and ill-advised ruffles, a hat that matched. Her eyes had to have been fixed on the help, throwing the fear of God into those who didn't measure up, he figured. That or she was dreaming up a new level of hell for the artist who'd had her corseted into the dress.

Son/father Cyrus gave the appearance of someone who recognized life's bank shots and played them. His dark suit, patterned vest, tie and stickpin recalled a painting of Diamond Jim Brady Shawn had stood before in the DeYoung Museum. He looked for Catherine but the only vestige was the eyes, intense blue that appeared to be calculating the obstacle presented, Shawn concluding that the same might be said of any of them.

"If you're wondering why there's no painting of my mother, she died young," Catherine Mulvhill said from behind him. Denim dress similar to the one she was wearing the night of the reception, string of amber beads in sizes descending from the centerpiece, the charm bracelet.

He looked again at the painting of Cyrus, the prospect of a life with the man. "I don't see much of you there."

"On that at least we agree."

"The other two were a pair to draw to."

"Seneca built her this house when my father was born. I find it intriguing to think that they could come back today and feel at home."

Her meaning evident: *Things that are let be endure.*

Figuring it was time, he jumped in. "My father and mother came here after the war. Rosie the Riveter and G.I. Joe the Motor Pool Shmoe, to quote him. He owned a repair-and-service station in Lakewood. Now he fixes what the neighbors bring him for pot roast or whatever."

"No shame in pot roast," she said. "And your mother?"

"My mother died in 1987."

"Shortly after your brother…"

Side note on Catherine Mulvhill, if it wasn't abundantly clear: *Watch your ass – more importantly, your mouth.* Trying not to sound defensive, he said, "Are you always this thorough?"

"I'm sure you can think of worse things. Now if we're through here, I'll show you why I asked you to stay."

She led him to the stairwell, up past a landing with a painting of a just-completed Stonehouse, the inscribed date 1866, to a wide-branching hallway, landscapes and old photographs of people.

"Aunts and uncles among these…?"

"None beyond infancy." Looking back. "Most were stillborn."

They were almost to the end, Catherine Mulvhill at a door on what would be the lake side, when he moved to the portrait of a young girl in a western-style riding outfit standing beside a pony.

"This is you?"

"It was." Coming back to it. "The horse years."

He was about to tell her that he had that to look forward to with Elizabeth but decided on the hand less played. "Sweet pose," he said instead.

"Aren't they all at that age."

"Some are. Not all."

She was silent a moment, then, "What was he like, your brother? Cortland, right?"

"We were sworn to call him Cort," Shawn thinking *from out of nowhere;* but, of course, nothing with this woman was out of nowhere.

"If you'd rather not answer, I understand."

"Handsome, charming, talented, loved," he said after a too long beat. Aware that she was filling in the blank, the one that gave her *everything my parents wished I'd been.*

Think, he told himself: *Surprise her back southpaw, Rocky to Apollo Creed. Do it.* "Were you and your father close?"

"That's an odd question."

"I'll withdraw it, if you like." *Touché.*

"Mr. Rainey, my father was fifty-six when he had me. Does that answer your question?"

"In part. You never had children?"

"Not when you're widowed and as busy as I was."

Needle flick, the deep rumble of stone grinding to powder.

"I can imagine."

"I doubt it," she said. "You have two, I believe. A boy eleven and a girl eight."

"Of course you'd know."

She ignored it. "At their ages, it must be especially hard."

Talk about it and feel better...where's the harm? "Look, Mrs. Mulvhill," he said, low on body shots and feeling the walls closing. "I hate to cut this short, but I'm due someplace at noon."

"South Shore, Lake Inn, plenty of time." His touché returned with interest. "Humor me. It might even help."

He let out a breath so as not to reveal the need in it. "When you put it that way..."

She opened the door.

Dark room until she brought up the lights, no window.

Central to the space and unmistakable was the glassed-in model, highlighted by recessed spots. Six feet long within its standing case, the ship was the most perfect he'd ever seen: *Constance, 1896, Echo Bay, Nevada,* etched in the brass base plate followed by a list of the designers, boiler men, engineers, woodworkers, machinists, and ship-fitters who'd built her. And, with a space to separate: *For Holmes Transportation Company; Seneca DeWitt Holmes, Chairman; Cyrus Chandler Holmes, President.*

Shawn bent to the detail: length-to-beam ratio of almost 10:1; white steel hull, upswept and lined with portholes; raked deckhouse with contrasting mahogany and teak; wood pilot-house and white-lattice railing; single cream stack rising from the upper deck. It felt as if her lifeboats could at any moment swing out on their davits, searchlight scan the shore, bow crane and windlass swing baggage aboard, props begin turning. Fore and aft, her starched pennant and American flag said the wind agreed.

On the opposite side, spot cutaways revealed her boiler and firebox, engines and ballast tanks, main salon and galley, ladies cabin and smoking lounge. As if you could board with an excursion party, spirit a dance partner with fragrant hair and sunglow around the deck to the sounds of string and woodwind, her laughter in your ear, and never look back.

Never look back.

"She was built in San Francisco, disassembled and hauled here by rail and mule," Catherine Mulvhill said. "Were you aware of that?"

Shawn had almost forgotten her. He told her he'd read it, throwing in the watertight compartments that virtually guaranteed she wouldn't sink by herself.

"Unless," she came back, "someone with a heavy heart at the rusting hulk she'd become decided to put an end to her suffering."

Smiling at how adroitly he'd been maneuvered, Shawn cast for inspiration in the framed and spotlit wall photos. He saw *Constance* with passengers in mid-wave, scenes of her at lake landmarks: Emerald and Echo Bays, long-gone Tallac Resort; her launch down narrow-gauge rails; stern and bow shots; profiles that made it seem as if she'd materialized from the lake, so integral was she.

Lock and load. "You mean the same someone who rejected the alternative solutions that might have saved her?"

Her laugh was short and sharp. "Solutions based on the value of her weight in scrap – if you know what that means."

"And the company's resources? Or his own?"

"Check your facts. It's documented that my father's company faced periodic shortfalls. Not to mention his recognition that without a market, her agony would only be prolonged. In other words, though he viewed her as more than a ship, he was not a fool."

"From what I read, you had no objection to the survey dive by another group. Why not its logical extension?"

"Mr. Rainey, my father told me only once about that night, but I've never forgotten it – how he sent his men to open her cocks, compromise her compartments, how the rain came in torrents. How she drifted in from the deep water he'd intended for her, back to Echo Bay where she'd been launched. I suppose you knew that, too."

Cease firing. "No," he said, "I did not."

"Then let this in: I have shown this room to few souls. My hope is, it's made an impression on you."

"How could it not?"

"Then you reject this attempt to exhume her for profit?"

"Perhaps if I were to hear a reason beyond the subjective."

"Too bad. Mr. Rainey, are you a fan of films?"

"Older ones, I am."

"An intriguing subject for later. In a recent one I saw, the hero, a Roman general facing the prospect of being overrun, tells his troops, 'At my signal, unleash hell.'"

"And does he?"

"He does. May we also assume the point is clear?"

"I think so. All but the overrun part."

"Well, Mr. Rainey, I tried. That's more than I've done with most."

"Am I permitted a final question?"

"Only since the opportunity will not arise again."

"Thank you. What is that?" Moving toward a piece he'd noticed against the far wall, occupying its better portion. Clearly old, it was of very dark wood, yet it glowed in the light. It was inlaid with mother-of-pearl, its base made up of storage compartments, some with doors, others meant for display. Flanked by tiered shelves was a flat workspace bearing the marks of time and use.

"That is a Chinese ancestral altar. In it were found symbols of life and business, wealth and health, family matters of conse-quence. It came from an estate sale."

"Arresting to find it in such a dedicated gallery."

"Much of what my grandfather and father achieved is the result of Chinese effort. I find it only fitting."

He checked closer. Its contents looked like an immigrant his-tory of California – small glazed jars, square-holed coins, an incense burner, Chinese writing and artifacts. He threw a glance at the wall above it where, judging by the hook, a picture had hung.

"Out for restoration," she volunteered before he could ask. "And won't you be late for your function?"

"Sounds like my exit line," he said.

"Coming to terms with your conscience, Mr. Rainey, or find-ing out if you have one. And now, goodbye." Killing the lights, brushing off his thanks, escorting him to the head of the stairs, where Millicent stood waiting to escort him to the double doors.

Which, without a word, she did.

Outside, the sky was cloudless, the lake a blue inland sea: breeze to clear the head of tight spaces, sun with a push beyond the shade. No sign of Frank Love on his walk back to the Cherokee.

It was only on his way south, traffic moderate and the experience that was Stonehouse lapping at him as the waves to shore, that Terry's comment – *ones that think it's a shrine, even though nobody died* – resurfaced strong. Which got Shawn to thinking that the room upstairs, its nature and focus on the goddess under glass – her residual power to seduce even him – more than fit the category.

16

THE LAKE INN PARKING LOT WAS A WORLD OF ITS OWN. Frustrated drivers cruised in search of parking places. Behind a police line, protesters announced their opposition to the *Constance* project and their affiliations – Mother Tahoe; Kit Carson Brigade; Fallen Leaf Vigilance Committee; Friends of Washoe Billy – the ones Terry warned him about who might be sensing the tide turning and not in their favor. Moving in a large hand-held circle were: GREEN AND BLUE, WHAT ABOUT YOU? PROFITS ARE POLLUTION; OUR LAKE, NOT THEIRS; and A QUEEN, NOT A WHORE.

What saved him from parking off property and hiking in (as a stream of others was doing) was a sign reading S. RAINEY strung between two stanchions. Shawn nodded to the guard who checked his ID, walked in at ten after twelve to a flutter of 8X10s. He signed, apologized for not being able to chat, moved inside. The crowd had to number four hundred, with a big room set up for cocktails, the mobile bars packed.

Bob Lamont spotted him and looked relieved, herded him to a fivesome he'd been proselytizing. In order of introduction:

Ernest Dyer, President, Nevada Chamber of Commerce; State Senator Charles Steele, Nevada Commerce Committee; Diane Butler, Assistant Comptroller, State of California; Martin Myoshi, Board of Equalization; Refugio Castillo, Assistant Speaker of the House. The former two were up from Carson City, the latter three from Sacramento, Shawn envisioning the scent of lake money wafting down into the capitols.

As they shook hands, entourages wending his way confirmed it: Nevada and California were interested in preliminary discussions re revenue sharing; more to the point, serious mention of investing. And yet the conversation still ran to his skiing career, Shawn trying not to think *pimp* where it applied, without success.

It struck him, then, the coin's other side: If there was a time when he felt he *was* the *Constance* Project, it was now, oddly welcome after so long down. Double strike was the parallel, himself and Catherine Mulvhill in lockstep. He shook it off, trashed the thought as Pathetic Identification Syndrome or Dramatic Impulse Concurrence, whatever his college psych professors might have called it, Shawn at the time the older pupil trying to understand himself after the limelight had winked out.

Before he'd hooked up with Terry.

He snapped to voices, faces anticipating a reply; with his best sheepish look he asked for a repeat, thinking, *Stay alert, no time to blow it.* Because *their* feelers surely were out.

The politicos ginned his words for clues; questions led and followed and doubled back again. Figuring it worked to his advantage to earn their respect, Shawn gave as he got, the Q&A half-resembling duels. More than once he confessed to not knowing something, would research and get back. Answers he'd memorized – donations to date, funds needed, deposit information, projected expenses and income – he outlined with sources. Time frames, then, technical questions regarding the dives, Shawn breaking the announcement of the open house and exhibition broached with Mal, the ramrod having responded with *Just do it*.

Staff slid back separators, revealing a dining room with lake view and themed tables via Suzanne Padget's coordination, Suzanne waving back as he worked the room. Intros and business cards; clipped sentences, buzzword-loaded; offers of whatever, whoever, *be in touch*. From a far corner, Joe Don grinned and made a halo gesture above his head for Shawn's benefit.

Following lunch and Bob Lamont's pared-down intro, Shawn rose to speak: Marcourt rally talk plus keep-it-loose remarks brought forth on the way over. Casino, contractor, and lodging association heads smiled as he acknowledged them from memory, his old trick. He finished up by inviting them to the dive demo, calling their attention to the literature laid at each setting, the donation envelope in particular. His ending pun about it being bread upon the waters drew laughter, then applause.

He stepped down.

Yet no one seemed prepared to leave.

Heated talk followed: Catherine Mulvhill's opposition, the loosey-goosey coalition that greeted them (her flunkies, all agreed), the project's otherwise bright prospects. After an hour, Shawn was able to break free, flattened signs the only indication protestors been there at all. Despite the grade and its 10-mph switchbacks, traffic up 89 was minimal for summer approaching Labor Day, late afternoon golden on the ridge. Cedars gave way to the Emerald Bay view spot, its bouldered parking circle nearly full as he pulled in and found a place, walked to the edge, and took it in.

Far down and green as its name was the bay, respite from the hype: stone island with its stone teahouse, pleasure craft leaving wakes. Shawn recalled camping trips with his family, Cort later on, Robin latest of all: the fragrance of her cleansing lavender, her cries in the late sweet mornings. The more he tuned in, the more she came to him, a station he was trying to pinpoint: Robin, whom he'd left because he couldn't bear her knowing what she knew about him and Cort. Robin exchanged for Loren, Shawn knowing the two of *them* wouldn't work even as they drove away, elated at their getaway, Loren from her old man, Shawn from himself.

The Great Escape.

He realized he'd spent the better part of an hour reflecting and, with a last look, went for the Cherokee. The area had thinned to an empty SUV down from him, next space a van-family rounding up stragglers, other side a convertible with a man and woman about his age deep in conversation.

As he opened the door and got in, dropped the windows for air, his foot kicked something he hadn't noticed before. The cassette case was scuffed and jacketless, the cassette itself new and unmarked. Between the capstan holes was writing that read simply, *Shawn Rainey,* blocky and undistinguished. He turned it in his hands, wondering if it had been there since the Inn, no memory of seeing it.

Earlier than that?

Doubtful.

Later?

If later, it meant someone had followed him and slipped it in the window he'd left open a crack. Which meant...what?

He looked, saw no eyes, the few at the railing still facing it, no one walking toward the cars. Giving thought to the alternatives –

phone the sheriff and leave a message or, if he did get through, listen to disbelief followed by dial tone; toss it in the trash and forget about it; play it – he finally slipped it from his case, inserted it in the slot, turned the key, and waited. For a bit there was nothing, then…something faint.

Maxing the volume, he finally identified the sound.

Ticking, as in a clock…

As in a…

The sound of the explosion nearly blew Shawn out his door, deafening in the Cherokee's six-speaker setup and driven volume. *SON OF A BITCH!* Momentarily stunned. Then: *professionally done – had to be – flash-and-bang…but WHO?* He caught the family exiting the van wide-eyed, the two in the convertible rising up from duck-down, the man going off at him despite his mouthed and gestured apology: *"FUCKING MORON. YOU THINK THAT'S A JOKE? OUGHTA KICK YOUR DAMN TEETH IN."*

Rocked back and scared mad.

But the tape was still rolling.

A reach from the switch, from walking it off until the ringing in his ears stopped, his pulse returned to itself, his nerves to *them*selves, Shawn held up just long enough to catch the electronically altered follow-up whisper delivered in a sort of fade-down neutral menace:

"Anytime, anywhere. Back off or live it."

17

I T WAS DARK when Shawn made the cabin after back-to-back doubles at the lodge bar and saw a white station wagon parked alongside his unit. As he locked the Cherokee, he made out a shape, smelled cigarette smoke, heard salsa-fused jazz, and went over.

"What?" he said to the cracked window. "I blow it or something?"

Robin killed the sound, ran the window all the way down. "I don't know, did you?"

"It's happened before."

"No shit," she said. "You going to ask me in or just stand there?"

"I'm not sure asking you in is a good idea."

"Based on what?"

"Three guesses, you and me being two of them."

Robin more or less smiled. "You're not afraid of Joe Don, are you?"

Shawn leaned on the jamb. She was wearing tight jeans, white top, a loose-fitting suede jacket. He caught a waft of lavender under the cigarette smoke and rose to it.

"Because he's afraid of you, you know," she said, stubbing her cigarette in the ashtray.

"Right."

"You're not just a little curious about that?"

And so much for good intentions.

Shawn thought of the bar, rejected it as too public, crowded with eyes and ears connected to Joe Don. All he needed was to be seen in McCandless country with her. Finally he said, "Pull in under the far eave. There's brandy inside."

"If I need one, you mean?"

"I wasn't talking about you."

While she parked, he unlocked the cabin and, making sure the curtains were closed, turned on the lights. Everything looked the same: unmade bed, chairs, bureau, banker's box in the corner by the small table. He adjusted the bedding, threw the spread over the result. He'd pulled the pint out of the nightstand drawer when she said from behind him, "Decided you're not scared of me?"

"Remains to be seen, doesn't it?"

She closed the door, took off her jacket, sat on the bed. "Stuffy in here. You used to hate that."

He cracked the upper windows free of the paint in which they'd been frozen, lowered them, let the curtains fall back, asked her if she wanted ice in her drink. When she said no, he opened the brandy, poured hers into a plastic glass and handed it to her. He added ice from the small fridge to his, took the chair opposite.

"Salúd," he offered.

"I've always hated that toast."

Flashing on the few times he'd been around her family, her Mexican cousins in particular, gang wannabes now serving time, he had to smile. "Tough day at the office?"

"If you're referring to my real estate, I work out of the house.

Joe Don targets the properties, I go after them. Then I sell them. Hopefully before his loans against our other properties come due."

"I thought they'd cracked down on leveraging."

"Joe Don gets around it. The trick is all in who you know and owe." She sipped her brandy. "Doesn't make us sleep any better."

"You know anyone who does?"

"We used to," she said.

"Kids, Robin. Kids get a pass."

"Little Shawnie, all grown up."

"And yours are where tonight?"

"They're with my mother. Joe Don hates it, but so what? Time flies when you're having fun. Even when you're not, I've figured out."

"How's his hand?"

"Your guess. The cast lasted all of one day."

He drank, heard the explosion again, replayed his thoughts. Miles beyond Emerald Bay, he'd pulled off the road, played the tape to exhaustion, concluding finally that there were no identifying sounds. Which meant that anyone serious about taking him out would have plain done it. Which meant that a) despite putting him on his guard, it was just a warning; b) he might have more time than he'd first thought.

He drank.

"So why *did* you come back?" she asked, searching his eyes. "No more *Constance* bullshit, just honest-to-God, this-is-me why."

"Honest-to-God? Robin, I spent half the day with Catherine Mulvhill, the other with the friends and nonfriends of Washoe Billy. How about we give it a rest?"

She shook her head, which loosened a smile that became a laugh. "Washoe Billy," she said. "I've run up against some of those people."

"Something funny there, they fail to see it."

The smile faded. "Joe Don thinks you took the project on as a cover, that you really came back for me. That scares him."

"You are kidding."

"I look like I'm kidding?"

"Assuming I did, what about it would scare him? What I have in this room, my dad's place when he goes? I couldn't begin to offer you what Joe Don has."

"It goes a little deeper than that, *amor*. Plus, I know where the bones are buried. Running out on him would not be good for business. His words."

Headlights leaked in around the curtains, but it was just a car turning on the highway. Shawn leaned back, felt only fatigue. "It's gone that far, has it?"

She lit a cigarette, blew out smoke. "I'm leaving him, it's only a matter of when. Or who."

"Joe Don know that?"

"He cheats on me enough. I should worry."

Shit. Life as we know it. "Robin, I'm sorry. All around."

"But what the hell, right? Boys into men." She shook her head. "No, that's not fair, it's been coming for years, starting when you left. Joe Don and I never even liked each other until you took off."

"Robin, I didn't leave you to *him*. I just left."

"You left all right, without a fucking word. Robin, I hate you; Robin, I'll miss you; Robin, you're great in pickup beds and on camping trips and thanks for whatever it was we had, now go fuck yourself."

Shawn forced his eyes up out of his drink. "Tell me what to say, I'm asking. Did I mean to hurt you? You know the answer or you wouldn't be here. Would I have done different, knowing what I know? Of course I would. Across the river and through the woods."

Her smile was a knife. "Nothing like sixteen years too late."

"Maybe I couldn't convince myself that you wanted me instead of Cort. Not deep down, anyway."

"So you're the expert now."

"Robin, every year that goes by, I'm less an expert at anything. Back then, though, I knew enough to think it. Enough to go off with somebody I barely knew."

"Loren Slater, drama queen."

Crowded restaurant deck, sunlit hair, empty eyes, retreating speedboat. "Come on, Robin, be fair."

"Sorry if the meaning escapes me."

She held out the glass for more brandy. Cutting the flow off before she stopped him, he said, "Choosing me over Cort never made any sense to me – none. Best I could come up with was that you wanted us both and that was the way to pull it off."

"That is so fucked."

"It's also not how I meant it."

"Is that right? Shawn, you were like no one I'd met before. You were fun and fast and you liked me back, I thought. But you're right, I liked you in a different way, more lasting, obviously. Does that help?"

"I lived, he died. What do you think?"

She downed the whole shot, gasped, recovered. "If I told you it wasn't my choice?" Pause as if deciding. "If I told you it was Cort's?"

"No games, Robin."

"No games, *amor.* How it was."

Shawn felt the way he did when thunder rolled across the lake and ended up in his diaphragm. "For God's sake, why?"

"Oh Shawn, that look. You can't guess? Because there was someone else, that's why."

"I don't believe it."

"Yes you do, because you know it fits. He never told me who, and I'm not sure he felt the same way. He died before–" Swiping at the shine through which she was looking at him, reaching for her jacket to put it on. "Look, I just knew, okay?"

"Robin, you're too smart and I'm too tired for you not to say what you mean."

Turning up her collar, she said, "I never meant for you to hear who it was and neither did Cort. You have to know that."

"Goodnight, Robin. I don't know what else to say."

She turned at the door. As if the chains holding the thing had rusted off and finally it had surfaced, she said, "Who but a friend, *amor*? Think about it. Anybody but Arn Tennell ever hate you that much?"

What seemed like half the night after Robin dropped Arn Tennell in his lap – that whole time turned on its head, dots starting to connect even if he couldn't or wouldn't grasp the pattern – Shawn finally drifted into sleep. He knew it was sleep because, just before he went under, Cort was there and they were climbing.

Climbing...

The building is a city skyscraper, its crown lost in misting cloud: polished granite sides, wet-slick handholds they are able to find and exploit with increasing difficulty, the mist troublesome as a waterfall. As to why they are midway up a fifty-story building in such conditions, down having long ago ceased to be an option, Shawn has no idea. He only knows they have one chance and that is to complete what they started, whatever that may be.

They do not speak, for that would be a distraction. A universe below them, the traffic is a pale presence, secondary to the building's random drips and their own labored breathing. And something else, the reason they are here – the unseen thing behind them, no clue as to what, is gaining on them. Side by side, as though competitors, they reach-pull-steady-reach. As though only one can make his escape.

Above them in the mist a landing or step-in in the building's endless rise appears. It is a ledge rimmed by iron protective railing, handholds where theirs have become irregular, still no looking down, unthinkable at this height. Inches taller, Cort exploits his height advantage and reaches, reaches for the rail. He grips its base, begins to pull himself up. Within a hold of it, Shawn pauses, exhausted and waiting for the hand he knows will come…for even though he is a competitor, Cort is first his brother. *Isn't he…?*

Sure enough, there is the hand.

Shawn grips it as it grips his, a bond despite the slickrock between them, an implicit *You first, up and over.* But then the railing Cort grips collapses, pitches forward; there is a rusting screech as the thing dislodges, hurtles past Shawn, a violent jolt as he is separated from his holds and his full twisting weight hangs from Cort and he is bouncing-skidding against the wet side of the building, his other hand frantic for holds that are not there.

Finally the human pendulum comes to vertical and he looks up, sees Cort's hand L'd over the ledge. Somehow Cort is holding on, his fingers cramped and whitening.

Another few seconds, a minute at most…

But others are on the ledge now; they are saved. Shawn ignores the feeling in the pit of his stomach, wills himself not to look down, to breathe and concentrate, let the rescue play out. He glances up with wider scrutiny and sees that the dozen or so people bending down are not taking action, they are merely curious. At least it appears so because, in addition, they have no faces, only flesh-colored wrapping where a face would be.

The only face is Cort's, and his is smiling.

Shawn is aware that his grip on Cort, despite the willing of it, has loosened, is further loosening, that Cort is all that holds him now. His brother – his rival, but still his brother – is the only thing saving him from a fifty-story drop, likely an eviscerating rip from whatever it is that has driven them to it in the first place.

"We are not what we seem, Shawn, none of us," Cort says in a voice that is but a grave-sounding echo of the voice Shawn remembers. *"You of all people should know that."*

Then he lets go.

18

NEXT MORNING the dream was a bottom-dropping videotape looping on itself: looping as he rubbed life back into the arm he'd slept on wrong; looping as he showered off the dream sweat; looping as he tried toweling free of the terror-squared freefall that had brought him bolt upright, face to face with the clock-radio display showing four-thirty. It was still looping as he walked and bought coffee at the store, he and the morning man the only ones about at that hour. Fading to *We are not what we seem, Shawn, none of us,* once he got something in his stomach.

Elizabeth and Nate's cracked-frame photo grounded him, got him to the office, where he checked in with Suzanne, thanking her again for yesterday, the way her part had gone. For a while they went over the rest of the week, support for Mal's upcoming demo/open house, Saturday, ten to four the settled-on time frame. Recalling *She knows everybody* – Terry's comment – he asked if Suzanne had ever heard of a real estate outfit named Target.

Suzanne thought about it, shook her head, looked at him to explain; when he didn't, she asked, "How are you and Catherine

Mulvhill getting along?"

"We haven't done each other in yet, if that's what you mean," he answered. "Although there's still time."

Which seemed to satisfy her.

He read his messages: more invitations, lunch in Carson City with State Senator Steele and Chamber President Dyer the most promising. Beyond that were requests for appearances at group functions, for some reason the union heads he'd met chomping at the bit, Shawn speculating fund roll-over time; that or wanting to beat management to the punch, the ever-present dance. Looking up, he said, "By the way, C.M. liked the flowers, even though she denied it."

Suzanne gave a snort. "Sounds like her."

"You know her very well?"

"My mother does, or used to. They went to school together."

"Around here?"

"Up the hill, the historical museum housing records and such for the Gatekeeper's Museum. You know it?"

"The Gatekeeper's Museum I know." Native baskets, books, period items, old photos documenting Tahoe life…on display in the lake's former level-regulator's quarters, the man at the outlet gate to the Truckee.

The other one he did not know and said as much.

"It was a boarding school then, private. Apparently Catherine was a terror, always getting into trouble the old man had to bail her out of. Finally, he had to pull her out."

"Why does that not surprise me?"

Smile. "She's still a presence on this side. The bank and mall are obvious, but she also owns the title office, buildings the county has leased, condo and waterside tracts. Plus the museum."

"Thanks to Daddy."

"It's easy to think that," she said, "but you'd be wrong. Most of it she acquired. Mom said the estate was down to little more than taxes when Cyrus died. Have you seen a picture of him?"

"Big man. Flamboyant. Diamond Jim Brady."

Nod. "Wouldn't be surprising if they knew each other, the way they both went on. Catherine pops in now and then to read somebody the riot act. Doesn't give Mom any trouble, though."

"How so?"

Her eyes left her computer. "Mom runs the place. She says it's like never having left school, which makes her feel young. By the way, Mal's been phoning. You talked to him yet?"

"I'm on my way there now. I'll call you."

"Which reminds me, your friend McCandless, too. Said you'd know what it was about and that he'd be in the Lakewood yard today and tomorrow."

Shawn's immediate thought was of Robin, swearing under his breath at being so dumb...fucking *knowing* Joe Don's eyes were everywhere. "Maybe I'll stop there afterward," he said.

She held his eyes.

"What...?"

"He's a looker, that one. He married?"

"Wife and two boys."

"Happily, I mean." Scanning his face for subtext.

"Better ask him."

"You think I won't?"

Shawn let it pass.

"Then there's you..."

"Take my word," he said. "You don't want to know."

The start of a smile. "Heads-up for you. Saturday after Mal's thing I'm having a little get-together. Few friends, fiveish to whenever. Come alone or with somebody."

"Thanks, Suzanne. Can I get back to you?"

The smile went cat-to-mouse lip-smack. She said, "I mention that the lieutenant governor might be there?"

Shawn found Mal Kadich in the warehouse they used for gear just up from *Deep VI*. With him were team divers Duane Carper and Burl Ruttan, throwback types sporting beards; veterans, their look said as they shook hands and, with Mal, went over how they planned to work the dive event. Starting point would be a video tent showing surface and underwater clips, computer-generated explanations plus how *Constance* would look restored, rare footage of her á lá *National Geographic,* one member on standby for Q&A. Next in sequence was the equipment display facility in which they now stood, two members to demo the gear and discuss it. The culmination would come in a larger tent showing live video-feed from the site, three divers and two surface crewmen to support, decompression chamber and Mal standing by on *Deep VI,* footage to be edited later into a saleable promo and media vehicle, Shawn's contribution.

The thrust being *Here's how,* not *If it goes.*

Two hours they went over it: individual responsibilities, Shawn opening a speaker phone for Suzanne to participate. When they'd finished, he steered Mal down by *Deep VI,* where a crewman was installing something on the bow.

"You comfortable with this?" he asked Mal out of earshot.

Mal glanced at him. "If it creates the interest I'm counting on, hell yeah."

"But not ordinarily."

"How to put this?" Mal said at length. "We're working stiffs, not PR types. But if it needs doing, we'll do it. Point it out and turn us loose."

"Anything you need from me?"

"Yeah, my house out of hock. You and the old lady making magic yet?"

"Funny how everybody seems to ask that."

Mal grinned. "Can't say I didn't warn you out there."

"So you did. Incidentally, you were right, she did watch us. We sent her a VIP invitation. The courier should be arriving about now."

The grin fell off to starboard. "The hell you say."

Shawn's turn: "It's anybody's guess she'll come, but if she does, she won't bite. Not right off. Just be smarter than she is."

"Right," Mal said. "And that's worked for you?"

"Not yet, but there's always a first."

Mr. McCandless *was* on the lot, but the kid Shawn asked didn't know where, so he had him paged. Shawn was watching the kid maneuver a forklift among stacks of mill lengths, the customers appraising them, when he saw Joe Don in khakis and white polo leave the hardware shed and start for him, within hailing distance saying, "Well, if it isn't my old pal, Mr. Charm. Hell of a job you did yesterday, Mr. Charm."

Shawn knew immediately from the tone, half expecting one of Joe Don's patented bull-rushes: *Smash 'em all till you come up with the ball.* Putting up his hands, he said, "There is an explanation, if you care to hear it."

"Already heard it," Joe Don said. "Robin told me. Rather enjoyed it, I sensed. Course I doubt she'll be making any public appearances for a while."

Being noon hour, the customer count was higher than at other times. Shawn saw a number turn and watch. "The direct approach, that it?"

Measuring Joe Don's advance.

"Here's how it plays, Charm-boy: I don't believe in put-off. I believe you screw up, you answer for it then, not some tear-stained scene when the heat's off. My kids know that, those around here know it, and Robin surely does now. People understand an example."

Shawn watched Joe Don's foot placement, his right shoulder slightly back; he positioned himself accordingly.

"It was nothing," he said. "A talk."

"Old times, I imagine. The good old days?"

"Old, new, good, bad…talk. That's all."

Joe Don's grin was all business. "At night in your cabin, my wife and her old flame. You think I need a diagram?"

"No. I think you need somebody to help you put the acid back in the battery. Somebody other than you or me."

"Old Shawn, give with one hand, take back with the other. I should have known what was up the minute I saw you here. I blame myself for that."

Sailor take warning. "For the last time, Joe-D, you're talking yourself into something that didn't happen. Would not happen."

But Joe Don was past it, worked up and playing to the crowd, turning as if to say to them, "Nothing like making sure is there…?" Coming across with a weight-driven right Shawn ducked before stepping into one of his own, everything he had behind it.

It was like hitting a sackful of washers, the shock felt all the way up his arm to his shoulder, the bones and nerves in his hand as if someone had thrown a switch. But Joe Don had been on the business end. He saw Joe Don's eyes bulge, his wind leave him in a grunt; the rest of him become a puppet with cut strings: one minute standing, the next wide-eyed at the turn things had taken, the crowd equally so.

"Time to listen," Shawn said, bending to him, shaking it out, the feeling in his hand only just coming back, his arm still tingling. Knowing this was the only way to finish it – that if Joe Don chose to get up it sure-as-shit *was* over.

"Like it or not, *old pal*, we're stuck with each other. But if you hit Robin again you'll wish we weren't. And you still telegraph your right hand."

Joe Don grinned through gasps. He was reaching out for help up – like his sucker right, a trick Shawn had seen before – when Shawn turned and walked from the yard.

19

He'd had it.

Fed up with the bullshit crosscurrents and infantile jockeying, not excluding his own, Shawn pulled in at a pay phone beyond Mal's and checked the directory. There was no listing for a K.T. Ware.

He called the Marcourt and found she hadn't come in, her day off today. He dialed Bob Lamont's extension, caught him in a staff meeting, asked for his help locating the female bartender, the one working the night of the reception. His excuse: she'd found a pair of reading glasses she'd seen him using but forgot to leave her number with his office.

Bob chuckled. "The lost-glasses trick…I've used variations of it myself, no luck with her."

"Bob, do you realize how far out I'm having to hold this directory? My focal length is almost out the door."

"Forewarned is forearmed. All I'm saying here."

"So you are, and with all my thanks."

He dialed the number Bob gave him and got a machine: no

name but sounding like her voice. He'd identified himself and was leaving a message when she picked up.

"Sorry about that," she said, "late night. Working a private party." At least not sounding displeased to hear from him.

"Which must mean they're giving you tomorrow off…"

"Right, and I'm Catherine Mulvhill."

Recalling her pronunciation – Katie, not K.T. – he said, "Katie, would you mind if we talked about something else?"

"I suppose that would depend on what you had in mind."

Buck-up breath, the fear that things whipped up too fast didn't rise: "This wild thought I had you might like to do something together. Your choice of what."

Pause. "I see. When?"

"Had lunch yet?"

"I'm still getting used to being up."

"So we start with baby steps. My specialty."

Another pause. "It is a thought. Unfortunately, I have a ton of stuff I promised myself I'd do. Rain check?"

"What if it doesn't rain until tomorrow?"

"Or the next day…or ever again."

"You see my dilemma," he said, enjoying the banter.

"Job wouldn't be getting to you, anything like that?"

"The people I've been dealing with? You must be kidding. And if Bob Lamont brings it up, you returned my glasses you found."

Longer pause. Then, "Bob's where you got my number?"

Uh-oh. "I sort of pressed him. If it's a problem, I apologize."

"No. Some things you learn the hard way, is all."

"Another of my specialties. So we're down about the glasses?"

"I suppose," she said. "Except shouldn't it be you who found mine and returned them? Being the gentleman, I mean."

"Where are life's surprises anymore?" Having to smile, hearing her background stereo playing slack or steel guitar, melodic Hawaiian upcountry sounds.

Finally she said, "How's this for one: the girl who has a lot to do but changes her mind."

Her A-frame was in a neighborhood of modest ones, half a mile up the road he'd first come in on, half a mile in on a street named for a trout. She was on the porch, a caramel-and-white cat in her lap: jeans and trail shoes, scoop-neck top, red-and-white-checked shirt with the sleeves rolled up. She had tanned forearms he realized he hadn't seen before, brown hair brushed down and holding the sunlight, the effect causing a little catch in his throat. Closer in he saw she wore a flat silver neck chain and small gem pendant hanging from it.

"Katie Ware," he said, extending his hand.

"Shawn Rainey." Taking it, smiling.

Her grip was firm, warm from the stoop.

"Gemini," he added. "Born and raised in Lakewood. Sunsets."

"Sagittarius," she came back "Austin, Texas. Any food."

"I'm glad you were home."

"I'm glad you called."

"So far, so good?"

"No, I'm hungry."

They ate at a place she knew down the hill: burgers, spinach salads, tabouli with fresh mint. Half-banter, half-serious, their talk came easily: his post-knee-blowout psychology-major period before work in San Francisco (no Terry, that whole thing); her leaving Austin for Reno on the proverbial bus to shake a bad marriage, all that, once landing in Reno, feeling a nothing less than metal-tomagnet attraction to the mountains. Coming up on five years…

"You're telling me you actually left this place?" she said, trying not to sound incredulous.

"Too close to it," he covered.

"Someday maybe I'll understand, but I hope not."

"It's a long story." Draining the last of his drink. "So, what next?"

"My choice, right?" Her grin was conspiratorial.

"That's the deal."

"Then I want to meet her."

Shawn was imaging Catherine Mulvhill and wondering why in hell Katie would want to when she threw in, "Not *her*, HER." Brown eyes looking straight into his. "The one you told me at the reception you knew. Your hill with my initials."

They made Squaw Valley just before three.

Because the best overview was from the aerial cable car she hadn't yet been up, they bought tickets for High Camp and caught the waiting three-o'clock. As the car rose, Lake Tahoe angling into view behind them, the valley fell away to don't-look-downs, sheer rock walls, peaks connected by saddles fringed with glacier-melt meadows, conifers shaped by the January gales.

Seeing it both in summer-present and winters-past – blink and change the scene – Shawn pointed out landmark runs: Headwall and Cornice, Mainline and Siberia, Silverado and Broken Arrow. The peaks, then: Squaw, Granite Chief, Emigrant, KT-22 – the afternoon shadows making them appear far more treacherous without snow. They docked at High Camp, where Shawn charged a pair of walkers like Katie's, shorts, a water bottle, fruit bars, a tube of sunscreen for the 8200-foot rays.

They set out across the meadow, its mule ears rustling in the breeze; as they did, dust rose from their footfalls and the sun felt warm. Katie spotted a pair of good-sized birds riding thermals – eagles, Shawn thought. They crossed green-banked seeps and rivulets, drank from one, tried naming the wildflowers still in bloom, the dried-spring and early-summers now whitened by dust. Squirrels shucked the nuts from cones or dashed up trees.

Midway up KT's lower third, Shawn's knee still cooperating, they stopped to take it in. Broken and steep, KT-22 simply *was* – near-vertical entry, chute gradients from hell, screamer straights, bumps big as gold-rush tailings – Shawn seeing it from the time he'd first dared it to the last. No margin, no quarter, just speed and buffet and torque and hope to God the prayer you said lasted to the end.

They picked out a rock near the closed chairlift, sat in easy silence. Shawn stretched his legs, lifted his face to the sun, closed his eyes. Not a good idea: As if waiting for the moment, it came again, the gut-wrenching separation – body from hill, soul from body, everything and everyone lining the course.

Tilt…blur…impact.

"You all right?"

He opened his eyes, nodded, passed her the water bottle.

"Haven't been back since the day it happened. You forget how different it looks in summer."

"And back then…?"

"Overcast. Flat light."

"I don't quite understand. Hadn't you already qualified?"

"That was the Giant Slalom. This was the Downhill, going for a double. Not the brightest thing I've done."

She drank from the bottle, passed it back, eyed the railroad-track scar tissue on both sides of his knee.

"You said that it was near here?"

"Up a bit. There's an old joke: The ski patrol never ventures up for bodies, it's so steep they just wait for them at the bottom."

She frowned. "This *was* a good idea, wasn't it?"

"Coming here with you on a day like this? How could it not be?"

"That's nice to hear, and please don't take this wrong. But any time you'd like to tell me what you're really feeling instead of the old Shinola, that would be okay, too."

He smiled at her directness, drank and capped, slipped the bottle back in the pack. "You ever consider that what your life is now hinged on a single moment?"

"Oh, once or twice."

"And...?"

"What, the rest don't count? That's what you're telling me?"

Knowing she knew what he meant – the moment that transcended all others – he said nothing.

She regarded him. "You ever think it might be now?"

"Do you?" Not challenging so much as not knowing, so ingrained in him was the thought. And if he didn't know, how was he to make her understand?

She said, "I try to stay open. The idea anyway."

"There you go. And speaking of open..." He broke out the fruit bars, handed her a stack, started on his own, fixed on the mountain he'd walked in summer, battled in winter.

"Help me understand something?" she asked.

"I'll give it a shot."

"Up there – what makes someone do that? Let alone want to?"

He smiled. "Flat eyeballs and no sense?"

She just looked at him.

"Shinola, I know. Don't ask me, but it was there ever since I was about seven. Bad enough that you eat it and sleep it and wake up to it and hurt and bleed with it."

"Then the question would be why?"

"I suppose proving yourself factors in."

"Proving yourself to whom?"

"Everyone. Them. Myself."

She let a beat pass. "Your brother?"

Thinking he should have seen it coming, any number of human and online sources open to her, he said, "Interesting you'd ask about him. That is, assuming you're asking." Trying to keep the edge out of his voice and failing.

Which, of course, took the wind out of her sails.

"You're right, it isn't any of my business. Good example of a little reading being a dangerous thing."

Way to go, shithead. At least she gave a damn. "And maybe if I had it all sorted out, I wouldn't sound like that. I'm sorry."

"Me, too." And, at length, "Tell me, does it still hurt?"

"What, the knee? On and off. Lately it's been better."

She seemed about to say she wasn't asking about his knee, but thought better and switched gears. "What about now?"

"Not too bad. This is as hard as I've worked it in a while. We probably should keep moving before it seizes up and you have to carry me off the mountain."

They fell into step, glances upward at where he'd come flying down, that *moment,* real as bent time. He said, "About my brother, Katie…just not now. Okay?"

By way of answer she slipped her hand into his and left it there.

He took her to dinner at a West Shore restaurant, a Swiss place. She told him she'd had a child, a girl who had died before she left

Texas, Shawn not daring to wonder what that had been like. She asked about his marriage, so he took her into the basics: Shawn and Loren, two people with little in common except escape – a bit like in *The Graduate,* the final scene on the bus, Katharine Ross still in her wedding dress, Dustin Hoffman having saved her from an unloving groom, their smiles fading into *God, what now?* Rather than deepening what they had, only making more apparent what they didn't.

She nodded, sipped wine with him in silence, told him impulsively that her game was basketball. She'd been point guard on the girl's team because she was the only one who could dribble, most people in her high school believing the only ball that mattered was thrown by a quarterback. Or at least by the all-Midlands one she'd gone with and married the day after their graduation.

On the way back to her place, he asked if she hadn't anything planned for Saturday there was a barbecue after the dive demonstration and would she like to go with him, offset the kind of party and people he anticipated being there. Meaning it to sound flattering before seeing her frown.

"I don't know," she said. "Can I let you know later?"

"Sure." Glancing at her, oncoming headlights illuminating her face, once past them returning it to darkness. "It was just an invite. No big deal if you're busy."

"Shawn, I could bullshit you, say no wonder people call you Speed, but I think more of you than that. It's some things I have to think over."

"Anything you'd like to bounce off a friend?" Not believing he'd said it, the example he set by his own life: floor-to-ceiling crap waiting for someone to open the closet door, death by avalanche.

"No," she said. "But thanks all the same."

They let some jazz she dialed up take them the rest of the way, not speaking even when he stopped in front of the A-frame and she kissed him on the cheek. Saying as she got out of the Cherokee, "I had fun today, Shawn, more than in a long time. But I've trusted my heart before and had it handed to me. Can you understand that?"

"I think so."

"It isn't you, at least not how you're thinking. Okay?"

"Rain check," he said. "At least I hope so."

She didn't answer.

"Five-six-one, oh-oh-three-one, twenty-four seven. Leave a message if I don't pick up. Want me to write it down?"

"No. Goodnight, Shawn." She closed the door, and he watched her go inside without looking back. As he drove away, he could see the curtain part, her backlit and unmoving shape at the window.

20

A DRIZZLE MOVED IN DURING THE NIGHT. Without the sun, Shawn slept till seven-thirty, was working the stiffness out of his knee – predictable after the hike, no real pain – when he noticed the envelope that had been slipped under his door. He was sure he hadn't noticed it last night but not altogether, as pre-occupied as he was with thoughts of Katie. Late afternoon sun bringing up the red-gold in her hair. The restaurant candlelight in her eyes. Her response when he'd asked her to Suzanne's shindig, that she'd had her heart handed to her and asking if he understood.

No, he had no idea about that.

Not much, he didn't.

Half-expecting his friend the tape-explosion crazy, he picked up the envelope, prepared for the same childlike block letters – read untraceable. Instead he opened it to:

SOME PEOPLE JUST KNOW A PERSON TOO WELL TO STAY PISSED. WHICH APPLIES TO YOU, I HOPE.

AT LEAST I'M A CONSISTENT ASSHOLE.

—JD

After checking in with Mal, the diver telling him they were going to run a test of Saturday's video-feed system – *Constance* to the shore monitors, a chance to test some new dive adjustments – Shawn dialed McCandless Lumber, the Lakewood yard. Bounced from extension to extension, he finally got his party.

"*Yeah?*" Joe Don over the whine of a power saw.

"Never had a quarrel with your consistency," Shawn said, "just your timing."

He heard Joe Don yell for someone to cut the thing off, then: "Pretty sorry spectacle, huh?"

"Oh, I don't know, the crowd seemed to like it. Beats *Survivor* reruns."

"Sorry, man, sometimes I just lose it. Like lately."

"Not to start up, but I was serious what I said about getting help."

"No need to push, *compa.* I'm looking into it."

Right, Shawn thought. *Quando puercos vuelen. When pigs fly.*

"So," Joe Don said. "We copasetic?"

"The way you swung, you're lucky I'm able to say yes. What about Robin?"

"We're working it out."

Which could mean any number of things, all of which led to *butt out* and which Shawn agreed were none of his business, that only drove the wedges deeper. Going on to explain what Mal had in mind, he asked if Joe Don wanted to preview the system, Joe Don sounding relieved at the peace offering, agreeing to meet him at the storage facility at ten-thirty.

Shawn hung up, got himself together. He was about to have flowers sent to Katie's house, something simple like daisies, but in light of her comment about having to think over his invitation, the advisability of *him,* period, he thought better of it.

Better to respect her intent, leave her with the action step.

Hoping she'd taken note of his phone number, tempted to call and leave it on her machine as a reminder, he willed himself to put the cell phone away and head for the storage building.

Joe Don met him at the empty *Deep VI* slip. Inside the building two crewmembers – Thad Axtell and Al Lydecker, systems-hookup/tent-duty watch for Saturday – shook hands, said they'd been told to expect Shawn, welcome Joe Don. They went back to tweaking the equipment until Mal in shorts, pullover, and ball cap came up on the monitor, saying he could see them fine on his.

Shawn introduced Joe Don as friend and Chamber brass; Mal greeted him, added that Duane Carper and Burl Ruttan were already in the water and getting set. He then panned to them in their vests and full-body dry suits – Carper in black, Ruttan in red, Ruttan with mini-cam headgear. Along with another crewmember, they waved at Mal and the camera.

Shawn and Joe Don un-stacked white plastic outdoor chairs, sat watching the divers double-check masks, gauges, meters, weight belts, then thumbs-up and turn tail in a swirl of bubbles. The gestures made Shawn wonder if Catherine Mulvhill was watching through her scope. Mal cut back to himself, explained the dive as a trial run on a number of systems, not just the cameras, then announced that he was switching the feed to Ruttan's mini-cam.

Carper came up in soft green; they saw Ruttan's arm extend, his hand touch Carper's shoulder, the diver nod and point. Carper descended until the light faded, his flash becoming the only light, Mal explaining the underwater floods already were at depth from a previous dive.

While the descent progressed, he went into detail: duration of dive, twelve minutes max, moment of descent to start of ascent; bottom temp a frigid and strength-sapping thirty-nine degrees; lake altitude adding at least a hundred-twenty feet of added pressure; dedicated computer software dictating the oxygen-helium-nitrogen mixtures and decompression times – two-plus *hours* in the ascent to avoid the blood bubbling known as bends.

Just then the screen flared white, the lens adjusting to the activated floods. They saw Carper hoist the light carriage, direct it upward, saw Ruttan's lens come in tighter, tighter on something: in focus, then, an image that made Shawn's scalp prickle. It was an angled white stern with the letters C-O-N-S-T-A-N-C-E; beneath that in smaller letters was E-C-H-O-B-A-Y. Above the lettering was the diamond-grid railing he'd seen in a thousand shots of her, Mel's voice saying, "Gentlemen, I assume you can read."

"Have some goosebumps," Joe Don said.

"Every time," Lydecker said, his eyes not leaving the screen."

"Let's hope the goosebumps are catching on Saturday," Mal came back. "Especially in the checkbook department."

Ruttan's camera began drifting along the port side gradient, up and over the deck rail, the overhead awning to the upper deck and its intact air scoops and fallen stack, down again to slowly pan the row of salon windows, some still with glass that reflected the light. Up and over the pilothouse to a bow overview, a true goosebump shot: ghostlike crane, deck gear, anchor davits, Shawn envisioning her captain looking down as he headed the queen and her buzzing subjects toward South Shore, wind in her pennants and her whistle wide open in salute.

That feeling of the world in your hands.

Then…something else.

It came across as confusion. Ruttan and his camera swung instead of panned from the lit bow shapes around to black – the bright-adjusted lens reading it that way – as if something had caught his attention. The pilothouse came into focus, its three bow-facing windows, vertical black frames against the lighter wood background. Carper's light bathed the pilothouse, details emerging as he realized Ruttan and his camera were fixed on it: house and deck rail, missing searchlight and life preserver mounts, those three dead eyes.

But Ruttan wasn't fixed on it anymore...

There was a downward yaw, a blur of motion at Ruttan's waist, the camera seeing what he saw, followed by the pilothouse and Carper and the light and everything dropping away and blackness closing in, broken only by a pencil beam of light.

"The hell," Lydecker said as Mal's voice crackled over the image: "Burl, what is it? *Burl – come in.* Duane? What is Ruttan doing? Why's he headed up? He *what?* Well get after him, for crissake."

"Mal, what's happening? Mal?" Axtell.

Mal with static, breathless: "Ruttan's dropped his weights and blown his suit. Carper says he has no clue, but from the screen it doesn't look good."

"Son of a bitch." Lydecker.

There was more of Mal trying to contact Burl Ruttan, set to black screen, pencil beam, water particles conveying ascension into night snow. With Joe Don, Shawn sat transfixed; he felt the mounting sense of dread until it was a tangible thing in the room. At least the screen had begun to lighten now: charcoal to gray green to green.

"Duane, *goddamnit,* can't you catch him?" Mal said into his phones. *"Son of a bitch!* Shore, Ruttan's through 340 and on the main line. Carper has to stop there or he'll be just as fucked. We're standing by to decompress, but…oh, man." Then, "Burl? I know you can hear me. There's still time, but not if you keep on. Red light, Burl, you have to stop. *Burl, you're killing me here…*"

Mid-green, then pale: Ruttan's camera still transmitting, Mal not having thought to cut in his own. There was a shimmer of approaching surface, Mal shouting instructions against a new sound, this rising, guttural hum. Then the mirror broke apart and Ruttan's camera was looking at three crewmen and Mal reaching down; topsy as Ruttan was pulled aboard and stripped of his gear, extreme close-up of duckboards lurching into sky and faces, hands in motion. And, as Ruttan's mouthpiece was extracted, the worst scream Shawn had ever heard.

It was a moaning, grinding, rising, falling *thing*. Finally it was muted by the clang of the decompression chamber, Mal's camera at last cutting in to reveal Ruttan's face through the chamber's thick glass window, his mouth in a rictus, something that resembled cherry soda foaming from his nose and ears.

Joe Don's cuddy cabin was tied up nearby; they took it while Lydecker and Axtell hightailed in a backup boat to be there when Carper surfaced. Between the Four Winns running at flank and the wind's buffet, there was no point in talk, so they didn't try, if only to distance themselves from the image of Ruttan's distorted face and scream.

Replaying one, feeling the other.

Twenty minutes out, through binoculars, Shawn made out *Deep VI* well along toward South Shore, the larger hospital there; pulling alongside the slower boat, he saw Mal nod at him. In what seemed like hours they were pulling up to a dock with a winch and hoist, raising the cylinder with Ruttan in it, lowering it to a waiting pickup with an ambulance standing by. Shawn told Joe Don, who had to get back, that he'd brief him. He then hopped a lift with Mal, two of the crew, and the paramedics.

At the hospital the chamber was muscled onto a dolly and wheeled in, the crew volunteering to stay with Ruttan during decompression, Mal to check in and out. Over burnt coffee in the cafeteria, Mal told Shawn that Ruttan had been with him since day one, that he didn't understand it, any of it. Shaking his head as he stirred in milk.

Shawn blew on his absently. "Why, do you suppose?"

"You're asking me? Hell he's seen things, they all have – I have. You get narcosis at depth, that's why the gas mixtures are such a deal, to prevent it. Not interfere with your judgment."

"You think that's what it was, a malfunction?"

Mal took a breath, hissed it out. "Paul's going over the tanks now. That Carper had no problem tends to clear the calibrations and software." He took a sip, set the cup aside. "*Son of a bitch.* Whatever Ruttan thought he saw sure put him into override."

"Don't answer if you don't want to – he going to make it?"

"Depends on what you mean by make it. Bubbles can put a man in a wheelchair, or worse. Docs can't even evaluate till he stabilizes." Noting Shawn's look, he added, "I came up like that once, though not as deep. I came through okay."

"I keep hearing him."

"Which is how it feels, you want to know. But the bubbles leave in time. It's the ones that lodge in places like your spine and lungs…"

Shawn said nothing, just *heard.* They sat; then Mal said, "We need to talk about Saturday, where we stand."

"No shit. So where do we?"

"Nobody goes down until we finish our check, that one's in stone," Mal said. "But we can still bring it off, it's the reason I wanted today in the can. Technical difficulty prevents a live feed, so we run the footage up to Ruttan's losing it. If we're lucky and it doesn't get around, everybody goes home happy."

Shawn let a beat pass. "Okay so far as it goes."

"Man, don't tell me that."

"Now or Saturday."

"Fuck it. You got a better idea, let's hear it."

"All right." Hand on Elizabeth and Nate, the cold broken frame, he said, "Stonewalling is out, it'll be around the lake like *that*. We preempt: statements from us, human error, no way is the project affected, back diving Monday, whether we do or not. If Ruttan's up to it, we run a live feed, him saying it goes with the territory, assuring the friends he's made and the public that he's looking forward to getting back to it. *Then* we run the *Constance* footage, leave them with that."

"Damage control…"

Shawn nodded. "Personal calls to everyone with a stake. You to your list, me to mine."

"And if Ruttan doesn't make it?"

"Plan B, whatever that is."

Mal said nothing. Then, "I tell you what I've got riding on this?"

Gripping the frame and thinking *You're not the only one,* Shawn settled for a raised foam cup.

"More than once," he said.

It took two hours in a room the hospital gave them for the purpose: laptops to draft the statements, calls to principal donors and players, Shawn outlining what he had in mind, Terry confirming it after some give and take. At four a doctor appeared to tell them Ruttan was out of decompression, they had some tests to run but it looked as if he'd make it. They might be able to see him around six, but he'd likely be too groggy to answer questions.

In response to Shawn's query, the doctor allowed as how they could quote him.

Incorporating the Ruttan update, Shawn e-mailed the statements and sat back for his cell phone to go off, which it did for another hour and a half around a call to Joe Don: questions he answered with a *just-wanted-to-keep-you-in-the-loop* insouciance – use it or not, no change in status, Saturday or otherwise – by and large the callers sounding satisfied with the explanation. Yet when it was over, when the bullet they'd appeared to dodge finally hit him, Shawn had to grip the picture in the cracked frame with both hands to hold himself together.

21

THEY GOT IN TO SEE BURL RUTTAN AT NINE: a few minutes only, doctor's orders, visiting hours already bent. First in due to limited space were the two crewmembers, then Shawn and Mal.

Ruttan was raised slightly, his eyes swollen almost shut, face puffed from fluid accumulation, cotton taped in his ears. IV tubes ran from drip bags — morphine for one, they'd learned from the doc — while a monitor ran vital signs. So far they didn't know the full extent of the damage, but from senses detected in his extremities there was optimism. As to what happened, Ruttan was able to communicate an overwhelming panic that he suddenly couldn't breathe, couldn't get air, had to get to the surface or drown.

Nothing then but the pain.

"Carper?" he asked when Mal told him to rest, that he'd see him tomorrow.

"Carper is fine. Al and Thad picked him up."

"Put him at risk, too." Barely moving his head. "Sorry, Skip."

"You know better. Just get well."

In the pulse, Shawn asked, "Burl, you up for a question?"

"Try…"

"From the monitor it looked like something around the pilot-house caught your attention. Anything to it?"

"No. Nothing."

"You're sure about that?"

"Sure. Mal?"

"Right," Mal said, head-gesturing to Shawn they were done. "Save it for the nurses, Burl. We need you out there."

The night air was like something from a premium-champagne bottle. Later, on the way back in the *Deep VI*, lights showing around the lake, stars but no moon, Shawn asked Mal what might have gone wrong now that he'd had a chance to think.

Mal focused on the instruments. "Hard to say. Paulie said the tanks checked out – mix, regulators, seals, everything the same as Carper. Ruttan never would have made it up if that was the problem."

"Narcosis, you think…"

"Put it this way, I've seen stranger things. Had a deepwater guy come up once who swore there was a giant squid around his neck – took five of us to get him under control. Guy was checking the mirrors for days afterward, shipped out after a week." Mal looking as though he still saw it. "Some things you chalk off."

Shawn said nothing. Mal peered into the darkness.

"Then again, some things you don't want to know."

Shawn sat in the Cherokee, thinking over what came next, the one day they had left to regroup. Mal was right: All things considered, they were in good shape. A final briefing on possible questions, points to stress, Ruttan's Saturday hookup and hospital feed at this point looking like a real possibility. He reached

Terry, still in his office, and updated him; Suzanne, who told him she'd been besieged by interview requests, closing the office finally and turning on voice mail.

He punched up the messages, heard among them Katie's: "I tried getting through, guess you had your hands full from what I heard on the news. Call me when you get in. It doesn't matter how late."

He dialed her number, told her that Ruttan would make it, that he was plain beat, the truth. She asked if he'd eaten, told him she had leftovers but would understand if he just wanted to crash. Twenty minutes later, he found himself at her door, Katie in jeans and a Texas Rangers sweatshirt, telling him to come in before the bugs around the light came in with him.

The interior basically was one big room, knotty-pine paneling and eclectic furnishings, with a wood-railed loft where she slept under a ceiling fan. On respective chairs were the caramel-and-white cat he'd seen her with yesterday – Ben Affleck, so she could josh people that's who was waiting for her at home – and a brown rabbit named Ihop she'd found in the restaurant's Dumpster and who sniffed his hand with enthusiasm. Two beers and the leftovers later he felt better and said so.

"Am I glad you were home." Leaning back in his chair.

"I took a day to get my head together and figured work wasn't the place," she said. "Bartenders aren't supposed to seek advice."

"There something on your mind?"

"You could say that."

"Worth the effort, I hope."

"It remains to be seen, but the prospect looks not too bad." Eyes not leaving his.

Feeling their warmth, he said, "But you still have reservations."

"The very reason I've been consulting with my advisers."

Shawn looked down: Ben Affleck was on one side, Ihop on the other. Both were looking up at him. "Other than tuna and carrots rule, they come to any conclusions?"

"One, they barely know you. Two, they don't much care."

"Easy for them to say," he said. "What about you?"

"It took a while, but I went with the majority."

"I see. There an action step here?"

"Already switched my shift for the eight-to-three AM. That is, if the barbecue invitation's still open."

"You bet." And to her look, "Do I see something else on your mind?"

She smiled. "As a matter of fact, you do."

At first they made love with Ben Affleck on the bed, nudging for attention, Katie noting that Shawn was in Ben's usual spot, Ben curling up as it became clear they had other fish to fry.

Which they did.

Katie, predictably, asked him about the tattoo on his shoulder, Shawn explaining that *Ski to Die* was inscribed in reverse so he could wake up to it in the mirror that summer when he and Bill Johnson and some others had gotten them. Mindsets for the 1984 Olympic Downhill Johnson ultimately won. As she kissed it, gradually branching out, he tried not to think of how long it had been, just to go with it, easier said.

After a bit, she stopped, smiled, pointed, and he saw Ihop making himself comfortable in his discarded clothes. She used the laugh to touch his face and tell him to relax, that it wasn't an audition, they had all night and she was fine with it no matter what.

So he did, and they had, and she was.

22

FRIDAY WENT BETTER THAN EXPECTED: breakfast first on Katie's patio behind the A-frame, Ben and Ihop working cleanup.

Then he met with Mal and crew at the storage building, where they went over responses, responsibilities, finally an edit of Ruttan's videotape, which Shawn agreed was as good as they could have hoped. And though he didn't tell the divers as much, he had a feeling the sudden media attention might turn out to be a windfall.

Stranger things...

Ruttan still hurt, but there appeared to be no permanent damage; local media was working on arrangements for his live feed in exchange for an exclusive, another bonus. Joe Don brought down a contingent of Chamber members and brass eager to volunteer; Bob Lamont matched with casino and hospitality association staff. Then a number of union members showed up, an embarrassment of riches.

The only downers were three: reported plans for larger protests, Katie's having to work later, and the condition of Shawn's cabin when he finally did arrive home.

Whoever had searched it had been thorough, though not enough to detect the things Shawn had placed after becoming sure he was being followed: banker's-box angles, toiletries, bedside articles, a curtain just so. For a while he pondered what to do about it, then he made a call.

Rings, then: "Pop, it's me."

"Hold on while I turn this thing off." After his father had turned off whatever he had on: "I'm glad you qualified or I'd never have known. I assume that means you're all right?"

"Sorry for not calling. It's been nonstop."

"So I got from the radio." Pause. "Let me guess: somebody's on your tail or you're finally tired of wasting money over there."

Oh boy, Shawn thought.

"Pop, if the offer still stands, I'd appreciate it."

"It's not rented yet, if that's what you mean. We don't even have to cross paths."

Shawn took a breath, figured what he said next would be taken just as wrong, so what the hell. "You're right, it would be in and out, mostly out. Per diem, no arguments."

"That'll be the day. When?"

"Tonight. I'll bring dinner."

"Don't go out of your way."

He let it pass. "Any chance there might be room in the garage for the Cherokee?"

"So it is somebody on your tail. Any idea who?"

"Not as yet." Thinking no point in denial.

"Figured it probably was that. Now that you're made of money."

"Pop, I'm hardly–"

"Never mind, I'll move the truck so you can slide in. And Shawn?"

"Yeah, Pop?"

"Shotgun's where it always is, behind the water heater."

He had to admit the thought came as mostly welcome. Still he answered, "Pop, this isn't—"

"I'll be looking for you."

It took two hours to settle up, head for Truckee, loop around to make sure he wasn't being followed, pick up KFC and stow the Cherokee next to Liam's pickup. By then the sun had started down. Shawn tried explaining to his father he wouldn't be needing the shotgun, plus what was going on with the project, but with the game on radio, he wasn't sure it made much impact. After several attempts they simply listened, the crack of the bats and the cheers as if from a more predictable time.

In bed in his old room later, wondering if he'd done the right thing, he told himself it was only temporary, a cosmic puppet-master's absurd twist. He half expected Cort to barge in, his mother to appear with a glass of milk, his old man with some new thing he'd read about in *Popular Mechanics*. And he wondered if it had been waiting for him just this way, or if he'd ever truly left.

The crowd started lining up at nine-thirty, two hours after Shawn, crew, and volunteers began final prep. The tents were up, most of everything inside arranged, the burlier volunteers posted to head off disrupters, though no protestors appeared until ten. Then what seemed like the Lake Inn crowd tripled arrived with their signs, chants, and circles. Shawn saw Arn Tennell and a knot of deputies and nodded to him, but it wasn't returned.

At eleven, the building and tents cranked up and the rest was a blur: people, volunteers, deputies, protesters, questions, hands to shake, glossies to sign. At noon they broadcast Ruttan live and each half-hour from then on. Perhaps the biggest crush was at the tent showing the edited *Constance* footage, old timers relating their own tales of her, the sacrilege it had been to put her down.

Shawn wondered how much knowledge they really possessed, but the effect was to fuel another rush on the pamphlets and donor envelopes. Their ground-floor offer was linked to the website: videotape or DVD with each donation over $200; vintage photo book – the work of a local collector-photographer – for those over $100. More impressions: the media sound-biting the crowd, Mal chatting up Neville and Neal Autry and other Chamber boosters, Phil Van Alden of Ways and Means up from Carson City, reminding Shawn he owed them a lunch appearance they weren't forgetting.

The most heated it got outside was when the protesters outflanked security and set a Dumpster on fire, flames and shouts before the stand-bys put it out: four arrested and hauled off, not many crossing Arn after that. On it went, four, four-thirty, all the way to an hour past scheduled shutdown. Still people stuck around, talking, gesturing, full of the promise of the queen's return, while Shawn worked the crowd until his hand pulsed.

"Jeez!" Mal said, as they collapsed into the first empty chairs in six hours, last visitors bound for the lot where groups still talked, some jawing with holdover protestors. "You getting the sense of this I am?"

"Too early for champagne, but a few more like it…" Caught in the moment and not trusting it, the sea change from their near disaster.

He stood to hit the road: Katie picked up first, then to Suzanne's, Mal's congratulatory grip before waving him off. He was beeping up the Cherokee's locks, wondering how Catherine

Mulvhill was reacting to the day, Joe Don earlier telling him that he'd seen Frank Love talking into a cell phone, when he saw Arn closing in, hand on his baton. Shawn regarded him.

"Even you aren't that stupid."

Arn regarded back. "So you won a round. Not sure I'd let it go to my head just yet."

"This all part of the service, Arn?"

"It is for deadbeats like you."

"What are you talking about? You saw the crowd today."

"That so? Word I'm getting is a little different – like a whole lot of past dues piled up by the project, like creditors getting antsy. Anything you'd want to tell me about that?"

"Yeah, Arn. I'm late."

Arn smiled, popped a toothpick between his teeth. "Late could be arranged," he said.

Suzanne's house was on the West Shore, an architect's knock-down and rebuild, lower half stone, the upper half redwood-stained lapboard. The sloping roof and window mansards were sheathed in copper a weathered shade of green; the window glass was expansive enough to look as if it were actual trees and sky. Grapestake fencing surrounded the property.

Shawn left the Cherokee to the valet parkers.

Katie had been waiting for him in a white dress and shawl, sun-browned shoulders, a head turner. Bummed that she'd missed the open house for the few bar customers who hadn't also attended, she pumped Shawn for details, her pleasure growing with each anecdote. Beside him, then, walking up the drive and around to the source of the music and what must have been several hundred people holding cocktails who chatted under

Japanese lanterns while the sun topped the eastern mountains and lit the high clouds.

"This thing you have with sunsets," Katie said after a waiter left them with champagne flutes. "Did it start up here?"

Shawn sipped from his. "You'd think so, wouldn't you?"

"But not…?"

"New Mexico," he answered, "Jim Beam and beer backs, whatever went down first."

"And the sunset part?"

He took a moment to frame it. "Always reminded me of a spotlight fading out, giving you permission to stop tap-dancing and slip into the wings…just cease." And to her look, "Hey, you asked."

"It can't have been that bad."

"That good now." Leaning down to kiss her, feeling it come back with heat. "It's turning, Katie. You, *Constance,* all of it."

"Including your two faces in the frame?"

"That close. Just hold the thought."

She squeezed his hand, which began a parade of well-wishers: Suzanne, whom he thanked in brief remarks they requested he make; local politicians; other contributors; California's lieutenant governor, a personal friend of Suzanne's, telling him they were keeping watch, that all stood to gain, two states, five counties.

Terry appeared in the company of a model type Shawn recognized from the volunteer pool; up for the day to background schmooze, which was why he hadn't come in on Shawn's moment. After introductions, Katie left for the powder room, the model type for an actor she thought she recognized.

"Bob filled me in," Terry said. "In all modesty, you're making me look better than I deserve."

"Meaning you must be close to phasing me out," Shawn said.

"Meaning if it's getting fixed, don't break it." Scoping the crowd. "Meaning I'm not sure I'd have turned around that little dive thing as well as you did."

"Elizabeth and Nate, Terry. Remember?"

"Doing well, thanks."

"Soon, Terry."

The grin "That wouldn't be a threat, now, would it?"

"Juice is everything, whoever it was told me that. You, as I recall."

Terry watched Katie come out and wave; he waved back, bent to say, "That little thing you've talked into feeling sorry for you – maybe I should have a talk with her on your finer points."

"Talking out of your ear might be a problem."

The grin died. "Some guys never learn, which is why there'll always be guys like me. In short, now that it's rolling, don't fuck it up."

Shawn bought time by draining his flute and thinking how much Terry sounded like Joe Don telling him the same thing the other night. To sidetrack it, he said, "I was approached on a number of late-pays, Terry. There anything to it?"

"Hell, we owe everybody and his dog, but not for long. Just keep the donation train going the way it is and you're home free."

He drifted off in the direction of the model.

Shawn was tossing off his second flute when Katie took his hand and led him up to the dance area where the combo was returning from a break. "Think you could get any more tense?" she said when the music kicked back in. "Robots aren't this tight."

"Sorry. He has that effect." Trying to will himself to relax.

"Maybe we can loosen you up later." Then, "*Hello...*earth to Shawn."

Shawn shook it off, snapped to. "Anybody ever tell you that's a killer dress you have on?"

"Only about half the men here, if you'd notice."

"What you get for dating a slow learner." And when Terry, leading the model-type out on deck, winked at him, "You wouldn't want to get out of here, would you?"

They were in the loft, Katie sleeping and Shawn trying to instead of replaying Terry's grin and wink, when the call came on his cell phone. Telling her to go back to sleep, he took it out on the patio, Ben Affleck deciding there might be something in it for him, hanging by his bowl until Shawn spooned out open tuna, the phone to his ear.

"All right, you can talk now," he told Terry.

"Domestic bliss, Shawn?"

"Before I stuff this thing under a lounge pad, is there a reason you're calling?"

"As it happens, there is. Wasn't that you at the party making noises about getting phased out?"

Shawn's heart flipped. "What of it?"

"All leaves cancelled, son, Catherine Mulvhill's gone to the mats. Bob Lamont just called. She's gotten her legal team to petition the State Supreme Court."

Shawn felt ice. "On what grounds."

"That state law regarding *Constance* is unconstitutional, that it doesn't fit the definition of abandonment, that the environment will be harmed, that I don't give a fuck. Bottom line is we've been enjoined, read hosed."

Think, he told himself. "She have a case?"

"These days of judicial activism? What do you think?"

"You'll forgive me if I'm not up on my constitutional law."

"Wrong answer, Shawn-boy. All she has to do is tie us up in court: momentum gone, hope gone, lots of things gone, if you hear what I'm saying."

The ice became an ice pick.

"Why didn't she do this at the beginning?"

"Knowing her, it was to save fees, wait and see what you brought to the table. Which means you impressed her, at least you can take that to heart." Horn blare: *"Motherfucker. Stay in your lane!"*

"What do you want from me, Terry?"

Deep breath, the struggle for control that audible. "It's simple, Shawn, I want you to take her down. And when you have her down, I want you to take her apart. And when you have her apart, I want you to feed what's left to the goddamned fish."

"That wasn't our deal. Forget it."

"Our deal is what I say it is, sport. But fuck it; I'll add another point to your share, no problem. Feel better now?"

Shawn was vaguely aware of Ben Affleck rubbing against his leg, the spread of stars through the trees, not enough air. He said, "Keep it, Terry, I'm not in that business anymore. Better yet, do it yourself."

"Myself, Shawn? Well, here's a thought: Rio might be just what the kids need to further their education. I tell you we were thinking that? No? Well, we sure are. Now kiss off your little punch and get on it."

23

THE WAREHOUSE WAS A MORGUE, smoke from a nearby Sierra wildfire settling in and adding to the pall. Shawn had been up the rest of the night, Terry's call to a 7-Eleven for cigarettes, barely aware he was smoking until his throat turned raw. Katie had noticed him gone and gotten up, mulling with him when he returned, making coffee they drank in silence. At seven he'd phoned Mal, already aware of the situation, the upshot a 9 AM meeting, all divers and crewmembers.

Mal spoke first, spelled it out that they were officially on the beach and why, that the only fair thing was not to lead them on with false hope, release them to pursue other work. That's what he intended for himself, no option other than to pick it up and lay it down someplace else. Then if things did break their way, he'd contact them, each his job back if he wanted, understandable if something else came up.

For a while everyone just sat.

Finally they shook hands and filed out.

"Some fucked twenty-four hours," Mal said when he and

Shawn were the only ones, engines starting up in the lot, tires peeling. "So what do *you* do now?"

Shawn regarded his hands. "Work the cracks I find, if I can find some. I haven't decided."

"But you're sticking?"

"You mentioned options, Mal. This is mine."

The diver nodded. "Me, I spent the night packing, it was that or walk into the lake." Pause. "You saw the crowds, you felt what they did. How in hell can she do that to them?"

"Getting too close, I suppose."

"To what? Aside from her not liking it?"

"I don't know," Shawn said. "You tell Ruttan yet?"

"Yeah, and I'll spare you what he said. Hospital's releasing him later today, so I told him I'd swing by and pick him up."

"I'll do it, if you like."

"Done. Give me a couple more hours to clear out the boat and this place, get going by dark."

"How's Ruttan doing?"

"He'll be back down somewhere in a week, his kind always are. They're like corks in reverse." Mal cracked his knuckles, blew a breath. "You held up your end, you know that? I wasn't sure about you to begin with, but you did."

"Mal, I'll do what I can. I know what it means."

The diver flashed a grin. "Hell, I've been bust before, that goes with the turf. It's just that for some reason this one got under my skin. Maybe it's because I saw myself on her bridge, felt her move under me. I should have known better. Come right down to it, she's just another rust bucket with a boiler for a heart, a cold one at that."

Looking at Shawn as if daring him to dispute it.

On the way over to pick up Burl Ruttan, the lake hammered copper in the smoky light, Shawn thought about where he stood with Catherine Mulvhill's halt of their operation. Zip and zero about summed it. Money talked and bullshit walked, and right now he was the one with the holes in his soles. And yet, to extend the metaphor, he still could lay one down in front of the other; he just needed to step around the rocks and puddles, stay poised for the glass.

Waiting for him at the hospital front desk, Shawn could hear Ruttan bitching to the nurse wheeling him. Including Shawn then: The whole thing was a crock, hospital policy didn't mean he wasn't able to transport himself, all the way out the double doors. The black around his eyes had faded to a yellowing purple, Shawn saw; that and taking it slow getting into the Cherokee were it for outward signs, Ruttan not volunteering much to him beyond, "I was better yesterday," reference to the Mulvhill news.

Shawn waited until they were through the casino-fringe sprawl, past Zephyr Cove and up the Nevada side, to take a deeper cut.

"You heard I'm staying?" he asked Ruttan.

The man nodded. "Mal said something about it when he told me you were coming. Only question is why?"

"Hope springs, I suppose."

"Hell, more power to you."

"You mind a question, Burl?"

"Not so far."

He took a moment to phrase it. "In your room Mal asked you what happened down there. I asked what you might have seen, because the camera tracked a certain way. You said nothing. Do you recall that?"

"Vaguely." Shields rising.

"I had this sense about your answer and thought I'd try again. That is, since the job isn't at stake anymore."

Hesitation. "You saying I held out?"

Shawn said, "That job means something to you. No point a man saying something his employer might take wrong."

A mile passed in silence. Then: "Something like what?"

"That's what I need, Burl. I don't know."

"Told you, I'm listening."

"My theory is it's something a man might be more inclined to let out if he was guaranteed it wouldn't get back. Here or anyplace else."

Ruttan steadied. "You trying to blackmail me? Because if you are, pull this thing over. I'm not so out of it I can't kick your ass."

The lanes merged and Shawn fell in behind a truck. Thinking at least now the man could relate, he said, "Burl, I'll let you in on something. It's me who's being blackmailed. By Terry Dahl. Either I turn this thing around, no idea how yet, or I lose my kids. It's the reason I'm here, the only reason. And now you know something nobody else knows because I have to start somewhere."

"That no bullshit?" Ruttan finally asked. "About your kids?"

"No bullshit. Taking them to live out of the country came up in our last swell conversation."

Tire hum. "And you want what from me?"

"Everything that happened. Doesn't matter how small."

Ruttan thought, started to speak, thought better, leaned back. Shawn gave him a minute. "How about this? If it's still nothing, forget I asked. If not, let me worry about whether it's relevant."

"Nothing to anybody?"

Cherries in a beautiful line, the sound of silver downspouting.

"Not that will get back to Mal, my word on it." Silence; sensing Ruttan drawing back, he jump-started: "Burl, you said you felt as if you were drowning, yet your gear checked out. Any idea why?"

Ruttan's eyes locked on something down the road. "You ever had a feeling like that? Like all you could draw in was water?"

Shawn nodded. "In a pool once when I was a kid."

"Try it at five-hundred feet, dark as a grave. Your life running down this long tunnel and you fucking trying to catch it."

"Narcosis?"

"Hell, I know narcosis like I know a hard-on." Hesitating before adding, "You ever seen things that didn't belong there? It's called sight. Sometimes it's described as a gift. Some damned gift."

"Then you did see something?"

"Answer my question."

"Only read about it. But Mal said you have before."

Ruttan swallowed, cracked his window, caught a breath. "It's like this rash starts, and the hair on the back of your neck stands up, and you turn, and instead of what was there when you looked, something else is."

A pale sheen of sweat had formed as it played in the diver's mind.

He said, "All right, fuck it, you want it so bad. We're down there and I think I hear something, maybe my name. So I look that way thinking it's Carper and instead, there it is, this fucking glow, this *thing*. It's inside the pilothouse, staring out at me, I don't *know* what. And the cold, fucking freezing – inside-out cold, colder than a mother – and I get this feeling like I'm drowning and the bends don't matter and nothing matters, not Carper, not Mal, not the mission, not anything but get the fuck out of there. Just *fuck* it."

Shawn waited. "Could it have been lights off the glass?

Air bubbles?"

"Bull*shit* it was lights or bubbles. I *saw* it."

"Sorry. I just don't know what I expected."

"*Sure you didn't*. Point one: I'm finished with Mal; they don't ask divers back who do what I did. Point two: Even if he begged me, ain't no way in hell I go back down there, end of story. That what you wanted to hear?"

"I don't know, Burl," Shawn said. "But I do know what it took. Thanks."

Ruttan, however, had pulled the plug. He looked away, sagged against his side, stared out at the smoke and haze, the pale sun lurking in it, as if something there had caught his attention.

Shawn dropped Burl Ruttan in the warehouse lot, Mal still loading up his RV. After promising to stay in touch, he drove up to the A-frame and found Katie getting ready for work. He told her about Mal, about letting the divers and crew go, about Ruttan, minus his revelation, such as it was. He then told her of his decision to bunk in with his father for a while.

"Sleep at your dad's…?"

"Long as he doesn't throw me out."

"Any particular reason?" Setting down the tote bag she was rummaging through, Ben Affleck and Ihop looking up from their spots.

"Nothing you need to worry about."

"So what do I tell them? They've been asking when you were coming back ever since you left."

Shawn kissed her, pulled back to open eyes.

"Tell them that's the problem, that for a while I have no idea where I'll be or when. That I wouldn't put them through that."

"What if they don't mind?" Returning to the bag, retracting

her keys from it, looking at him.

"Look, I'll call you, come by some morning. We can go to breakfast or something, catch up."

She clutched the keys. "*Catch up...* That's good, Shawn, nice and polite. But I've been around enough to know that if you have something to say, I'd appreciate hearing it now."

"It's nothing like that."

Her eyes narrowed, lost their light. "We wouldn't be talking about Robin here, would we, the return of the native?" Then, "God, listen to me. As if I had some right to ask."

He held her, sat her on the couch, felt Ihop nose his shoelace, Ben Affleck his hand. He said, "Katie, in the business I was in before I had to do things that weren't so nice. That's the position I'm in now, except I don't even know what they are."

"And that means what? That you're going after Catherine Mulvhill?"

Breath. "It's come to that, yeah."

"For a boat that hasn't seen daylight in sixty years?"

"For what it represents to a lot of people."

She said nothing, all that needed saying.

"Katie, it's the game, playing to win. This happens to be the next move." Hating the way it sounded, that Terry couldn't have said it better.

"That's BS, and you know it." And when he didn't respond, "Maybe you should tell me what you mean by not so nice. Maybe it's something I need to know about you."

"Trust me."

"Why not let me decide?"

"Because you don't want it. You may think you do, but you don't."

"Is that no shit? Well, try this: My ex-husband liked belts, all sorts of uses. His father taught him. You think I couldn't have used that particular bit of information? You think my daughter couldn't have? Don't patronize me, Shawn."

"Katie, I'm trying not to hurt you."

"Great job so far."

"All right." Hands under his thighs as he compressed and edited. "We had a client whose company made cosmetics. One of *her* clients used a product she made, a skin defoliant, only it burned her face, scarred it so badly she had to wear a veil. She sued. I found a doctor, a psychiatrist, who for money swore this woman had a tendency toward self-inflicted injury. Court-mandated analysis, psych profile, the whole nine yards."

"I don't believe it. You knew going in?"

"What does it matter? She had a history of instability and I turned him loose on her, this Josef Mengele clone. It didn't take Jerry Lizardi long, either – you've heard of him? He was our lawyer. But it was the doc who turned it."

She took Ben Affleck into her lap. "So what happened to her?"

Seeing it again, her disfigurement on the stand, wounded eyes finding him wherever he sat, flashbulbs in his face outside the courtroom, he said, "She was found in her pool the day after my client was cleared and counter-sued. She'd drowned herself."

Katie just stared.

"Will you listen to me now?"

She let Ben down, walked to the window, turned from it. "Shawn, whatever you were, *if* you were, you're not that now. I'll never believe you are."

"I'm about to be again, Katie. That's what I'm trying to tell you."

"You don't know that."

"Unfortunately, I do."

"You *don't*. Listen to me, if it's your kids, we'll find a way."

"What makes you think they're involved? Because they aren't," he lied. *Shit,* he couldn't even lie anymore.

"*Whatever it is.* Don't you understand? I don't care."

He took her shoulders in his hands, was aware of their warmth, her eyes, his own racing pulse. "It also doesn't change anything. Look, I'll call you, or you can leave a message with my dad. He's generally there." He let his hands fall, wrote down Liam's phone number on her pad.

"Trust me, Katie, you're better off." Turning to go.

"Right," she said. "Like I haven't heard that one before."

He was on the front steps, hating himself enough for both of them after shutting the door behind him, when he heard her open it and say, "Who winds up in the pool this time, Shawn? Catherine Mulvhill or you?"

24

NEXT MORNING THE SMOKE WAS GONE, blown out by a night wind that still shook the trees. After perfunctory questions about Shawn's plans now that his project was in limbo, his father left the breakfast table to work in his shop behind the garage while Shawn left for the office.

He found Suzanne Padget boxing up desk and wall items, pamphlets, the reverse-biography glossies Terry had sent. He handed her a coffee he'd brought, sat down with his own, popped the lid, added half-and-half.

"No point wasting rent money," she said, stirring sugar into hers. "The landlord has somebody who wants the space."

"Makes sense," he said.

"The media were here earlier, they're panting for a quote. The machine is full of messages."

"No doubt."

They sipped, listened to an incoming request for an interview from a Sacramento TV station, the machine click off.

"Nice party," he said. "I didn't get a chance to thank you."

"Made me jealous is what you did. What's her name?"

"Katie. Katie Ware."

"Seemed okay for a younger woman, if you like them, and what man doesn't, ask my ex." Then, "You're not blaming yourself for what happened, are you?"

Shawn lifted off an elbow. "More wondering which I took more seriously, Catherine Mulvhill or myself."

"Maybe you should ease up a little."

"That might have been the problem," he said.

"What? Like you should have seen it coming?"

"It sure wouldn't have hurt."

"Look, I'm telling you this as a friend because I think you are one. Catherine Mulvhill is who she is and always has been, what I told Terry from the beginning. You just bucked the odds a little longer."

He looked up from his coffee. "You knew she was going to do this?"

"I'm not surprised. And now you have to do what, save the day? Save *you* would be my advice. One time she killed a project my ex-husband sweat blood over to get approved. Studies, permits, you name it – only up here. She cut John off at the knees, came near to breaking him, and not just financially. Nothing's beneath her when she wants something – or doesn't. It might as well snow in August."

For a while they just sat. She began filling the boxes again, Shawn pitching in at the low chest with the sliding doors. Reaching in and pulling things out, thinking it was unbelievable how much stuff they–

"Like snow in August…"

She raised up from a box. "You say something?"

"Thinking out loud. What you just said."

"Don't stop on my account."

"Money feeds politics, and right now she has the support. But if there were a way to melt that support, make it harder for the people who back her to justify it… Suzanne, you mentioned your mom went to school with her. You think she'd talk to me?"

"Mom? About what?"

"I don't know yet. Something, I hope."

She broke a smile. "Sweetie, the problem is not whether she'll talk, it's what she'll say and when she'll stop. Other than her condo and me, she has the museum and the few researchers who basically smile and find their own way around. This, in a museum Catherine Mulvhill pays for in a building she owns, a job Mom wouldn't have if it weren't for Catherine. Plus she's no spring chicken and hates it that I'm on the other side." Shaking her head as if hearing her mother say it. "Is this making sense?"

"As much as anything."

"Aha. But you have to start somewhere."

Shawn nodded, had a hit of coffee – lukewarm now, like his idea after the initial flare. "That's what I keep telling myself."

Strategize: His one chance to come out.

Phase one: Lull Catherine Mulvhill into the confidant state his had been before her bombshell. Phase two: While her guard was down, get something on the woman he could use as juice.

He asked Suzanne to keep packing boxes, be there with him when the media showed up. Rather than duck their questions, they'd present themselves as forced to abandon a worthy cause but gracious in defeat. His reinforcing message when they did show: a) they had the utmost respect for Catherine Mulvhill, b) they knew she had the interests of Lakewood and the other communities at heart, c) they felt she was making a mistake that would cost a heritage the project wished only to preserve.

Shawn did the return calls; they were there in minutes. On the basis that the heart trumped the wallet, at least in reporterland, he shunned the prosperity angle – underdog high ground, something to keep his outside chance alive. By two-fifteen, the last were gone to deadline.

"God, how do you do it, stay even like that?" Suzanne asked when they were alone.

"Keeping other things in mind helps," he said.

"Whatever."

"I appreciate your staying."

"Best supporting actress in a soap opera. Still want me to let Mom know you're coming?"

Shawn rubbed his neck to loosen the knots in it.

"And do that for you?"

"Probably not the best of ideas," he said. "Your mom, I mean."

"Theda's her name. Sandstrom. The museum is by appointment, but she's always there. I left the number on the desk."

"Thanks, Suzanne. For everything."

"Don't be a stranger, hotcakes. And good luck – you'll need it"

The museum was up the hill, a three-story stone building with a windowed bulge of dark brick and a view of the lake.

Son of Stonehouse, Shawn thought as he parked in back. The heavy oak door had a port with curtains that parted moments after he heard the doorbell echo inside. The woman who opened to him looked older than Catherine Mulvhill: white hair severely cropped, posture that had seen better days, thick glasses. Behind them, sharp eyes looked him up and down.

"You're the one who called?" she asked.

"Yes, ma'am. Interested in the *Constance*."

"Who isn't these days? This way."

He entered, followed her past a staircase, through wood-panel doors into what was once a drawing room: rosebud-cream wallpaper, converted gaslight fixtures, post-Victorian furnishings. Other than his Cherokee through the corner-bulge window, it could have been 1912.

"We encourage donations," Theda Sandstrom said as he sat across from her.

Shawn deposited a ten in the jar so marked.

She waited.

He put in another ten.

She said, "Have you an area you wish to explore, or is your interest more general?"

Crunch time: not the least of which was whether she recognized him, though it seemed as if she didn't. He said, "I was wondering if you knew – if you might know – of any passengers or crew who died aboard the ship."

"Died…"

"In transit, fallen overboard. Anything like that."

"Well," she said, drawing it out. "Her first captain did, Captain Glenn R. Bledsoe, December of 1919. They found his footprints in the snow and him in the water. He'd slipped and struck his head. Would he be who you mean?"

"Possibly. Anyone else?"

"Maybe you should just tell me what it is you're after, Mister…"

"Malcom Ruttan. I'm researching anything that might be construed as paranormal for a book on ghost ships. Of course, I'd credit you."

"Well, I've never heard of *Constance* referred to in that sense. But we can certainly look, can't we?"

"You'd find me grateful."

Two hours later they'd gone through ship's logs, passenger lists, yellowed newspaper clippings, microfilm transfers, volumes by lake historians, articles, even the narration track of a video made for tourists. In forty-four years of service, there had been nothing but a handful of overboards, all rescued, one drunk and showing off who'd died ashore of pleurisy.

"Would that qualify?" she asked.

"I'd say the captain is a more likely candidate."

"Young man, three captains succeeded Captain Bledsoe and not one reported seeing anything like that. Unless, of course, you're writing fiction."

"I'd have no idea how. But thank you. You've been very generous with your time."

He was getting up to go when she said, "Do you believe in them? Ghosts, I mean."

"I confess my interest is rather recent."

"Is that an answer?"

He sat back down, beginning to wonder where the woman was Suzanne had described. "I believe in something. I'm just not sure what."

She said, "One morning a young woman in old clothing passed in front of that mirror there and disappeared. Some forgotten consort of old Mr. Holmes, I expect. He's the one who maintained the house for such purposes. In short, I believe in ghosts after working here."

Thinking of a kid with black hair and a smile that could separate you from your reason, *R.I.P. Cortland Matthew Rainey,* he said, "Maybe we're the ones who keep them here. At least keep alive the ones we can see."

"At my age that's comforting and it's not. What did you say your name was?"

Shawn repeated it, to which she said, "I do have one more possibility, the woman whose family built *Constance.* Catherine Mulvhill, that would be. I could ask her."

Shawn could see the woman describing him to Catherine Mulvhill, the shit hitting the fan for real. He said, "Thanks, but from what I've read, she has enough to worry about right now."

"Knowing her, I wouldn't bet against her."

"I'm afraid I wouldn't know how to do that either."

"Well, it's no trouble," she said, closing a volume. "Leave a number where I can reach you."

Shawn was about to beg off, instead made a snap decision, asking Theda Sandstrom, "What is she like, your Mrs. Mulvhill?"

It was coming up five when Shawn told her he *had* to leave then, Theda showing no signs of slowing: meeting Catherine when the house was converted to a school for high-spirited young ladies; despite the rules and supervision, sneaking out to smoke and drink gin with young men who had cars and some who didn't. Overall, Catherine was a friend to have and an enemy not to, who used to come back from trips full of the new things she'd learned.

"She belonged in San Francisco or Paris, not here," Theda said. "But, then, who didn't? I certainly thought I did."

"She never went away to college?"

"Not while her father was alive. He was afraid of what she'd do that far off the leash. We lost track when I went to Stanford and got married. Then I came back a widow with a daughter and we picked up again, though she was different."

"Different how?"

"Adult. Responsible. By then her father had died and she had her hands full running things. She never wanted to talk about how we'd been, those times. She's still pretty serious."

Shawn nursed the thought. "You say she did go to college?"

"While I was gone. Her mother went to University of Wisconsin, so she did as well. Her mother had died by the time I met Catherine, which might explain why her upbringing was so unstructured." Pause, a look: "Regrettably, I had no such excuse."

Random chips in a mosaic, no pattern yet but early. "I see. Well, if there's nothing else…"

She followed him with her trifocals. "I suppose there is one thing."

"Ma'am…?"

"The name you picked. It's a good enough composite, but it doesn't fit." And to his expression, "Our secret, Mr. Rainey. I won't tell Catherine you were here, you don't tell my daughter I went along like this. The way Suzanne yaks, I'd be minus a friend and out of a job in no time."

He was about to say something but stopped himself.

Shut up, Rainey, it's a gift.

"Thank you, I won't," he said instead. "With apologies."

"Catherine is my friend, it's true, but she's wrong in this. That ship *is* the lake. Whatever you came for, that's the reason you're still with me and not in Arn Tennell's sheriff's car. I mean, how would it look, you trying to fool a poor old woman?"

25

SHAWN STRUGGLED WITH A TIMELINE, Catherine Mulvhill's life according to what he could glean from his banker's box and the Theda chronicles. He was planning a visit to the newspaper archives – things he'd start with that might lead to something – when his father turned down the ballgame. San Francisco-Atlanta, promos calling the Braves America's team to snorts from his father.

"Forgot to tell you," his father said. "Your friend called, the crazy one. The McCandless boy."

"Pop, he's chasing forty."

"That mean he's growing up?"

Shawn let it go, dialed Joe Don from the extension in the garage, heard, "What? You're so busy now you can't stay in touch?"

"Figured you'd make me an offer I couldn't refuse. Not that I couldn't use a job about now."

"Steaks tomorrow, my place, boys night out. What do you say?"

Shawn waited him out.

"All right, you win," Joe Don said. "Robin and the kids are at her mother's for a while."

Shawn recalled his and Robin's talk, Joe Don's *I doubt she'll be making any public appearances for a while.*

"Her mother's…"

"That's what I said. There some problem with the meaning?" Then, "Sorry, but I'm climbing the walls around here. Just thought it would give us a chance to talk."

"Why not? Anything I should bring?"

"Salad, if you want. What's in the reefer doesn't look so hot." Then, "Your old man still the same as when he used to run me off?"

"Funny, he was asking the same about you."

Shawn hung up.

That night he dreamed of water, the hand-rising-from-the-filling-lake ending in *Deliverance*. As had Jon Voight, whom it had risen to haunt, Shawn woke wide-eyed and sweating. Only he knew it hadn't been a hand, and whatever it was hadn't yet broken the surface; it still was rising, rising. Bloated faceless and white.

"That you I heard bumping around last night?" his father asked at breakfast. "You look wrung-out."

Around sips of coffee, Shawn mumbled about it being a tough week.

"You spent more time on my grandkids instead of that dead ship, you might sleep better."

"I'll keep it in mind, Pop."

"Like everything else I say, right?"

His father rinsed out his bowl, set it in the rack, turned at the screen door. "Here's another, for what it's worth. Living alone doesn't do much to file the points off a man. However I come across, I want you to know it's good having you here."

Before he could respond, Liam's footsteps were fading on the walk.

The rest of the morning Shawn spent with a psychic recommended by Suzanne, *don't ask*. After an hour, he left knowing as much as when he'd started; or as she'd stated up front, believe or don't believe. Yes, spirits/energies/phenomena were known to hang around places identified with in life or where sudden acts had ended them – the evidence was too documented to ignore. Confused, vengeful, afraid to move on, they drifted, neither here nor there. Yes, some people simply were more in tune, a gift you neither asked for nor stood to return.

Shawn left, thinking Captain Glenn R. Bledsoe, late of *Constance,* was the most likely candidate for Burl Ruttan's episode.

As big a given as *that* was.

Broad daylight made him feel foolish heading for his next appointment, a lawyer Suzanne also recommended. Vincent Satterfield basically confirmed what Terry had said and the papers ran with: They were on Catherine Mulvhill's home clock and turf, and she knew all the soft spots.

Unless something broke their way.

Right.

Next was Lakewood, where he met with Sheldon Spring, the local newspaper editor leaving him alone with his laptop and the files he'd broken out for him. Four hours sandwiched around lunch yielded the following notations under Mulvhill, Catherine Constance Holmes:

Born: November 26, 1921, Echo Bay. Delivered by Li Chen, midwife; Dr. Richard B. Hull, examining physician.

Mother: Eunice Dexter Holmes (dec. May 7, 1930).

Father: Cyrus Chandler Holmes (dec. December 14, 1943).

Education: Grades 1-8, Echo Bay Elementary (Shawn noting her approximate ages as 5 to 13, years 1926 to 1934); grades 9-12, Lakewood School for Young Women (age 13 to 18, years 1934 to 1938, dates confirmed by the debutante news, Ladies of the Lake); higher education, University of Wisconsin (age 19 to 23, years 1940 to 1944), finance major.

Married: June 17, 1940, to Landon Graydon Mulvhill (dec. December 31, 1940).

Shawn halted there, found the obit: self-inflicted gunshot wound. Total duration of wedded bliss by Shawn's calculation: six months, two weeks. Never married again: confirmed. *Note to himself:* Reason(s)?

He moved on, each year accounted for in some manner – social events, charitable and environmental causes, endorsements – up to the *Constance* dustup. Notable by their absence: trips; no *Catherine Mulvhill returns from,* the sort of thing that might have passed for social calendar then. His casual speculation: Her trips had been sandwiched around the events; either that or she had no love for travel. For certain: Money wouldn't have been the deterrent.

Overall assessment of the files: a start.

Specific fact assessments: more needed, but which?

Bleary from it, Shawn quit at five, showered, picked up salad makings and insurance beer at the supermarket across from Holmes Bank and Trust. He was at Joe Don's hillside split-level at six.

"Open," he heard in answer to his ring. "Use it or lose it."

Shawn walked in, set down the grocery bag. Following TV sounds to the den, he found Joe Don watching family videos, empty highball glass in hand.

Joe Don froze the frame on Robin laughing, waving off the camera with a stage grimace; he rattled the ice in the bottom of his glass. "You're just in time."

"You all right?" Shawn asked.

"Can't live with 'em, can't live without 'em. It's all bullshit anyway."

Great, Shawn thought. *Welcome to the dream.*

Joe Don levered up the recliner, killed the VCR and TV. "Fuck this shit. You want a Crown Royal?"

"Beer's fine."

"Not the first one, my man. You got some catching up to do."

Thinking what the hell, the price of admission, he accepted the belt, watched Joe Don pour himself the same double shot and power down half. "Can't very well catch up if you don't slow down," Shawn said, sipping his.

"That old dame really fixed us, didn't she? Me, for sure."

"I have an idea. How about if we eat and talk?"

"God, you sound just like my wife."

Joe Don turned on the grill, the exhaust vents beside it on the Jenn-Air. He shook ground pepper seasoning on the steaks, laid them on the grill as Shawn got out the lettuce and began breaking it.

"So," Joe Don said, draining half the remaining whiskey. "You have a plan to turn this misbegotten mother around?"

"More a direction. Dig until I come up with something," he answered. "Decide then how to use it."

"Don't you mean *we?*"

"No, and be glad I don't." Cherry tomatoes and the dressing. "Just like that..."

"Try me with a better idea, I'm open."

Joe Don refilled, drank, let out a sharp breath. "It might be a tad more direct than yours."

"So I remember you saying about Robin."

"I figured you'd get around to her."

"Direct sometimes comes with a price."

"Yeah? Tell me what doesn't. And I thought we were talking about Catherine Mulvhill."

"We are," Shawn said. "Look, it's not as if she doesn't have the bases covered. She does, a lawyer I talked to confirmed it. For once, the papers got it right."

The steaks flared; Joe Don slopped Crown Royal on them. "We're not talking nine innings anymore, Speed, the game's changed. In case you hadn't noticed."

"Whatever you're thinking, forget it. Right now we've got a solid base of opinion."

"For all the good it's done us."

"Think you might want to scale back a little on the firewater?"

Joe Don grinned. "I have a better idea, clear something up we can clear up. You and Robin – once and for all"

"Watch your fire," he said, and when Joe Don did nothing, poured his own drink on it and turned off the gas. "I think these are about done, don't you?"

"Fuck 'em," Joe Don said. "I want an answer. Are you doing my wife?"

"Thanks for the booze. I'll be going now."

"Not this time, you won't."

Shawn heard the drawer open, looked back, saw the gun Joe Don had pointed at him, a black semi-automatic pistol. He stood very still.

"That's your answer to this?"

"No, that's my question put another way. You and my wife – yes or no?"

"No. N-O. Clear enough?"

Joe Don thumbed back the hammer. "Bullshit, nothing is

clear. It's like you're in every room, that ghost in the old TV series. It didn't work you trying to forget her, and you fucked up your own deal, so here you are working in on mine. You must have thought it would be easy, old Joe Don hanging by a thread. Now who's hanging?"

The gun tight-patterned to Joe Don's pulse, Shawn feeling it as much as tracking it, conscious of his sweat. "Listen to me, and this time hear it. I came back because Terry Dahl has me by the balls – his project in exchange for my kids. Robin and you and anybody else you care to name have nothing to do with it."

Joe Don's grin went off, a crayon smile by a kindergartener. "You think I'm a complete fool? I've seen you together, the way she looks at you, then at me. Tell me that's nothing."

"I'm telling you the truth."

"When's the last time you even *knew* the truth?"

"Robin knows it. You bother to ask her?"

Straight-ahead, no let-up: through the flashing red. "Now *you* listen. She's all I've got, her and the kids. The old man's dying – bone cancer. Nobody knows it yet, but I'm putting the other store up for sale. The house if the Echo Bay Monster wins."

Son of a bitch. "Joe-D, I'm sorry. As a friend, I'm sorry. But this is not the way."

Joe Don noticed the gun as if for the first time; a light seemed to dawn, clarity of purpose. Slowly he backed the gun into his mouth, held Shawn's eyes, and pulled the trigger.

The hammer snap was louder than a shot.

At least it was to Shawn.

Joe Don drew out the gun, held out the handle to show Shawn no clip was in it and, with his other hand, the full clip itself. There was a moment when neither spoke, then Joe Don let both drop to his sides.

"Get out of here – *friend*," he said. "Before I do something even dumber than believing you were one of mine."

26

SHAWN HAD THE CHEROKEE OUT and was heading for the gym, then another round with the archives, when the call he was expecting came through on his cell phone.

"Rainey," he said punching on.

"Shawn? Jesus, I can't believe I did that last night. You okay?"

"Try the act on somebody else, Joe Don, I'm done with it."

"Sorry if you think we're making a habit of this."

"We?"

"Would it help knowing I feel like crap this morning?"

"There is a solution. It's called help. You have to ask for it."

"You are cold, bro."

"Try up to here with my own problems. You ever think of that?"

"Your kids…"

"Get help, Joe Don. End of story." Pausing to let oncoming traffic clear for his left turn.

"Had you going there for a while, though, didn't I? I can hear it in your voice."

"If that's your big score, I suggest you have a look at the

markers you're using."

Pause. "Look, I drank too much and it happened – *mea culpa*. But it got me what I needed to know. At least *you're* not coming on to *her.*"

"Lose the thought, Joe Don. It's a zero play."

"That's real good advice, Shawn-o, I appreciate it. But don't tell me you're any different. I fucking know you."

Still no break in the traffic. "The hell does that mean?"

"Just what you think it does. Next time you decide to lecture me, keep your own past in mind."

Chill wind, the sound of a horn: "You want to spell that out?"

"Lighten up, Speed, we all got things to live down. Yours just happens to be your brother." And when Shawn didn't respond – trucks, cars, and campers he didn't see anymore coming at him and around him – Joe Don threw in, "But like you say, keep digging. Who knows whose shit you might turn over. Might even be your own."

Bike and free weights followed by a long shower finally turned Shawn's thoughts around. As big a prick as Joe Don could be, the man's loyalty and into-the-fire-beside-you bent still counted for something; you just had to know there was more to Joe Don than last night, put up or shut up. At least you knew *where* you stood – something that used to be a virtue. Too often now you got the shaders and sliders, the kind who never showed you a full-on profile.

With Joe Don you got what was there, undiluted.

For that you forgave some things.

Already Shawn had decided to create a context around Catherine Mulvhill's laptop history, so at the newspaper, in addition to the general files, he requested those specific to Cyrus

Chandler Holmes. Concentrating on 1930 to 1943, the year of his death, he culled out:

1930 – Sells joint-venture hotel when Lakewood partnership dissolves.

1931 – Loses wife Eunice Dexter Holmes in boating accident, Catherine age 9.

1933 – Repurchases former company steamship Peregrine *(utility and passenger) for pennies on the dollar; orders it decommissioned and sunk. Cites stated plan and a "fitting end to her years of service."*

1934 – Launches resort venture with local businessman Ling Chen.

1935 – Repurchases former company steamship Mirabelle *(mail and passenger – see* Peregrine *disposition).* Rainey Side Note: C.C.H. big on "fitting ends."

1937 – Defeats creditor attempts to replace him as company head and install financial mediator.

1939 – Spends better part of year in San Francisco seeking capital while accepting hospitality of prominent socialite.

1940 – Posts worst annual loss in company's history; dissolves partnership with local businessman Ling Chen. Sinks Constance *á lá* Peregrine *and* Mirabelle.

1941 – Faces allegations of mismanagement of company funds, dismissed upon suicide of <u>Landon</u> <u>Mulvhill</u> *(underline by S.R.; see* "Catherine")*.*

1942 – Files for protection from creditors, is granted same.

1943 – Dies at Stonehouse of liver failure.

Overall impressions: The Stonehouse portrait nailed him – a hedonist, high-roller, financial dodger who nearly sank his own company. *Otherwise stated:* not a minimum risk as a business partner.

Questions to address: Landon Mulvhill, ill-fated husband – what role and why? Fall guy for Cyrus's ineptitude? Who took care of young Catherine during the old man's jaunts, which seemed most of the time? What effect had it on her?

Shawn called the museum, but Theda wasn't in, leave a message. He did, then on a hunch about the coincidence – Cyrus's business partner and the midwife who'd delivered Catherine having the same name: Chen – he asked a newspaper staffer if there might be a file on the family. Specifically, on Ling Chen.

No, the staffer thought.

But there might be one of a general nature.

The *Immigrant-Chinese* file she located yielded old photographs and documentation: railroad, flume, and road construction; logging-camp and hotel labor; retail and service business. Ling Chen's name appeared toward the latter third, an immigrant-camp baker who'd set up shop first in Truckee then Lakewood, later branching into mercantile and money-lending. At first, he'd lent money to his own, subsequently giving the banks a run.

Bingo. Cyrus needed money; Ling Chen sought opportunity and, with the Alien Land Act prohibiting ownership then, the legitimacy of a name like Holmes. Further on, Shawn found their joint-venture resort. It had been built on a remaining company parcel that boasted undeveloped hot springs and lasted but five years after completion. Leveled by fire of suspicious origin in late 1940, the land was sold by the company during Catherine's tenure in 1952.

Shawn kept reading. Beyond Catherine's file, there was no further mention of midwife Li, just Chen-family tragedies: a nephew missing boating back from the casinos, his motorboat found stove-in and half-submerged; a granddaughter killed in a head-on returning from Reno; two sons lost on Tarawa and Kwajalein; several members lost to immigrant-community smallpox prior to the old man's death in '47; a great-grandson dead in Vietnam.

None of these addressed the issue at hand, the millstone that was *her.* He needed a fissure into which he could drive a piton, inch his way toward something at which he could even chip away. *Anything...*

His phone trilled: It was Theda Sandstrom returning his call, saying she'd be straightening and organizing files if he wanted to come over. But if he did, come prepared to help.

"Best offer I've had all day," he told her.

"Try getting out more," she said as he hung up.

She was in a dust smock when she let him in. The next half-hour he pulled out books and files, brushed a duster over them, sorted according to her instructions. At length she asked, "So you're back for what, exactly?"

"Questions I'm only beginning to know to ask." Repeating from his list: Landon Mulvhill...the old man...who took care of Catherine...the effect had it on her...

She said, "Am I incorrect, or was this originally about Captain Glenn R. Bledsoe, rest his soul. Early timber contracts over there, please."

Shawn complied. "It was and is and was."

"Let us not be coy, Mr. Rainey. It's about my friend, isn't it?"

Roll the dice, fuck all. "The friend you consider wrong in this?"

"Misguided is one thing, hurt is another. I won't have that."

"Your call, Theda: If something goes beyond what any researcher might ask, I leave, no further questions. That fair?"

"Donner Party over here. And you'd leave regardless."

She busied herself with a file; he passed her a book on early Indian settlements, said, "This may seem forward, but does your daughter have any idea what you're really like?"

"I have no idea what you mean." Pause. "But if I did, the answer would be *over my dead body,* which would mean yours.

And don't give me that look, Suzanne drove me crazier than I ever drove *my* mother, and that's bad enough. Rubicon, this pile."

Shawn banished Cort, the lake, the cold. "What was the old man like?" he asked.

Her distaste was apparent. "To a child growing up without a mother? Frightening, luckily gone more than he was home. Have you seen a picture of him?"

Shawn nodded as she went on.

"Catherine hated him. She always believed he drowned her mother to get at her money. As to who took care of Catherine while he was gone, they had a housekeeper, May Chen. May had a daughter the same age as Catherine. Lily, her name was. May used to bring her along so they could play together. Railroads go here."

He handed her the file. "Was May Chen any relation to Ling and/or Li Chen?"

"You have been busy, haven't you? Li Chen was Ling's second wife. May was their daughter, or one of them. The old man had his fingers in a lot of pies. They had this funeral for him when he died at ninety or so – bigger than Cyrus's. She never said, but I think Catherine got a kick out of that."

Shawn made note of the names. He asked if she knew if there was anything left of the family.

"I assume you're familiar with old Truckee?" And to his nod, "The original bakery and store is just off the tracks. It's a small brick building with dark-green trim and a historical-interest plaque. Someone there might be able to tell you."

He added to his notes. "In your opinion, did any of this have an effect on Catherine?"

"Say what you mean: What effect?"

"Just trying to understand."

"Then tell me which Catherine you mean? The little rich girl who lost her mother, the hell-raiser who liked gin and boys, or the business woman who salvaged a bankrupt mess and turned it into what it is?" She slapped a volume on top of a pile. "Or would it be the Catherine with you on her case trying to back her into a corner?"

Shit. "Theda, if I misspoke I apologize. But I thought you told me that you–"

"And stop throwing my own words at me, I hate that. Who knows what I'll say next."

27

SHAWN THOUGHT OF LOOPS, of closing at least one before another opened. With light left, he took the route along the Truckee, families on rafts enjoying the slow-moving current and warm late afternoon, cyclists the bike path. He found the brick building twenty minutes later, parked the Cherokee, walked back. Except for the Chinese characters on the sign and the plaque, founder Ling Chen and the businesses he'd run from it, the building looked like its neighbors from the railroad era: narrow-deep two story with a tin roof and vertical iron-shuttered windows.

He stepped up to the porch and went in.

The interior smelled of spice and age. Shawn took in ornate scales, pharmacy globes filled with colored water, dust lazing in the window light. A blackened counter fronted repository squares filled with herbs in glass; a gold-rush-era register overshadowed a contemporary model. Coolered bok choy, ginger, and cilantro; shelved teas, woks, fans, and condiments – all said the store still sold things.

He smiled at the young woman behind the counter, picked

out a carton of sandalwood soap. When she'd rung it up, he said, "Great old place. You part of the original family?"

"Distant," she answered. "Cal student up for the summer."

"There anyone around who might be? I'm writing a book."

She gave him a look like *Right, another one.*

"Wait here."

She went through a partition, came back with an older woman in loose-fitting navy silk pants and a mini-floral top. Graying hair overshadowed burnt-almond eyes under arched, shaped brows.

"You're the one writing a book on the Chen family?"

The faintest of accents. Nothing faint about the laser gaze.

Shawn touched the cracked frame in his pocket hoping the book-writer front wouldn't prove too often to the well. "It's on the Chinese contribution, which would include the Chens. Would that also mean you?"

"I am Mrs. Yue. I work here. And you would be…?"

"No one you've heard of. Shawn Andrews. It's my first book." Extending a hand she ignored.

"The name is Irish in origin?"

Few lines, those eyes: up close it was still impossible to age the woman. North of sixty, he guessed. "Irish. Yes, ma'am."

"I see. Have you a business card?"

"Next item on the budget." Sheepish. "Cash is tight."

"If you wish to be taken seriously, I would advise it. Meanwhile, are you prepared to correct some misconceptions about us involving anti-Chinese bias?"

"I believe the truth is the truth wherever you find it." Careful not to draw blood on the frame this time.

She seemed to come to a decision. "Very well. Though I am

not the family historian – she died a number of years ago – I might be able to assist. This way, please."

He followed her through an office done in dark woods and brocades to a brick patio surrounded by bamboo in glazed containers, a koi pond with water hyacinth. The Cal student, as if by remote control, appeared with bottled teas and cups she set down before disappearing.

"A niece by marriage," the woman said, as if for the girl's lack of manners in not pouring it. "The young don't even know what they don't know."

"I appreciate the hospitality." Opening hers for her, pouring it, then his.

"Have you specific questions or should I just start?"

"Mrs. Yue, I've been introduced to Mr. Chen's accomplishments. It's the way in which they became accomplishments that I hope readers will find interesting."

"What you mean by that might be helpful."

Touché. "The details and inner workings. For instance, the people he did business with and in what manner."

"Mr. Chen did business with a good many people. If you've studied him, you must know that."

As offhandedly as he could, Shawn said, "I'm particularly interested in his interaction with Cyrus Chandler Holmes."

She said nothing, so he went on.

"I'm aware they were short-lived partners in a hot-springs resort. I know that his wife Li and daughter May worked in the family home, and that her daughter Lily was a playmate of Mr. Holmes's heir."

Koi roiled the surface of the pond, the ripples spreading out.

"Catherine," he added. "Mulvhill."

The eyes lasered him. "Are you aware that Mr. Holmes cheated Mr. Chen? That his deceit was ultimately responsible for Mr. Chen's death?"

At age ninety...? "No, ma'am, I am not."

"It's not surprising. From the beginning there was bad blood. When Mr. Chen learned he'd been cheated, Mr. Holmes's response was to burn the resort for the insurance money. Mr. Chen's name did not appear on the papers."

"Mrs. Yue, with all due respect, Mr. Chen didn't seem the type to allow himself to be cheated."

Mrs. Yue drank from her cup – delicately – then set it down. "At that time, things were much shaded toward Caucasians. Mr. Holmes had able lawyers. It was a hard lesson, but the family was never cheated again."

Redirect. "Yet his daughter, May, continued to work at Stonehouse during and after?"

"That would be correct." The eyes seeming to dissect.

"And she was fond of Catherine and vice versa? As was Lily?"

"As I understand it."

"Would they still be alive?"

"Oh, no. May was the family historian I mentioned. Her daughter left and hasn't been heard from in years. We believe she died in Los Angeles in the forties."

Note to himself on the phrasing: *Her daughter* rather than Lily. Language, most likely. "Her death was confirmed?"

"A reliable source."

Something about her answers: almost, but not quite. "Would you know anything of May and Lily's relationship to Catherine? To expand, I mean."

"Only that they were close and that it ended when Catherine

went away to college after Mr. Holmes died, and if I may, this seems quite a narrow area of pursuit."

Sound recall. "Then let me broaden it. The family seems to have had its share of tragedy. Do you think there might be a legacy there? Good luck, bad luck, that sort of karma angle?"

She straightened in her chair, finished her tea. "Mr. Andrews, I had hoped you were a different sort of writer. I can see, however, that I was wrong." On her feet and moving toward the door. "I suggest you not bother us again. You'll find a way out between the bamboo containers."

And so much for loops. Shawn took it, the bamboo brushing his face as he slid through. He started the Cherokee and drove home.

Home, he thought, starting up the grade.

Like *family,* there was another one.

Thursday nights Liam went bowling with a neighbor, so Shawn ate dinner alone. Afterward, he returned a call from Suzanne Padget.

"So," she said when she heard who it was. "How was our Theda?"

"Couldn't have been nicer, Suzanne."

"Hey, this is me, not somebody you have to butter up, although it's a thought."

"She was sweet as pie."

"What kind, rhubarb?"

"Goodnight, Suzanne."

He tried reaching Nate and Elizabeth, but the answering machine was on; knowing that whatever he said would be intercepted or worse, he left no message. He called Katie's number, told the machine he missed her and was thinking of her, that if she got in before midnight to give him a call. Then he went in and lay down without undressing.

Staring at the ceiling, he retraced his steps: Joe Don's craziness, Chen's Store, Cyrus's timeline and where it intersected with Catherine's at her mother's death. Which had to have been a painful time except for May and Lily Chen, her friendship with Theda Sandstrom. Theda saying, *She always believed he'd drowned her mother to get at her money, even though nothing was ever alleged.*

Which sounded like Catherine.

He pictured her with her father: Mohammed and his daughter-mountain, an endless test of wills. More importantly, he tried picturing where any of this was heading, time running through the hourglass. Weighted by fatigue, his thoughts went random, replayed the Q&A with Mrs. Yue.

Him: *And would May and Lily still be alive?*

Her: *Oh no. May was the family historian I mentioned. Her daughter left and hasn't been heard from in years. We believe she died in Los Angeles in the forties.*

That odd phrasing again: *Her daughter* rather than *Lily*.

Him: *Would you know anything of May and Lily's relationship to Catherine?*

Her: *Only that they were close, and it ended when Catherine went away to college after Mr. Holmes died.*

Echo: *After Mr. Holmes died...*

Shawn flipped on the light, opened the laptop, booted his notes, the Catherine timeline under schooling: Grades 1-8, Echo Bay Elementary, *dah, dah, dah.* And there it was, last entry, the thing that had kept spinning subsurface:

University of Wisconsin (years 1940 to 1944).

After Mr. Holmes died.

Cyrus, who'd died in 1943.

Big deal, he told the flutters: third-hand information at best,

Mrs. Yue admitting as much. After sixty years it was off by three, so what? Telling himself further if that was the best he had, he might as well fold the hand, the tent, the works.

Snapping the lid shut, he turned off the light and lay back, thumbed the frame's cracked edge, saw his kids the way they'd been that day on the deck, then waving goodbye from the boat. Last thought before sleep came: *Folding the hand was not remotely an option.*

He was dreaming again.

How else could Elizabeth and Nate be holding up electronic minute-second signs as he whipped past them, his father and mother stretching out the finish-line tape below? But they were on skis, too, and they kept backing away, matching his speed as Joe Don and Tam and Sonny and poor dead Jake with a crusted hole in his chest laughed like mad clowns at his panic that the others had finished and he might not, not ever.

Now his father and mother were gaining because the moguls were as big as houses, no getting around them and having a chance of winning. Catherine Mulvhill was standing on the one directly ahead, waving him off. He crested it anyway and there was no other side to it, just straight down and he was falling, falling, that awful bottom-dropping feeling in the pit of his gut, nothing now but gray swirl and the echo of Joe Don's laughter and someone else calling his name...

"Wake up, you're having a bad one," his father said from far off down the mountain. *"Shawn."*

He opened to residual gut-drop, soaked-through T-shirt, his father's hand on his arm. "Pop...?"

"You all right?"

"Yeah. Time is it?"

"Four. I want you to see something."

Shawn rose up, fought the dizzies, swung his feet over to cold floor. "What is it?"

"Couldn't sleep, so I had the radio on low and heard about it. Figured you'd want at least a look, even if you didn't come along."

Shawn slipped into his loafers, followed his father outside. The night air was cool on his sweat, yet the garage's window facing the street glowed a hot red, the same color as the sky beyond the trees to the west.

"My God, that's close," he said, slipping on the pullover he'd grabbed. "Where did they say it was?"

But Liam Rainey was heading for the garage.

28

L IAM PARKED AS CLOSE AS THEY COULD GET, a far corner of the lot. By the time they threaded the emergency lines and got up to it, the bank was fully involved. Even the Holmes Bank & Trust pole sign was burning, melting into the inferno as the fire crews shot water onto the roof and a small crowd watched, the air thick with burn. Then Liam Rainey recognized a fire supervisor named Whit Thiessen who happened to be a neighbor, and they walked over.

Thiessen nodded back; radio commands crackled from the unit he was holding. Without taking his eyes off things, he said to Shawn: "Seen you come and go and know your work for the *Constance*. Can't say I agree, but most people seem to. Watch the hose there."

They moved to avoid it.

"Some fire," Sean said. "Any idea how it started?"

"Not yet. Sure went up, though."

Shawn held his next question while Thiessen answered a radio call, then, "Meaning it had help?"

"Meaning it's rare to see this kind of intensity without an accelerant. Which doesn't necessarily mean there was one. It had a while to get going without being spotted."

"What about the alarm?" Liam asked.

"Can't tell until we knock it down. All I know is, we didn't get the call off the alarm, it got phoned in. Sorry, but I'm going to have to ask you to move back."

As they did, the roof sagged and fell in, sparks shooting out like a mill burner. A hotspot broke out in the dry grass and pine saplings beyond the fence, touch and go before they helped run hoses to it and start dousing. By the time they did, the fire team was gaining ground saving the businesses around the bank.

Sooted, reeking of smoke, they were getting into the pickup when the darkened sheriff's cruiser an aisle over hit its lights, growled its siren. Arn Tennell got out, killed all but the parking ambers, pointed to Shawn, motioned him over. Shawn nodded to his father that it was okay, to wait at the truck.

"Come to enjoy your handiwork?" Arn said as Shawn drew within range.

"If you expect a response to that, Arn, I'm not up to it."

"Maybe a night in jail would help." Leaning against the unit's door.

"What's the matter, too many witnesses to do what you'd really like?"

"Firebugs get off on the burn, Shawn, but then you know that. Why else would you be here?"

"With my dad for company…"

"Your accomplice for all I know."

"He's over there, Arn. He's not hiding."

Arn smiled around the toothpick he had going. "And maybe

he's your cover, the way he was for you with Cort."

It might have been the lack of sleep, the nature of the crack, or the way it was said; whatever, Shawn was left chasing the words leaving too high and tight. "Arn, I heard an interesting theory about you and Cort from someone with a stake in it, somebody close. Didn't quite ring true, but it made me put a couple of things together I hadn't before. Obvious things. You want to hear them?"

"I hope that means you're threatening a law officer."

"Not a law officer, Arn, you – the part I always wondered about. How Cort planned to get away with it."

Pause, Arn thinking it over, Shawn's eyes not leaving his, Arn finally saying, "Like this far down range, my history and yours, somebody would believe *you*. Your old man, for starters."

"Chips fall, Arn, it's already in letters to the sheriff and the media. That is, if you do something stupid to see they get mailed."

"You're full of shit."

"Am I? Right now or you're out of my face. One way or another, it ends."

Arn Tennell tossed the toothpick, pushed off the side of the car. "I should have run you off when I had the chance. *Whatever* it took."

"You know, you're right. The tape in my car just wasn't up to it."

"What tape? What are you talking about?"

Throttle back. Breathe.

"Nothing – different conversation," Shawn said, turning away.

He was almost to the pickup when a newer one, a white F-250, bucked the dip into the mall lot. Frank Love got out of the driver's side, helped Catherine Mulvhill down from hers; without a glance at Shawn, she walked to Arn Tennell, who'd left his unit when he saw her.

"Is it as bad as it looks?"

"Yes, ma'am, I'm afraid so, though we don't yet know the full extent."

"Deliberately set?"

"Accidental fires seldom burn that hot or that fast," he answered. "Plus there's the matter of the alarm."

"Have you arrested this man? Is that why he's here?"

"We were just discussing that," Shawn said. "Isn't that right, Arn."

"Mr. Rainey wouldn't say why he's here, ma'am."

"You mean there's some question – with my bank and shopping center an inferno? If he didn't do it, he knows who did."

"Well, Arn? Are you in *her* pocket, too?"

"Exactly what do you need, sheriff, the match in his hand?"

"One more word, Shawn… Ma'am, I can't just–"

"*Can't* is what I thought I heard you say. Are you going to do your job or do Frank and I have to do it for you?"

Shawn was conscious of Frank Love edging closer: leather jacket, stitches replaced by light scar tissue, the smell of hair tonic. He said, "The short version is we saw it burning and came to see what we could do. Not much, it turned out."

Catherine Mulvhill's look was matador to inexperienced bull. "This from the young man who likes old films and robbing graves. And now, burning me out when he doesn't get his way. You said we. You and who else?"

"There some point to all this?" a voice said from behind her.

"Who is that?" Turning toward it, squinting to see.

"Hello, Catherine," Liam Rainey said, stepping into the light. "Been a while, hasn't it?"

They sat at the table with the chrome legs and yellow Formica top, coffee steaming against the pale light of dawn. Liam Rainey slowly turned his mug, his eyes glued to it.

"She used to bring her car into the shop. We'd talk about anything, nothing, whatever was up. Have coffee when I made it. After a while I made it as a matter of course."

Shawn blew on his. "What about Mom?"

"Son, you get that judgment out of your voice, and you do it now. At most, your mother and I got along, and less and less of that. If you didn't notice, you weren't looking."

"How old was I?"

"Ten, twelve. Off winning races."

"Meaning I should have been looking."

Liam Rainey slammed his hand on the table. "Enough. You want to take this outside?"

Shawn tried to picture it, father and son on the lawn at six in the morning trading punches, and couldn't. He ran a hand through hair singed by the fire's heat.

"No, Pop, I don't want to take it outside. I'm listening."

His father was silent. Then, "Hell, about all we ever did was talk and feel guilty, if it's any of your goddamned business. Neither of us was young. She made it plain her heart belonged to some boy who'd left her a long time before. That wasn't going to change."

"She ever say who?"

"No, and I didn't ask." His voice tightening a notch. "Figured if she'd wanted me to know, she'd have said it."

"So what happened?"

Liam Rainey drank coffee, clacked his mug on the Formica. "She stayed in that house that's now the museum, upstairs in her old school room. She said it had been a happy time for her, that Stonehouse and Echo Bay were full of ghosts. We'd meet there sometimes. After a couple years, she stopped coming. I'd call, but she never called back. It hurts a while, then you find your way. Whatever we were or weren't to each other, at least your mother and I had a fallback. Someone to go home to."

"You knew why I'd come back here, what she represented to it and to me. Why didn't you say something?"

"You have a son. You tell me." And, when nothing came, "It happens, Shawn. Or need I remind you?"

Still nothing, the barbs hitting home.

"I'll tell you another thing," Liam Rainey said. "The more I see of you and her in action the more I think you deserve each other."

Shawn let a cooling beat pass before he asked, "What was she like then?"

"Why? So you can hammer it into another spear to throw?"

"Two reasons, Pop. All I can tell you for now."

His father stared at him.

"Pop, please, I need it. I'm asking."

Liam Rainey looked as if he were about to say something, only to change his mind and say, "Lonely…warm in her way…a listener. She knew things you wouldn't expect a woman to know. At least I didn't."

"What kinds of things?"

"I don't know – how the Golden Gate was built, how an internal-combustion engine worked, the board-foot cost of lumber and how it's figured. She'd been places I'd only dreamed of. I'd never met anyone like her."

Shawn felt a wash of sympathy for his father, who had wanted out no less than *he* but hadn't made it. Instead he'd stuck it out in a low-watt marriage and a fifty-one-percent job, with sons who'd taken much and hadn't much given.

"I'm sorry," Shawn said suddenly.

"For what?"

"For all of it. For any of it."

"Son, you need to tell me something," his father said. "I need to know if you had anything to do with tonight."

"No," Shawn told him.

"But you know who did."

He shook his head.

"Any idea who *might* have done it?"

"Try half the lake."

"Which tells me nothing."

Shawn shoved back his chair and stood.

Then yes," he said. "I might."

29

S HAWN WOKE AFTER THREE HOURS, his intention a quick lie-down. He showered, ate, and was out of the garage by ten, driving by the shopping center, most of which had been cordoned off, the road thick with lookers. Waving at a woman who slowed for him to cross, he pulled into an adjacent lot and walked back along the lakefront to the bank mall.

The bank was for all intents bombed: blackened walls, caved-in beams, charred joists, mangled and melted conduit. A single fire engine stood by to quell any undiscovered hotspots; department vehicles sat angled on the perimeter. Personnel in protective clothing poked around in the remains. One spoke into a pocket tape recorder while another photographed burn details with a flash camera.

Shawn spotted Whit Thiessen propped against a green Bronco and caught his eye. Thiessen stared a moment, then came over.

"Liam's kid," he said.

"Shawn." Extending a hand that Thiessen shook. "Hell of a shift."

"Tell me about it."

Shawn asked if he could bring him anything – coffee, food; Thiessen shook his head. "Getting ready to take off, but thanks. Appreciate the help last night, too. Could have been a lot worse."

Sun off the lake was bright, the smell of burn a shadow.

"Anything you can talk about?"

"Four flashpoints and a cut alarm wire," Thiessen answered. "Somebody wanted to send a message."

"Or trump one up. Hide something and blame the other side."

"I wouldn't know about that. More a fan of the obvious myself."

"You're probably right."

"Take it easy," Thiessen said, moving off. "And thank your dad. Tell him he can volunteer anytime."

Shawn walked back to the Cherokee, rejoined the stream of traffic headed east. Before and after his turn he kept one eye locked on the rearview: no car he recognized. He circled the hillside streets until he was convinced no one was on his tail. At that, he parked a block up from the house.

No one answered the bell, so he went around to the rear deck and took the steps, the sun warm on his back. As he did, Robin lifted her head off one of the lounges where she lay on a towel, her bikini top untied, hair up in a clip. Before she put on her sunglasses, he saw the remains of a bruise around her left eye.

"Hey," he said. "Didn't think I'd find you here." Despite himself, his gaze running her length.

She regarded him lazily. "Foolish me, I ran out of listings. You change your mind about anything?"

"Looking for Joe Don. He around?"

"Nope." Leaning over to sip from a straw. "Too bad. Or is it?"

"Would you know where he is?"

"Down at the yard – which happens to be the only reason I'm

here, I'm sure you've heard. Mom's is a madhouse. She still thinks I'm sixteen."

"How could she forget?"

Her look was one old lover to another. "So you do still think about me. I'm touched. Speaking of which, tie this for me so I can roll over."

He did, the smell of her tanning oil, the sun on her skin going deep, a barbed-ten Eagle hook. He backed away.

"You have any idea where Joe Don was last night?"

"We aren't exactly keeping track." Adjusting the cups, nipples showing through the thin cloth. "You want to go inside? Have a drink, hold my towel?"

"Thanks, but no thanks."

"You're afraid of me, aren't you?" As if suddenly in on it. "Fearless Shawn, my big heartburn."

"Haven't we done this? I'm afraid of a lot of things, not the least of which is your husband."

"Meaning mainly yourself." The smile faded. "What you might do if you lifted your foot off your own neck."

He let it pass, shielded his eyes from the glare. "So you didn't see him last night?"

"Who wants to know?"

"No games, Robin. I need to talk to him."

"Why, I don't believe it," she said, more as though she did than didn't. "You think he had something to do with the bank fire. His old pal Shawn. Some pal."

"Did he?"

"Fuck you. Go play with whatever it is you're doing now that Catherine Mulvhill put you out of business. Give us all a rest."

"Robin, there is no rest if he did this. You have to know that."

"Is that so?" She released her hair from the clip and tossed it. "Well, thanks for the concern."

"You know he has a gun, don't you?"

"Yes, Shawn, I do. Plus a few other things about him. Like how much he likes you to think he's unstable, when he's really just a scared kid, up against it – just like you. Now get off my deck."

Shawn hit the lumberyard, same eye on the rearview for a tail, nothing turning up. An assistant manager told him Joe Don had been in but had taken an early lunch; no idea where, not sure if he was coming back, might be reachable on his cell phone if it was urgent.

Shawn thanked him, punched up the number, got no answer.

With an eye out for the red Dodge Ram, he drove by several lunch-spots – even the partially cordoned-off bank/mall lot where the bank had set up a temporary headquarters tent to calm customers. No luck. He called Door and Hardware, heard Joe Don was not expected there, which didn't mean he might not show, keep calling or they'd leave a message.

He declined, picked up market-deli sandwiches, thinking Joe Don might have wanted to get off by himself – parks, then the public beach lots: no Ram. One last place before write-off: a utility district recreation area where they'd driven to neck while double-dating back when – he with Robin, Joe Don with Chantal Somebody-or-Other. Chantal, who'd had too much rum-and-Coke-in-a-can and thrown up on Joe Don's shoes, he and Robin arguing about it after they'd pumped coffee into her and dropped her off.

There, in the shade, was the Ram.

Shawn pulled in beside it, spotted Joe Don on a far picnic

table, leaning on his knees and facing the lake and its refracted spangles, boats and shoreline sweeping away to the west and south. As he came closer, Joe Don picked up the sound, turned, and nodded. Between his feet on the bench seat was a brown paper bag, its neck obviously crimped around a bottle.

"Thought you might like something to go with that," Shawn said, setting down the sandwiches.

"How'd you find me?" Faded Nevada Wolfpack cap over sunglasses.

"Checked everyplace else first. You okay?"

"You ever think I might not want to be found?"

"Say the word." Holding up his sandwich before he'd taken a bite.

"Nah, sit down."

Shawn sat; Joe Don sipped from the bag, offered Shawn a swig. He shook it off, started on the sandwich. "Pretty spot," he said. "Reminds me of rum and Coke."

"Daddy's back in the hospital," Joe Don said. "Doc says he hasn't got long."

"Damn. I'm sorry, Joe-D. There anything I can do?"

"It's not even that we're close. Fact is, he never much approved of me for better reasons than he knew, and God knows he beat on me enough. It's just...he's always been there." Another swig. "I didn't think I'd feel this way. Cut loose or something."

Extending the thought to his own situation, Shawn accepted a hit, the whiskey burning as it went down neat. A hundred yards out, a sailboat cut across their line of sight, one kid working the lines as the boom came around, the helmsman ducking. Watching the sail fill, the jibe complete, he heard Cort's voice, strained and gasping:

Let go of me. Damnit, I mean it.

Joe Don's voice broke through.

"Hey, it was going to happen, it's just a shock to hear it. Shawn?"

"Yeah," he said. "Here."

"Sure didn't look like it. You want another belt?"

"No. Thanks."

Joe Don's gaze drifted. "You know yesterday was Conner's birthday, and she didn't let me near him? One phone call. Like I was in jail or something."

"You hit her, Joe. Run it on somebody else."

He sat very still; without looking at Shawn, he said, "My frame of mind, I wouldn't go pushing my luck."

"Of course. You'd rather I blew smoke, told you bad Robin, poor Joe Don. Grow up. Dumb I know from. You're looking at it."

The sailboat beat west; wind ruffled the aspen leaves, the light on them like platinum. Joe Don said, "So why *did* you bother? Sooner or later I'd have been back at the yard."

"Forget it. It can wait."

"No shit, I'm okay." Lowering his glasses to prove it. "You going to make me guess? That long face, I have a fair idea."

Shawn tossed the top slice of bread to a gull, which took off with it. Pushing off the bench, he said, "Look, I'm sorry about your dad. I'll be around if you want to get serious."

Joe Don hit the bottle-bag, let out a gasp.

"But so you know, I was there last night. I watched it burn. I was there this morning when they were poking around. Four hotspots, somebody who knew how to cut the wires. You want to pretend this is some kind of high-school prank, that's your business. Just don't expect me to crank up the laugh track."

Joe Don half-smiled, shook his head as if seeing a train

approach his stalled car: *So this is how it feels.*

"Shawn, Shawn," he said.

"No bullshit, no patronizing. Tell me it's not true."

"Why? So you won't become an accessory if it is?" The smile now squint. "You know the difference between me and you? Somebody fucks with me, I fuck with them. I don't look for a magic flute that'll charm the snakes into princes, I take it to 'em." His eyes left Shawn's for the lake. "At that, it's not near enough. Not compared to what people like me are going to lose if she doesn't let up."

"Fuck," Shawn said. "I am not hearing this."

"Yeah, it's a bitch. And maybe you ought to take off before I start sounding like you."

"Like a friend, you mean."

"So *be* a friend and back off."

Tempted, thinking better they at least keep talking, Shawn said, "Anybody been around about it?"

"Aside from Deputy Dog dropping by and telling me he knew who it was and was going to prove it? No, nobody."

Damnit. "What'd you tell him?"

"Told him to come back either with a warrant or his head out of his ass, whichever came first."

Scenarios raced, all of them bad. "Man, oh man…"

"Welcome back, huh?" Joe Don grinned, took another hit when Shawn waved it off. "Hey, don't take it so seriously. We're all fucked one way or another. Now I want to hear something from you, Pinocchio. Tell me you want to bring down the Loch Monster less than I do. And while we're at it, the high-and-mighty difference between your road through her and mine."

All he needed, Shawn thought, *the Great Mandela gone hyperdrive.* He was walking away, hand in a frozen wave, when Joe Don threw in, "Hey, Pinocchio, your secret's safe with me. See, I love you as much as if you were a real boy."

30

SHAWN DROVE TO ECHO BAY, Joe Don's words still banging around like shoes in a dryer. He parked on a fire trail above Stonehouse, settled in on the wooded hillside with his remaining sandwich half and the binoculars he'd purchased at a sporting goods store. What he hoped to accomplish remained to be seen, long odds on anything useful.

At least it gave him time to think.

And what had he so far to show? Catherine Mulvhill's time-line that might or might not have a three-year gap (*Note to himself:* Clarify.); a somewhat better understanding of her father's dark tendencies; a youthful romance that ended in a youthful fashion (*Note II:* With whom and why ended?); a six-month marriage, casualty of a suicidal crooked employee. (*Note III:* Why marriage at all? Cyrus must have suspected Landon Mulvhill well prior to the fact.) And the grand prizewinner: Try a psychic line on a ghost that might or might not have captained *Constance* in her reign. For that matter, ghosts period.

Nice bag, Rainey.

Each American-crafted tool complete with lifetime warranty.

Then there was Joe Don's defining act of stupidity, to which he was now a party. And yet, what did he, Shawn, really know? Not what you'd call an outright admission, nothing that would stand up in court.

Great take, he thought, *garbage in, garbage out, Terry somewhere smiling.* He ate the sandwich half, watched a crested jay defend its turf, a woodpecker tapping for grubs, chipmunks and a squirrel working a half-shucked pine cone, the sun through the trees. Then, in sequence: Millicent coming out to sweep the front porch, steps, and part of the walk; Sheldon Spring and a young woman strapped with cameras arriving and leaving; Frank Love backing out the F-250 and taking off toward town; Arn Tennell pulling in and, a half-hour later, departing; Frank Love reparking the pickup in the garage.

He was set to leave when Catherine Mulvhill came out onto the porch and stepped down, began walking among the trees. Through the binoculars, she disappeared and emerged, her figure the only constant. At one point, as if it were a friend, she put a hand on one of the big cedars. She looked up into its branches, held the position momentarily, then she slowly walked back to the house and went in.

Shawn lowered the binoculars, surprised at its hold on him, the tightness it had left in his throat.

He stopped at the Marcourt on the way back, but the lobby and bar were packed with conventioneers. Beyond their brief initial eye contact, tempered at that, Katie could have been on the moon instead of behind the bar. He ordered a beer, camped at one of the far tables, watched her.

He wrote *Miss you. Tonite?* on a cocktail napkin, asked the waitress to deliver it, saw her do it, saw Katie scan the note, shake her head, but not look up. Before the waitress could return it to him, Shawn tossed off his beer and left.

After dinner he picked up, some neutral conversation with Liam, he drove to the A-frame, got there by ten-thirty. Ben Affleck joined him and was sitting in his lap, a pre-fall chill in the air, when she drove up in her Corolla.

"Finally run out of beer?" he said as she got out and took the steps.

"Catherine Mulvhill finally go to bed?"

Back at him, no more than he deserved. "Just wanted to make sure you heard it from me that I didn't burn her bank, despite what you may hear or read. And you will."

"That's reassuring."

"Exactly how Ben felt until I explained it to him." Flashing the can of tuna he'd brought and opened, now empty.

She sat down; Ben started nuzzling her hand from Shawn's lap. She said, "A funny thing happened at work. Bartender got this note, some guy who didn't know how to spell *tonight*. Like she's supposed to roll over for that?"

"Probably a dropout after a sordid fling."

"Her first thought, too."

"Either that or he lost his head."

"That mean he got it back and might open up to her?"

"It means his heart's in the right place. As you'd see, if you gave him a chance."

"Not much of a deal." Ben Affleck now at the door, looking at her then up at the knob. As if to say, *What empty tuna can? Come ON.* "But I suppose it's something to build on."

"You won't be sorry. Ask your advisor."

Wind shifted the treetops, a waxing moon showing through the breaks. "Just so this guy knows she's no pushover. Only that she's tired and wants to go to bed. She thinks."

"Already been made clear. No uncertain terms."

She stood looking down at him, her hair haloed by the porch light. "Well?" she said. "He going to sit there all night, or what?"

31

He was at the newspaper when the staff opened the doors, Sheldon Spring walking in after he did.

"You ever have people's mail forwarded here?" Shawn asked him.

"Good as you and Catherine Mulvhill have been for circulation, I'd deliver it myself," the editor said. "Want some coffee?"

"Already got it and padded the kitty."

"The magic word. Speaking of which, you catch this morning's fire edition?" Handing him one of the papers. "We tried to find you for a quote, but no luck. Cell dropout or something."

Obviously it was the reason he'd seen Spring and his photographer out at Stonehouse. He could have hit them with a rock, let alone a statement for inclusion. He scanned the front page: Catherine Mulvhill accompanied by an open letter. Before reading it, he asked, "Any chance you might put out another? Like tomorrow?"

The editor turned, grinned. "Actually, she wants us to. The bank vault wasn't badly damaged and they need to let their box holders know. If we do, you'll get a chance to respond instead of firing blind."

"It's that bad?"

"Don't take my word."

Shawn read, pictured her saying it, the photo that persuasive.

To our bank customers, lake citizens, and the person or persons who perpetrated this act:

We will not be deterred by violence. Nor will we hesitate to rebuild. We answer to this family of communities, not to thugs and criminals. Our history here runs too long and too deep to abdicate our responsibilities. Indeed, our on-site tent is already up and helping where we can.

As I reflect on recent debate, it has become clear this senseless act stems from my determination to prevent Constance from becoming a circus act. That is the very aberration my father wished to prevent when he consigned her to legend in the waters in which she served.

So, to whoever did this: You have not only betrayed your friends and neighbors, you have made a grave mistake, incurring not only their wrath, but mine.

For shame,

Catherine Constance Holmes Mulvhill

Shawn turned the page: Among the photos was a letter from the manager assuring customers that records were on data file and in no way lost. Next was a long list of deposit-box holders, with advice to relocate the boxes to other institutions while the bank was under reconstruction. Holmes Bank & Trust would reimburse any such security charges upon their return.

The winner on all cards…

Shawn scanned the notice for his father's name, found it and made a mental note to remind Liam of the offer, then sat and composed on his laptop *To all who, like myself, feel outrage at the burning of Holmes Bank & Trust:*

We who support the Constance *Project burn as well at this injustice. Such actions have no place in our lives; we condemn them. We also stand ready to assist in whatever way possible.*

But on another front, we burn at the inference that those of good faith were somehow — directly or indirectly — involved. Surely that is what the investigative process is for: reason and restraint and patience.

Facts and truth.

I was born and raised here. Like you, I hold only her interests. But when we cannot agree to disagree, that truly is the fire next time.

In support,

Shawn Andrew Rainey

He stepped back from it: not as good as side-by-side in this morning's edition, but sufficient if it ran tomorrow. Time would tell. Which, of course, was the fool's way of stating the obvious: In the late rounds, they were down and bleeding.

Shawn asked a staffer for the files he'd been going over.

He revisited Catherine Mulvhill's timeline and confirmed printed dates for the University of Wisconsin as 1940 to 1944, plus a subsequent notice he'd considered inconsequential. *Dateline 1947:* MISS HOLMES RETURNS FROM SOJOURN. *Europe:* the years following her graduation, magna cum laude...respite from rigors academic and those brought on by her father's death...Miss Holmes quoted as being "happy to be back at Stonehouse and eager to apply my newfound knowledge."

He heard Mrs. Yue again on Catherine's relationship to Lily, house-woman May Chen's daughter: *Only that they were close, and it ended when Catherine went away to college...*

After Mr. Holmes died.

1943.

One way to find out.

He spent the next minutes outside on his cell phone, ultimately reaching a registrar willing to look it up if it didn't take long, normal procedure sending a cashier's check and waiting for the transcripts. His leverage: He needed the dates *now* if an innocent victim were to avoid a smear. One of *those* cases, if she knew what he meant.

Silence, the tapping of keys, then she was back on:

"Nineteen forty-three to nineteen forty-seven. B.A. Finance."

"Not forty to forty-four?" Repeating the spelling for her.

"Sir, I have M-u-l-v-h-i-l-l, Catherine Constance Holmes, four-three to four-seven. Now, if you'll excuse me." Hanging up before he could challenge her further.

So Mrs. Yue was right. It was the newspaper article that was wrong, it's source doubtless Catherine or someone hired by her. But why? The question rippled, triggered second interest in the Chen file – re-reading, more attention paid its misfortunes. The granddaughter killed in a head-on returning from Reno died in 1949, outside the timeline; similarly the great-grandson lost in Vietnam, 1967. The sons lost on Tarawa and Kwajalein were within the timeline but beyond its geographic scope, the members lost to smallpox vice versa.

Which left the nephew.

Thomas Jefferson Chen, age 24.

Shawn reread: Thomas Chen had set out to gamble at South Shore and not come back; reported missing August 27, 1940; his motorboat found stove-in and half-submerged by Labor-Day picnickers who'd almost struck it in their own craft.

Late afternoon, Monday, September 2, 1940.

Shawn turned it over, around, upside down – first tilt at a

Rubik cube. The odds on being a coincidence that the reported-missing date was two days before *Constance* went down, the motorboat-discovery date approximately five days later, seemed about equal to Catherine getting *her* dates wrong. And yet, beyond the coincidence, what had he, really? Without corroboration, nothing.

Sheldon Spring's door opened. He emerged with the photographer Shawn recognized from Stonehouse and another woman, who headed for separate cubicles. "Thought you'd like to know," he said over the top of Shawn's. "We decided to print tomorrow. The photos are that good."

"And the revenue?"

He smiled as Shawn closed the file, picked up his laptop, stood to go. "Come back anytime," he said.

Liam Rainey was running an old hand mower over the grass, the click-click-click evoking memories of his mother bringing him lemonade on warm days. Same mower for all Shawn knew, the hypnotic effect it still had. For sure, the same smell of cut lawn.

"Spell you with that?" he asked.

"Almost done," his father answered.

"At least let me dump the basket."

He composted the cuttings, Liam brushed out and re-hung the mower, then they went inside. While he opened the soup can his father had out, stirred milk into a pan with it, his father melted butter in a skillet, laid in bread.

"You're back early," he said.

"Wanted to see if you'd caught the deposit box notice in the paper."

Liam turned the bread, set cheddar on the toasted side.

"Been and back. Plain forgot that I had it, which shows you the value of what's inside. Nothing I can't keep here and save the money."

Shawn kept stirring. "Pop, they'll pay for it. I'll relocate it for you."

"What, I'm helpless now?"

"I didn't say that." Then, "You feeling all right?"

"Slept lousy. This crap going on, my mind won't turn off." Lifting out the sandwiches with a turner. "Long as we're at it, there anything else on yours?"

Shawn divvied the soup while his father set down the plates. "Pop, you remember telling me Catherine Mulvhill gave her heart to a boy who left her?"

"Lord, you're persistent."

Shawn blew on his soup. "I was wondering if you might recall his name."

"I look like memory lane to you? Besides, I told you—"

"Thomas…Tom? Like that?"

"It's still no. No, she never said; no, I didn't ask. Back then we respected privacy. Not like today, where everybody's a book they read from no matter who has to plug his ears."

"Good grilled cheese."

"So eat. You want a piece of the paper?"

"No, thanks."

Liam Rainey scanned the front page; focused, defocused, lifted his eyes. "The fire, Shawn, what we talked about. You know who did it yet?"

The reason his father was so jumpy, what he'd figured it was; he said, "Yes and no, Pop. All I can tell you right now."

Long pause, long breath. "All right, if that's how it is. You're a man now, I suppose with a man's reasons. Not that I feel better for it." The paper rattled. "You know banks are FBI, not just local.

You do know that."

"I know."

"And that your mother's watching? Putting in a word when you deserve it?"

Despite himself he had to grin. "Tell me something, all due respect," he said to his father. "Did you ever *lose* an argument to Mom?"

"Every one," Liam Rainey said, getting up to rinse his plate.

32

THE MUSEUM WAS CLOSED, but a light was on inside. Parked across the street was a car with a security company logo, the blue-shirt eyeing him as he approached. *Catherine Mulvhill's guard.* Not that he blamed her, still wondering what in hell he was going to do about Joe Don.

More to the point, when.

He stepped onto the porch, knocked, saw the security guard reach for something under the dash and talk into it. From inside he heard, "We're closed."

"Theda? It's Shawn Rainey."

The door opened a crack; she peered out. "You have the gall to show up after what's happened?

"Theda, I did not burn the bank. Read tomorrow's paper. My statement in it."

"I already told Mrs. Mulvhill you'd been here. The things we talked about."

"I understand. She's your friend and I have nothing to hide."

"No, you do *not* understand. You have to leave before—"

"One question?"

"One too many. *Please.*"

"A name, your reaction to it: Thomas Jefferson Chen, 1940. The year he disappeared."

She'd been backing away. Now the door stopped its progress.

"His boat was found, but he wasn't," Shawn added.

He caught a flash: her face gone white, movement behind her.

"I was thinking you might have known him. Theda?"

"Thank you, Theda. I'll handle this."

Catherine Mulvhill stepped around her and out, closed the door behind her: khaki pants, faded navy casting shirt with the sleeves tabbed up, leather hiking boots. She said, "Aside from the issue of harassment, Mr. Rainey, what is it you wish to know?"

Shawn bought time with a breath. "You sure it's not the other way around? I'd be gone if you hadn't heard the name."

"For the record, Thomas Chen was a nephew of our housekeeper, one of a series of helpers for the more ambitious chores. I recall the sheriff telling us he staged his disappearance because he owed gambling money to people he should not have. We've had our share of those up here. People who take and leave."

"Thomas Chen sank his boat instead of selling it to pay his gambling debts…that's the line?"

"I can only relate what the sheriff told my father. Now, let me tell you where you stand. Your friend, or should I say accomplice, burned my bank because he picked the wrong side and couldn't live with it. We are very close to proving that, even to implicating you. Despite a certain respect I hold for your father."

"I'm sure."

She shook her head, leaned against the railing. "You disappoint me, Mr. Rainey."

"Welcome to a long list, Mrs. Mulvhill."

"I've been thinking. You were never charged were you? And what might your brother's death have gained you, a more diligent prosecutor might have asked? A woman, formerly your brother's, now married to your arsonist friend. A woman you shunned."

"Old news," he said, feeling the same. "Old and tired."

"I think you'll find otherwise. Public opinion has a way of changing with our perceptions."

"Generous of you to warn me. Again."

The Stonehouse smile resurfaced. "Along those lines, it has come to my attention that this Ware person you're seeing is not what she appears." Pausing for effect. "Have I your attention? I thought so. She seems to have been incarcerated in the women's prison at Gatesville, Texas, for no less than murder."

Coup de grace.

Shawn just standing there as it tore through him.

"Not surprising it didn't appear on her employment application. Of course, she may have told you, which would lead to other issues regarding your judgment. Better you'd have listened, Mr. Rainey. And now I have work to do."

"Bullshit." Gripping her wrist as much to steady himself. "You don't just throw down something like that and walk."

She regarded the hand. "Do you think I would say it if it weren't true?" Eyes rising to his. "I'll show you the faxes. More to the point, ask her."

Goddamnit. "Why? She has nothing to do with it."

"The company you keep, Mr. Rainey – including, of course, the loathsome Mr. Dahl. And if there remains a question, it is because you are in my way. Take your hand off me."

Tires skidded in the street; blue smoke rose from the wheel wells. Frank Love slammed the F-250's door, rounded the tailgate, topped the walk in three steps.

"You okay?" he asked Catherine Mulvhill.

"It's all right, Frank, Mr. Rainey is just leaving." Pulling her wrist free of Shawn's grip.

"Bet your ass he is. I've been looking forward to this for too many years."

"Too many for both of us, if you have any sense," Shawn told him. "Back off."

But Frank Love kept coming.

Shawn sidestepped his haymaker, the man nowhere as quick as Joe Don but winding up for another. The second punch grazed his arm and shoulder, nicked his ear; recovering, he sensed a presence, a glimpse of blue shirt, then the guard's nightstick slammed into his calves.

He was down, clutching at the pain and the fire and the cramping, trying to shield himself from kicks aimed at his wind and kidneys, when he heard from somewhere, "Frank, that's enough."

"I don't *think* so." Grunts as the kicks landed. "Fools like this you don't *let* up. They keep *coming*."

"Frank, stop it! Call your man off."

He heard a snap of fingers. There was a final kick and it ceased, Shawn thinking through the pain, *Hadn't that been where it started, Terry's little dance on his knee? Before that, his assault on Terry? The go-around again in wide-screen 3-D.*

He saw Catherine Mulvhill's boots hesitate as though deciding their next move. Finally they stepped away with Frank Love's steel-toed ones. Shawn heard the pickup start, saw it blur off, the security guard sheathing his nightstick and rolling behind it. His own future up in Joe Don's smoke.

Then it all swam.

"Mr. Rainey?"

Slap of lavender. Theda Sandstrom's face looking worried.

"I'm all right," he managed.

She capped the smelling salts. "Can you get up?"

"Yeah…just need a second." He pushed up to a sitting position, head forward to let the dizziness pass.

She said, "I saw what happened. It was terrible. She was wrong to let them do that to you."

He stood, took inventory: pain, but nothing broken, his knee aching but not re-injured. She said, "Come inside, I have tea on. I would have called the sheriff, but it happened so fast."

"Wouldn't have mattered. One way or the other."

She helped him inside to a high-backed chair in front of a claw-foot table. Set down china cups with saucers, poured tea from a china pot. Reached into a drawer and pulled out a bottle.

"Brandy in yours?" she asked. "I'm having some."

She poured liberal shots; sipping, he felt the warmth spread, distract the ache in his calves and ribs.

"Better?" she asked.

"Getting there."

She rattled her cup. "You don't have much use for my friend, do you?"

"And you do?"

"I'm telling you, she's not like this. I don't know who she was out there, but she's not herself with this thing."

"I've been known to have that effect on people. Somebody burned my bank and cost me a bundle, I might go off, too."

"Not just now, ever since it began. I tried to warn you she was inside."

"I know," he said. Forgetting to sip, he gasped at the bite.

"More brandy? I'm going to." Pouring into what remained of their tea.

"You knew him, didn't you? Thomas Chen."

Nod. "I knew him. Back then, we pretty much all knew each other, the young people anyway. Not like now. Islands in the stream."

"And Catherine?"

She looked out the window at early aspens turned yellow. "What did Catherine tell you?"

"She said he did occasional work at the house, disappeared, and didn't come back. Nothing I didn't know."

"Then I guess that's the answer."

"Such as it is." He thought better. "Sorry – this isn't your doing. You've been nothing but kind."

"It's all right."

They sat in the quiet of the museum. Shawn said, "Catherine knew him, didn't she? I mean, the way you said kids did." Pushing what luck remained off a cliff. "Maybe better."

"Drink up, tea's no good cold."

Shawn reached for the bottle, felt like downing it, topped her cup. "Theda, I know you're torn. I would be, too. But I'm going to ask one more question, and if you say nothing, I'll consider it answered. Then I'll leave and not come back. Okay?"

She looked down at the cup. She nodded.

He said, "Your friend Catherine had a thing for Thomas Chen. Or they had one for each other, and it didn't play well then, so they had to keep it quiet. Anywhere close?"

Her eyes stayed with the cup.

"Thanks for the tea," he said, touching her hand, getting up to leave. "And you're right. I do feel better."

33

He CAUGHT HER LOCKING THE DOOR OF THE A-FRAME, Shawn rolling up to face her: vest and black pants, tie not yet tied, hair swept up but wisping. He felt the rush that was becoming familiar whenever he saw her. Second nature.

"Hey," she said, turning the deadbolt. "Good timing."

"Katie, I need to talk to you."

"Some of us have to work." Then, to his expression, "You're serious, aren't you?"

He reached the porch. "Can we go back inside?"

"I'd love it, but I need to be on time. If not, I'll have to call in, see if Barney can hold over. If he can't—"

"Call him," he said.

"About what?"

"Please…"

"Shawn, you're pissing me off. Your schedule's fine, but mine isn't? It might not be much, but it's—"

"Gatesville," he said.

The flush fell away and she was a sapling into which a

woodsman had driven an axe. Not looking at him, she straightened, unlocked the door, went inside, Shawn feeling leaden and guilty, as if he were the one who'd revealed it to hurt her. And yet he felt betrayed by her silence, if that made sense, which it didn't.

He could hear her talking on the phone.

"Barney will cover," she said, hanging up, rounding on him. "For a while, anyway. How did you find out?"

"How do you think?"

It took her no more than a second. "I don't believe it. She can't be that mean."

"Guess again."

Her face was ashen.

He said, "What I want to know is, why now? Her bank's insured, its records are intact. Sure it's a loss, but she has the project in a hammerlock and sentiment running with her, thanks to the arson. All I can think is, I'm getting close to something she doesn't want me to find."

"So she's threatening you with my job."

"Katie, I'm sorry."

"Mr. Open Book. Not that you didn't want to know, anything like that."

Shawn thought of his father, how much like him he'd become during the affair with Cort, not to mention after. "Katie, I came only to brace you for it. To ask you what to do."

"Damn her, she has no right." Sinking into a chair beside Ihop looking up at her.

"Would you rather I left?"

"No, and there's nothing you can do. I'll tell Bob Lamont tomorrow. Tonight if he's there."

"Rule one, Katie: You don't just hand it to them. They won't even slow before running you over."

"House rule, this house: I will not have them using me as leverage. I will not." Then, "She didn't tell you why I was there?"

"No."

Leave now…go. But he couldn't.

She drew a breath. "Ever been to mid-Texas in summer? It's like you're the butter on burnt toast. Every direction's the same, hell-bent for the horizon. The noise you hear at night is the grasshoppers chewing."

Shawn said nothing.

"Swell place, Gatesville. After the trial, they ran me up with a real sweet group on a chain. Actually, I was lucky. Some women never get out for what I did. Only reason was, Austin's the capitol and I was within shouting distance of some people who took up my cause."

She stroked Ihop, her focus off; Shawn caught movement in the loft, Ben Affleck stretching before settling back. As if it physically hurt, she went to a drawer, pulled out a photograph, a girl of perhaps three who looked like Shirley Temple with Katie's smile.

"Her name was Alice. Alice Blue Eyes, my everything girl." Shaking her head as if living it again. "One day my swell pick for a husband comes home coked to the eyes and wants me to go out dancing with him and his pals. But I'm making dinner and Alice is fussy with a bug, so I say no, for him to go without me if he wants to so much. Darryl doesn't like no, or so I'd come to learn. Nobody much had said it to him growing up, for sure not his daddy, who owned a Massey franchise. Nothing but the best for his boy. Which is exactly what Darryl was." Texas softening her pronunciation, if not the rush of words.

"So daddy's boy waves off his pals, takes off his belt, and lays into me. Not with the leather end, this time with the buckle, this ugly bronze thing. But I dodge, and he…" deep breath, "he hits Alice. By accident, his lawyer said later, as much my fault as his, but that was Darryl, nothing was ever his fault. Anyway, it's like everything is in slow motion…her head is bouncing off the stove, and there's blood, and now she's on the floor, more blood, so much of it, and she's convulsing, my baby is…" Hands cupped to her forehead. "And then it stopped."

Jesus.

"Katie, you don't have to do this. For me or anyone."

"*No?* You'd rather wait for her version?" Fiercely, as if too many tears had preceded these latecomers. "I knew she was gone, my Alice was gone, but I kept trying to bring her back, Darryl standing over me. That's when the son of a bitch yanks me up by the hair, tells me I deserve what's coming next for making him do it." She swiped at her eyes. "But there was a knife I'd been using to cut green peppers with. Odd what you remember, isn't it? This time, I didn't dodge."

"And the cops came?"

"My mom did, she's the one who got the police. Three years, seven months, and four days later, my pardon came through. Darryl's parents made a huge issue of trying to stop it. His mother threatened to kill me."

"So you headed up here."

"Up above the world so high." She drank some water. "Not high enough, it turns out. But you know the thing I truly regret? Mom dying while I was in Gatesville, the stress on her. Had I known, I'd have let him hit me…"

Shawn put his arms around her, held her, felt the charge in her slowly ground off in a sigh.

"Katie, I'm so sorry."

"Yeah, me too. Which still leaves us where we are. I'll miss the job and the recommendation, but I'm good enough to get on someplace else. Who knows, maybe Lamont's got a past and I won't have to."

"I won't let you do this." Knowing she knew better, that Lamont would be the first to cave under pressure. "It's not your fight."

"And I will not be used against you – period – not when I think I know why you're doing it. Now come on. This late, Barney's going to kill me anyway."

Ben Affleck had come down from the loft, searching eyes trying to read him. "Will you at least think it over?"

"What? Start thinking now?"

She relocked the house, and he walked her to the Corolla, where she got in and rolled down her window, leaned toward him through it.

"Just promise not to waste it," she said.

Dinner and a fistful of ibuprofen, his aches giving him hell in earnest, Shawn packed it in early. He'd gone out hard, when Terry called, Shawn fumbling up the cell phone through his fog.

"Yeah...Rainey."

"You sound like a tape binding up. Tough day?"

"You could say that."

"Don't tell me. You're using her head as a tiki torch on the lawn right now. You were going to surprise me."

"There a purpose beyond your usual, Terry?"

"My usual is what gets it done, Speed. Now, what have you got for me? Lamont says you haven't been in touch."

Shawn rubbed his face, no help. "I wasn't aware Lamont was in the job description."

"You want to cut the crap? That lock better be close to yielding. Or do I have to tell you how well the kids have taken to learning Portuguese?"

Shawn bit back his anger and told him, long on concept, short on detail: still searching for the key, which right now was on Catherine Mulvhill's ring in a safe somewhere. At least he might have found the safe.

Maybe.

"She did have a good word for you, Terry. The word was loathsome. For once, we agreed."

"Why, the nerve of her, putting those thoughts in your head. I'm outraged." Then the tone changed altogether. "I'm also giving you a deadline: one week, next Monday. Deal's off the table then, and so are Nate and Elizabeth. Do we understand each other? I need the money machine up and running *now*."

"There anything else you want to tell me about that? A payment schedule I can pass on when it's needed?"

"Believe me, you'll know when there is."

Shawn let it go, said nothing.

Terry signed off with, "Hey, you there…? Want to hear 'em say *'sayonara'* in Portuguese? It really is a gas."

34

SLEEP CAME AND WENT, interspersed with dreams: a hodge-podge, nothing much remembered. By the time Shawn jerked awake to light slanting through the shutters, his father was through with breakfast and reading the paper over coffee.

"I made oatmeal," he said. Then, "You stiff from something?"

"Slow waking up." Cursing Frank Love and the guard; the truth was, he could hardly walk, though he knew it would loosen. He poured himself coffee, scooped oatmeal, added raisins and brown sugar, milk to both, eased into a chrome-leg chair across from Liam.

The paper crinkled.

"Photo of you in here. Along with your letter."

He handed Shawn the section. And there it was: same page as a three-column night shot backlit by leaping orange, the caption reading, *Residents Shawn and Liam Rainey help keep flames in check,* Shawn thinking it sometimes just came together, as often in spite of as because of.

Then he turned the page.

Lakewood. *Citing inadequate deliberation by a grand jury influenced by Shawn Rainey's skiing fame, the environmental activist group Friends of Washoe Billy demanded the investigation into his late brother Cortland's death be reopened. The younger Rainey, who recently has been prominent in local efforts to raise and restore the sunken lake steamship* Constance...

On and on, raising and restoring the issue as effectively as if he were being charged: guilty until proven innocent.

"You read this about Cort?" he asked his father.

"I read it. Now I'm going to go cut Jim Vogle's grass, maybe Whit Thiessen's."

"Pop, I'm sorry."

"You didn't try to reason with her? Tell her how little we have left to bleed?"

Shawn said nothing; could say nothing.

"No, I didn't think so," his father said before letting the screen bang behind him. "I just hope it's worth it. Whichever one of you is left standing when it's over."

Shawn ate without tasting; he read the story again, tried to compose a response, the words sounding flat and defensive. He was still coming up empty when his eyes roamed to the opposing page, the Holmes Bank ad with the list of safety-deposit-box names. He scanned it from the end, names he knew: Robin's mom, still Vasquez; John Sharpe Sr.; Jake's dad; Liam; old man McCandless (no Joe Don, he noted); Hardin and Engleman – imagining what was in their boxes. He was closing in on Autry, wondering if Neville and Neil had, like Joe Don, put their money where their mouth was, in some other bank, when his scan halted halfway up a column. At Chen, T. J.

No way, couldn't be…

But if…?

The question was, how long were the boxes kept? Likely not long if the rental fees ceased…unless it might be part of a service package, a perpetuity deal. Bottom line: *Cool it* – T.J. could just as easily be Teresa Joan or something like it, Chen a common enough last name.

He was up and out the door, limping, waving, calling over the whir of the mower: "Pop? Did they have phone lines set up when you were over there?"

The mower stopped. "Over where?"

"The bank."

"I should know? It's a tent full of people, everybody worried about their money." Starting back down a row.

Shawn went back inside, dialed information. Yes, there had been a number of rotator lines installed for Holmes Bank due to the fire, accessed by a single number she gave him. He dialed it, got a recorded message asking for his patience, that they would get to his call in sequence; ten minutes and he was ready to drive over, take his chances in line, when a young male voice came on.

Shawn asked him if he could find out whether anyone had picked up the contents of the deposit box in the name of T.J. Chen.

Pause, then the voice: "Sir, it does look as if that has been picked up."

"Would you know when?"

"Looks like first thing this morning. Some people may not have seen yesterday's notice or couldn't get in, but did today. We're as busy now as we were then." Laying the groundwork for a quick call.

"And that would be the Thomas Jefferson Chen box for certain?"

Fingers crossed.

"Sir, I hate to be abrupt, but–"

"Look, *my* name is Thomas Jefferson Chen. Those contents you released belonged to my grandfather, willed to me. They could be in the wrong hands."

"One moment, please." There was a pause that seemed forever, then: "That would be correct, Thomas Jefferson Chen. Sir, if this is some kind of situation involving misrepresentation, I suggest you–"

"Dating back to 1940?"

Pause. "Thirty-eight, sir."

Base hit: grand fucking slam. "And how is that possible?"

"If I follow the question, it's because the bank offered depositors lifetime boxes then. We don't do that anymore. Only with minimum average yearly deposits of two hundred thousand dollars."

"Story of my life," Shawn said. "Too little, too late."

But by then the kid had hung up.

35

S HAWN HIT NORTH LAKE, WEST TO **89.** At ten in the morning the river was packed with pre-Labor Day rafters, a brightly colored stream he barely noticed. Flashing out ahead of him in neon: Who had picked up the contents of the Thomas Chen box? What was in it? Had the pickers-up even known of it before the ad? Or was this yet another expired meter?

He drove past River Ranch, return busses waiting to pick up the disembarked rafters, on downriver, and into Truckee. Morning light had rendered the brick buildings a shade of red the envy of a more tumultuous age. And yet, he thought, was it less so back then? Not if he was guessing right about where this might lead, *guess* being the operative word.

The Chen store had just opened, the only person inside a young Chinese man: longish hair swept back, smoke-lensed glasses molded to contour his eye sockets; chinos and a form-fitting black T-shirt that showed off his abdominal muscles. "Help you?" he said.

Same intonation as *fuck you.*

"Looking for the older lady who was here a few days ago.

Mrs. Yue?"

"Sorry, no older lady."

Shawn eyed the kid, which got nowhere. "What about the younger one, the college girl? Slender, dark hair, pretty."

"You ever seen a fat blonde Chinese? You do, let me know."

"That your final answer?"

"She's back in school," he said, glancing up at the tone. "Anything else?"

"The older lady, Mrs. Yue. Please tell her that the man who was here before, the writer she spoke to, would appreciate a word."

"Dude, what's it going to take?"

"You're right, don't bother." Heading for the office door.

"Hey...!"

Shawn's hand was on the lever when the kid inserted himself between him and the door. "You got a jail wish, man? Cause I got it right here." Pulling a cell phone out of his pocket and punching in a three-digit number Shawn assumed was 911. Which is when the door opened.

She had on a blue embroidered top with wear spots and frog closures over utility pants, dark stains on the knees.

"David, that will be all," she said. "Leave us, please."

"You're going to let this mother—"

"I've warned you about your language. I won't again."

The kid went back to the cash register; when Shawn turned, Mrs. Yue was walking across to her desk.

"Thank you," he said.

"Close the door and sit down, Mr. Rainey."

It was like closing the gates to the Inner Palace. Despite the worn brick and iron shutters, the bars over the window, the room was more elegant than he remembered: imperial reds, greens, and deep blues; carvings and dark-wood furnishings; the faint scent of incense. The lone touch of present was the computer screen on which she'd been working.

She said, "I saw your picture in the paper. I also read your open letter. I'm glad to see you are at least able to write."

"I apologize for the rest. You're gracious to see me."

Her eyebrows arched. "We'll see. I will warn you it does not occur naturally in my veins. Curiosity, however, does. Why are you back?"

"The bank notice in the paper. I called them. They confirmed the contents of Thomas Jefferson Chen's safety-deposit box had been picked up this morning. I missed you, or maybe him out there, by no more than an hour."

She eyed her fingernails. "As it happened, you missed neither of us. My lawyer picked it up. Is that all you wished to know?"

Monday, Terry's bastard deadline: "What was in it might prove helpful. All due respect."

"If you call what you did respect. Thomas Chen is long gone, Mr. Rainey. What purpose would it serve?"

Shawn told her: the project, where it stood or didn't, Catherine Mulvhill. He watched Mrs. Yue lean back in her chair.

"Do you seriously expect me – us – to care about a boat our people were only hired to work on? Why would we?"

He took a breath and launched. "I can only answer with what I've found out: that by 1940 Thomas and Catherine were taken with each other, maybe in love; that Ling Chen and Mr. Holmes were enemies; that one night Thomas didn't come back from gambling. That the closer I get to all this the more Catherine Mulvhill views me as a threat, even though she has it all her way."

Her look pinned him. "This from someone who lies when it

suits him, lays plans to trap a decent woman in a sixty-year-old web she may or may not have spun."

"Mrs. Yue, I'm almost finished here – in a lot of ways for which I'm responsible. Do I like what I'm doing? I don't. Is it square in my lap and burning a hole in it? It is. I have one hope and it's this thread I intend to keep pulling until nothing or something is on the other end."

"You do realize the women of my family worked in that house?"

"Li Chen and her daughter May, then May's daughter Lily. Some odd jobs Thomas did at May's request. As you said."

A beat passed. "Mr. Chen was a great man. But like many, he was subject to his anger. After being cheated by Mr. Holmes, Mr. Chen was adamant we quit. Then reason took hold. We became his eyes and ears, though in turn Mr. Holmes became prone to silence around us. Except at those times he drank, which became more and more."

"You said 'we.' Would that mean you worked there as well?"

Mrs. Yue looked out the barred window; at length she brought out a lacquered box inlaid with mother-of-pearl, a bird in flight. She opened it, withdrew stacks of old casino-issued gaming chips. When she had finished, ten stacks of ten chips sat between them on the desk.

"The deposit box's contents, Mr. Rainey, twenty-five hundred dollars. Not a great deal by today's standards, but back then it could start a business. American-born Chinese could purchase property, as my grandfather could not." Pause. "Do you know how much this could have been worth had my cousin lived to invest it? Had we known of its existence? But American banks were foreign to us. Who would have guessed he had chosen to secret his winnings in Mr. Holmes's own institution?"

"Money that could have staked him and Catherine so neither family could give them grief, is that it?"

Her smile was oddly wistful; she brought out a faded brown photo-print, early Hawkeye size, set it on the desk. Frozen in time was a young man about David's age: Jason Lee-handsome in a two-toned pullover sweater and a straw fedora thumbed back. Smiling around a cigarette, he leaned against a large pine tree. Behind him was the lake, Tallac's notched peak in the far distance. Under his other arm, adoringly, was a Chinese girl of perhaps fourteen.

The resemblance was too striking for Shawn not to look at Mrs. Yue. He waited.

"You're assumption is correct," she said, glancing from Shawn to the photo. "The girl is Lily Chen. I became Yue later on. Tommy Chen was my cousin."

Lily Chen Yue, Catherine's housekeeper's daughter.

Someone who'd been there, seen it from the inside.

Shawn's thoughts raced, leapfrogging as Mrs. Yue instructed David via intercom to bring them glasses and a bottle of her wine, David in due course setting it down without meeting either one's eyes.

"To Thomas Jefferson Chen," she said when David had opened it and left. "My first real crush. Of course he had no eyes for me, a kid when he was twenty-four and I was his cousin. But I often thought of what might have been. It feels good to say his name."

Easy, Shawn thought, setting down his glass, *go easy.* "So what did happen to him? Did you ever find out?"

She held her wine to the light. "Except for the theory he'd run to avoid his debts, we had no reason to dispute the findings. Of course the chips rather prove otherwise. He would not have left without them. All these years…"

"Could he have set out with a few, left the main stake to limit his losses?"

"Tommy didn't lose – not often, anyway. But, yes, it's possible."

"Too bad his winnings couldn't help him in the water."

She sipped. Then, "From what I read, your brother was about his age."

It flashed, then: the real reason Lily Chen Yue had opened up to him after he'd lied to her. Tommy-Cort was their bridge, similar losses at similar ages.

"That would be right," he said. "Twenty-four."

"At least you were with him at the end. You were close?"

"Not as close as we should have been."

She let it settle. "Does that mean this Washoe Billy group is right?"

"No, it does not."

"Then why have they–"

"It's a long story. Part of my getting too close."

More wine; she eyed him. "Surely you don't believe Catherine had anything to do with their actions?"

"If she hadn't threatened it, I'd be less inclined."

"And if your positions were reversed?"

"The truth?" As if looking at himself in the mirror after a hard night at Quincy's. "I don't know yet."

Lily Yue sighed. "I loved her, you know. We all did, those of us who worked at Stonehouse. But she changed."

Shawn tried to see it. "And Tommy?"

Nod. "As she loved him. It's why she was sent across the lake to boarding school. Finances were such that her father couldn't afford one very far away and still travel. How she laughed at that."

Shawn pictured the dorm-room window sliding open,

Catherine letting herself out the lesser-drop side to a red glow in the shadows. "So she continued to see Tommy."

"Tommy's gambling came between them for a time, and they couldn't meet in the regular ways. But it was not the simple infatuation we first thought." Her look saying more.

Rivals, but not, he thought. *Sisters.* "And then it ended?"

"Her father found out. He took her out of school a second time. That's when everything changed."

"Catherine had a friend at school. Theda. I don't know her maiden name. Would Cyrus have found out from her?"

She thought. "I met Theda once when she was at the house, but I would say not. Even after it happened, she and Catherine were close."

"So how *did* he find out?"

"You spoke with her?"

Nod. "She runs the museum where the school used to be."

She swirled the wine, watched it run down the sides. "That's why I supposed you knew. The school nurse discovered it during a routine physical exam. Catherine was pregnant. Right then we were asked to leave the house."

Bingo, Shawn thought. *Double Bingo.*

"And you never saw her again?"

"By the time Catherine returned from her university and travel, I was married and working in my husband's business. In any case, she and I hardly walked the same path."

"So no one stayed on?"

"Only my grandmother, who had midwifed Catherine. Catherine got word to us she wanted Nana back to deliver her baby. Nana was afraid, but she did it."

"Why afraid?"

"Mr. Holmes's rages. Already he'd paid off the nurse and forced Catherine to tell him who the father was. It was not a time to possess knowledge of anything. Or to be Chinese in that house."

Think. "Do you know what happened to the child?"

She looked at him as if hearing someone else ask. "Other than they were putting it up for adoption, no. 'These things are not for us,' Nana would say. The fact is, my grandfather was ill and unaware she'd gone back at all. He'd have disowned her. As it was, she passed before he did."

"And Catherine?"

"We thought it best to lie low, even after her father died. I'd been sent to work in Los Angeles before returning to marry. When she made no effort to contact us, that became the norm. The pictures we saw later, the businesswoman rebuilding the estate, were so different from the girl we knew, it was apparent we'd made the right choice."

"And now?" he asked.

She finished her wine, let her eyes drift to the bamboo waving and splashed with light. "You never know, do you, Mr. Rainey?"

Shawn drove back over the mountain, thinking that Catherine Mulvhill had become as cold and hard as her house. Not only her house, but the father she hated yet, seemingly, oddly, had come to terms with. She had, after all, spent her life rebuilding her father's empire, though in different form. What did that say about her?

For certain, no less than that people changed.

Maybe Tommy Chen *had* staged the accident and disappeared, left the casino chips to cash in when he needed them. Maybe he'd left them for Catherine and she'd forgotten after getting over her anger at his abandonment. Maybe he and Catherine had simply fallen out of love, a sentiment wrung from her entirely when she'd lost Landon Mulvhill, the husband her father almost certainly forced on her so that if anyone found out she was pregnant, he had a cover.

Different era, different world…

Yet all of it fit, he thought. Look what *you* jumped into when Terry's little screw-job came down. Leverage ruled; you went along to get along. Or did you? He was mulling it, feeling the photo of Nate and Elizabeth again, running his thumb over the widening crack, when his cell phone trilled.

"Rainey."

"Shawn, where are you?" Katie's voice. "Have you had the radio on?"

"No," he said. "Why?"

"There's been a fire at Joe Don's house, the trucks are only hoping to keep it from spreading up the hill. From the pictures, it looks pretty much gone."

Goddamnit, Shawn thought, here we go again. Tit for tat just as he was getting somewhere. Up in smoke.

"The sheriff have anybody in mind for it?"

"News reports said they want to talk to Frank Love, but they can't find him."

Not surprising. "Okay, I'll turn it on. By now Joe Don must be howling at the media."

He heard her expel a breath.

"That's not what I meant by calling," she said. "Shawn, I'm sorry, truly sorry, but I don't know how else to say it. Joe Don is dead."

36

H E WAS AT THE TOP OF MAINLINE, *one of the gnarlier runs coming off Emigrant. He was thirteen, his size and appearance making him look younger, something that loomed large now that he was in junior high, Cort off to his freshman year at Holmes, none of his brother's cachet left to fall back on. New to Squaw, but not to skiing – champ-in-category two years running at Mt. Rose – he was sizing up the lay when three taller kids got off the chair, that late in the afternoon nobody much around.*

The tallest, a tenth-grader he'd noticed below, but who hadn't been on the bus, adjusted his snow glasses and loudmouthed, "Hey you – your mama know you're way up here?"

Laughs from the other two, Shawn fingering the bus and half-day pass hanging from his parka zipper.

"Question too tough?" the kid asked. "Maybe we should send her down a big snowball with you inside it. What do you think of that?"

"Not a lot," Shawn said, cold working its way down his spine.

"I think he'd make a cool snowball." Warming to his own idea. "What do you guys think?"

Nods all around.

"So let's find out."

They were coming for him, Shawn set to take his chances with the ice wall, nasty spill and roll if he landed wrong, when a ski pole crossed the tall kid's chest.

"He doesn't want it." Maroon anorak, amber snow glasses, not as tall as Tall, but solid. Off the lift while they'd been occupied with Shawn. "Or don't you get that?"

"I say he does and my friends make three. Only looking at one of you."

"True, but I fight dirty." The pole's tip going higher up the tall kid's chest. "Ask your pal there. He's seen some."

Tall looked at his cronies, who looked none to eager, the one nodding slightly. "What's your name?" he asked Maroon.

"McCandless: Dad owns the lumberyard. You don't dig it right now or you want to try my friend again, we're around." This odd light in his eyes, like bring it on. "Always happy to oblige."

For a moment they stood there. Then Tall said, "Screw it, I've got better shit than this going." Taking off down the road that led to a gentler entry before traversing the fall line.

"Jerkoffs," McCandless muttered, watching them. "Didn't even make JV football. Think they're hot shit."

"They would have been," Shawn said. "Thanks. You know me?"

"Maybe if you got your nose out of the ozone once in a while. We're in the same class. Joe Don — Joe-D to friends."

"Shawn…Rainey." Quick gloveshake, incredulous. "You're just starting junior high?"

"Big for my age, I know. You really know how to ski?"

"Some."

"No offense, but you don't look it."

"Looks, remember?"

Joe Don McCandless got the reference and grinned. "How about we show these butt-wipes how it's done?"

They swooped, avenging jets, two of the butt-wipes bailing out, then they hit it for real, Shawn taking a line he knew would get him there first. He was leaning on his poles at the Gold Coast complex when Joe Don slid to a stop, snow flying.

"Damn," he said, out of breath. "Nobody ices me like that. Two out of three?"

They were riding up the chair, last run, seven out of nine or some-thing, muscles screaming, faces lit from windburn, when Joe Don said, "Something else, Speed. You start at age two?"

"Six, and it's Shawn."

"Shawn, right. I, um…been wondering something." Quick glance over for reaction. "But I don't ask favors."

"What, you just do them and ride off?" Clacking the ice off his White Stars and watching it fall.

"Get out, that wasn't anything."

"I was there," Shawn said.

"Look, if I ask, promise you won't tell anyone?"

"Why would I tell anyone?" Puzzled at even the question.

"I don't know," Joe Don said, looking down. "People do weird shit."

"Okay, I promise."

They clanked through a stanchion, looped upward over the few skiers left while Joe Don found the words.

"I've seen you in algebra, front row. Stuff's kicking my butt, but you seem to be getting it. If I called you or something, you think you could help me out…?"

Then there was the time – much later on – they were Christmas-break slumming in Reno, bouncing one low-end bar to another, seeing how far they could get with fake IDs. After getting tossed from one, they were headed back to Tam's old Plymouth, prepared to write it off, when they saw a figure huddled against a chain-link fence.

Knees up, head on his arms.

Despite their protests, Joe Don went over, asked him if he was all right. To which the nodder, a kid not much older than they were, raised his head and asked if they had any change. Eyes bleary, face red from cold, breath hanging in the streetlight, torn vest leaking its stuffing.

Joe Don made them pony up, change plus bills, then gave the kid the leather jacket his dad had given him – six hundred bucks – made them promise not to say anything or he'd beat the crap out of them. Next day showing up with his own bruises after telling his old man he'd left it someplace, found it gone when he'd retraced.

"You about ready?"

Liam was talking to him from the bedroom doorway, slipping into the jacket of his too-big suit.

"Ready," Shawn said. "Just have to get my coat."

He got up too quickly, felt lightheaded on top of his hangover, nearly lost it. But the room steadied, and he met his father in the kitchen.

"You had anything to eat?" Liam Rainey asked.

"Thanks, Pop. I'm fine."

"Take the truck?"

"Sure."

They drove in silence. The churchyard was nearly full, but Katie had saved them aisle seats toward the back. She let his father get in first then sat between him and Shawn.

"You all right?" she whispered to him.

He nodded, squeezed her hand, glanced up the aisle at Joe Don's coffin, the flowers on it, Robin and the boys in the front row, Robin in black. Then it was under way, followed by people getting up in place to reminisce, Robin never once turning, though the boys did. Shawn barely hearing his own words, instead seeing their history scroll: shoulder-to-shoulder through junior high and high school, Joe Don the trench-jock Friday nights and Saturday afternoons, roadrunner Shawn on his graphite racing composites.

Different, yet friends.

Music snapped him to the present, Joe Don's words from days ago: *Now I want to hear something from you, Pinocchio. Tell me you want to bring down the Loch Monster less than I do.* And, as Shawn was walking off: *Hey, Pinocchio, your secret's safe with me. See, I love you as much as if you were a real boy.*

Arn Tennell came back to him, the day it happened, Shawn's command performance at the sheriff station: his whereabouts, dustups past and present between Joe Don and Frank Love; anything Joe Don had said about them, what Love said at the fire. Arn seated across a metal-edged table in a metal-edged interrogation room.

By then it was dark outside.

"You through with me?" Shawn finally asked.

"For the moment." Turning off the recorder. "Don't plan on leaving, though. I might take it wrong."

"Joe Don was my friend. Is that somehow unclear?"

Arn rolled his pen in his hands. "Sometimes it's friends you worry about. Wouldn't be the case here, would it?"

"In your dreams, Arn."

"Deputy Sheriff Tennell. Any reason you know of why Joe Don would do himself?"

"What are you talking about?"

"You tell me." Leaning back in his chair, gaze unmoving. "Guilt over something? The bank fire?"

"For that he'd burn his own house with him in it?"

"We know he had money problems, what that can lead to."

Shawn said, "It may come as a shock, but some people with money problems *don't* kill themselves." Doubts rising as soon as he'd said it, buoyant corpses.

Arn unwrapped a plastic-tipped cigar. "You're either an unusually good liar, which I know to be the case, or you really don't know."

"Know what?"

"Know the fire didn't kill him." Watching for reaction. "See, we got him out before that part of the house went up, lucked out for once. Wasn't much to look at, but…"

Shawn felt the room tilt.

"Hell, tomorrow's paper will have it. Your pal had a hole in his head, took off a good portion of his face." And, as Arn was getting up, pocketing his pen, "One more for you, hotshot, off the record. Ever wonder how things would have gone if you'd stayed the hell out of it? Come on, you've got an answer for everything. Is this what you came back for?"

The service was over and they were filing out, nodding to people they knew, Shawn getting into Katie's Corolla with her. Following his father's truck to where he'd stood sixteen years ago and watched them erect the stone to his brother. Horsetails of rain sweeping across the lake Cort would forever belong to, Shawn still seeing his eyes.

"Shawn...?"

He stood with her and Liam graveside as more words were spoken, pictured himself out there with Joe Don, doing three-sixties behind his old man's boat. The two musketeers, Joe Don once had called them.

Damn, Joe-D, you were two all by yourself.

And if you slipped along the way, you sure had company.

Robin laid a rose on the casket; the other mourners did the same. Then car doors were closing and motors starting, Liam saying he'd see him whenever. But the limo with Robin inside hadn't moved, her mother having taken the boys, and Shawn motioned to Katie he'd meet her at her car. He approached the smoked windows, hesitated, tapped; Robin's silhouette turned at the noise, put something down, lowered the window.

"Hello, Shawn." Dead and buried.

"Sorry we didn't have a chance to talk," he said. "There anything I can do?"

"You mean that you haven't done already?"

"Robin, I—"

"Forget it. You want a drink?"

He saw the bottle beside her on the seat, her empty glass, the driver's head facing forward behind the smoked partition.

"Thanks. Had my share already."

"Too early and too late. That's our Shawn."

He could think of no answer.

"Joe Don was a bottom-line kind of guy, Shawn, nothing you don't know. Well, here's a bottom line from me." The smoked glass rolled shut, the limo rolled out of the cemetery and down the hill, leaving Shawn with the lake and the sunlight, the trees and the wind.

37

S HAWN SPENT THE NIGHT AT HOME, hangover to bed early, bizarre dreams that kept waking him in a sweat. Next morning, he took his time in the shower – hot and cold till they were almost the same. He dressed, set eggs on to boil, toast to dark, poured himself coffee from the half-full brewer, then sat with the headlines, Liam already gone.

LOCAL MAN SOUGHT IN MCCANDLESS DEATH

FRANK LOVE SUSPECT IN MURDER

PAYBACK FOR BEATING, BANK FIRE, POSSIBLE MOTIVE

The article went into the bad blood starting when Love was a contractor, Joe Don's (and his) summer job, events that spun from it. It covered present employment, Catherine Mulvhill quoted as not having seen Love since a day and a half before Joe Don was found – now close to five. Of course, it covered Joe Don's project advocacy, his ties to Shawn, included a picture of Frank Love, one of Joe Don with his kids.

Shawn washed his dishes, read the article again, got out his cell phone. After a relatively short hold, he got through.

"Deputy Sheriff Tennell." Clipped. Rushed. No nonsense.

"Shawn Rainey. I'm looking at the paper, had a couple of questions."

"Lucky me. Take one, we'll see about the other. Which also includes the first."

"Frank Love I can see for Joe Don," Shawn said. "But why not Catherine Mulvhill? She pulls his strings."

"Aside from her personal standing in five counties and two states? The fact that she had no personal grievance with McCandless?"

"Joe Don told me you as much as accused him of burning her bank. Are you telling me you didn't inform her of it?"

Office sounds, then, "You just had to push, didn't you? So long, hotshot."

"Wait a minute, Arn, no excuse." Hoping he hadn't blown it. "I was out of line."

Longer pause. "Then yeah, that's what I'm telling you. No proof, no heat, whatever you think of me. The paper only had half the facts because we hadn't gotten Love's check back endorsed."

"I'm not following."

"Try listening. Catherine Mulvhill fired Love, she showed us the stub from his severance check. It only now worked its way back. He cashed it at a liquor store, Nevada side, South Shore. That coming through?"

"So far. When did she fire him?"

"The afternoon of the day before. Figuring McCandless bought it early morning and the fire at his place took a while to set up and get going, a day and a half apart. Why?"

"Just trying to get it straight," Shawn said, thinking that would mean Love was fired right after Love had set into *him*. Which made no sense whatever, considering his and Catherine

Mulvhill's history.

"Hey...you there?"

"Here, Arn. You really think Love did it?"

"What's not to like? Bad blood in buckets. McCandless torches his employer's bank – and don't tell me otherwise, you know it as well as I do. He makes Love look bad, since among other things Love is security for her whole operation. Plus, the guy's avoiding us, even though it's all over the news we want him."

Shawn fed it in, came up with, "You find the gun yet?"

"Killers tend to bring their own, which doesn't mean we're not poking around. Anything else?"

"No. Thanks."

"Then it's my turn," Arn said. "What you said the other day about knowing what you know, about your brother and me? Maybe I deny it, maybe I don't. Point is, I've been a damn good cop since that time. Ask the lowlifes, those still around. So weigh the two and see what counts, or go fuck yourself."

Washboard sky, faux-finish clouds strung together in ridges.

Shawn decided on the mountain route to Truckee, a short hitch first to see Katie. He found her on the sun side of the A-frame, working compost into her flowerbed, pink and white petunias set into worn brick. She'd pulled her hair back in a ponytail, halter and shorts revealing tan skin and flat stomach.

Ben Affleck was stalking the clods she was troweling up.

"Nice day for it," he said coming up behind her.

"Tell my back that," she said. "You doing a little better?"

"Sure."

"You want a tea or something?" Fixing on him. "I have time."

"Thanks. An errand over the hill."

"Shawn, you can only do so much. Can't you let the sheriff handle it now? Stay here with us?"

"Just following up." Lowering himself to one of the patio chairs. "Mainly I came by to see how your meeting went with Bob Lamont. It kind of got lost in the shuffle."

She sat back on her haunches, a move he felt in his own knee.

"That's the weird part," she said. "Lamont wasn't around that night and hasn't been since. No Catherine calls to personnel, either, unless they're sitting on it till he gets back. Are you sure she had that in mind?"

"I'm sure. So far, so good might be another way to look at it."

She held his eyes, let out a breath. "How much more, Shawn? I mean, truly."

"Katie, I've tried to explain."

"How about to yourself?"

He focused on the flowers, the smell of turned earth, Ben Affleck.

"Tell me you're not sick of it," she said. "Let alone what it's doing to us."

"Would it matter if I was?" Wind rose, swirled aspen leaves in the yard. Reaching out to touch her cheek, curl a runaway wisp around her ear, he said, "We've made it this far. Just a little farther?"

She turned from it. "It never goes away, does it, Shawn?"

"What's that?"

"The goddamn miserable past. It just finds a shadow and waits for you to walk by with your guard down. Then it drives an ice pick between your shoulder blades."

This time the kid had on a black polo shirt; looking up from a transaction, a florid woman carrying her own tote bag, he made a barely perceptible head-tilt toward the office. Shawn went to it, knocked lightly, poked his head in.

Lily Chen Yue glanced up from the computer screen, its light bathing her face. Loose burgundy top with mandarin collar and long sleeves, her expression revealing nothing, the thought crossing Shawn's mind he would not like to face her over cards.

"May I come in?"

She said, "I was under the impression we had finished with each other, Mr. Rainey. A prospect I was rather looking forward to."

"Something you said the other day that's been on my mind. It won't take long." He entered, shut the door.

"And I am not in the habit of dropping things on a whim, something I should have made clear the last time. Would you tell David when he gets a moment that I need him?"

"Why Los Angeles?" he asked. "Of all the places you could have gone then? Closer places...San Francisco."

She gathered the papers she was working on and shut them in a drawer. "Predictably, your obsession is becoming my annoyance. You must think I have nothing better to do than to rake it all up again for your benefit."

"Others now are part of it," he said. "A friend is dead."

"So I hw."

"Then you know he was shot before his house was burned down around him."

"Mr. Rainey, I'm sorry for your loss, as I am for his widow and children. But it has to do with me how?"

"Los Angeles," he repeated. "It's important."

"That remains to be seen, but you may as well sit." Waiting until he did, opposite her. "You want to know *why* I went there? Or why I went *there*?"

"That's the general idea."

She straightened in her chair, her bearing reminding him of photos he'd seen of the last empress of China. "Work was there, life was there," she said at length. "Los Angeles before the Second World War pulsed with it."

"As in the absence of death?"

"Do you plan to explain that, or would you have me guess?"

"You said your grandmother died before Mr. Chen did. What about your mother?"

"I fail to see the—"

"Will you please answer?"

Not a blink. "Mr. Rainey, I sympathize with your recent troubles. But if you persist, I will have to call David."

"If you do," Shawn said, "things will break and he'll get hurt."

"Perhaps not. David trains in the martial arts."

"And my friend is dead. Which of us would you put money on?"

She didn't answer, so he said, "What happened to your mother and grandmother that made you leave and go so far away?"

"Very well. It was a foolish move on my part. For all the good it did, I could as well have stayed with my family. Whom I'd never been away from before and missed terribly."

"Meaning they died."

"People die. People you love die. And you die with them."

Shawn stood, walked to the barred window. "They went together, or the same way or something, didn't they?"

"Yes, if it serves your purpose to know – on the way back from Stonehouse in my mother's car. They went off and rolled to the lake. Mr. Holmes was able to keep it out of the paper because the county hadn't maintained the road and feared a lawsuit."

Which accounted for his not finding it in the files...

"An accident," he said.

"That is what we were told." Eyes fixed straight ahead, as though hearing of it again.

"An accident that so frightened you, you fled to Los Angeles without telling anyone."

"You don't know that because you don't know me. And you certainly don't know what it was like then."

"At least I'm trying to learn."

"So you are. All right – first, lose everything. Live in fear that what little you have left may be taken from you. Then come talk to me."

He turned from the bars and the sunlight. "I *am* talking to you. Do you get that?"

"Words, Mr. Rainey, but I won't argue the point."

Change speeds, outside corner:

"Here's what I think. You left here to put distance between yourself and Mr. Holmes, what you thought him capable of – your cousin, your grandmother, your mother – even though you had no proof. You came back after he was dead and Catherine had returned home, and still you played it safe. Running this place from behind its walls, living under your husband's name, letting your relatives cover for you."

Pause. "That is only partly true."

"But you're still afraid, aren't you? The girl you once knew still makes you afraid because of what she became."

Lily Yue leaned forward, folded her hands on the desk. "How can you understand? With every headline that runs about China, every human-rights abuse or threatening gesture or negative sentiment, we are strangers in a strange land. What we were once to this country, we can be again."

"And your great-niece goes to university, maybe even David

out there, and Chinese-Americans own companies and serve presidents," he said. "You want to explain that to *them*?"

"What do you want from me?"

"Goddamnit, I want the truth." It hung there, a bird landed on the wrong wire and fried. He said, "I apologize for my outburst. It came out wrong. I *need* the truth."

"Then, Mr. Rainey, I wish you well. But if every fact were mine, I still would hesitate."

"Mrs. Yue, I'm not making myself clear," he said, spent, the words dead leaves. "It's more than that. It *is* all I have left."

She looked across the desk, across the motes of dust floating in the sunlight, across the years. She said, "Be careful what you ask for, Mr. Rainey. Sometimes the truth is the last thing anyone should have left."

38

SHAWN PARKED UP THE RIDGE. Stonehouse looked as ever – hulking and formidable, weighted by secrets. He pictured the portraits inside the main room, Seneca and Lila and Cyrus, imagined their imperceptible smiles at one another in the hours when no one was about, the only sound the clock's tick.

The squawking jay got him going, down the slope at an angle for a corner of the grounds. Alert for anyone on duty, he crossed the road, levered himself to the top of the rock wall, paused again before dropping down. Best to put nothing past Catherine Mulvhill, including her concocting the Frank Love firing. But if Love was still around, Shawn saw no trace of him; which didn't mean the security guard and his nightstick weren't standing by. Seeing no one, he wove his way through the mountain alders and dogwood until he reached the rear flagstone porch with its low-arched retainer.

No one.

He scanned: boathouse, lakeside patio, Millicent deep in a book, beside her on the wrought-iron table a bath towel and cell phone. Perhaps seventy yards out, a swimmer in a bathing cap, Catherine Mulvhill in the chill waters that fed her state of mind. He eased to one of the stone arches, to the glass doors, made out the faces on the far wall, no one else. Double check: Millicent hadn't turned and Catherine still was swimming, so he took the steps and let himself in.

The trio regarded him with disdain, eyes following as he headed toward the stairs, the house's silence as heavy as its stone. For a moment, outside the room with the *Constance* model, he felt as though he couldn't breathe – Ruttan as if he were drowning – Shawn telling himself he wasn't down there, he was up here, keep saying it. Deep breaths and he opened the door and went inside.

It was black until he felt the rheostats, brought up the track spots and the indirects, saw it come alive again: the six-foot scale model in all its detail, the ship photographs and memorabilia. And, on the far wall, the Chinese family votive altar, the space above it no longer empty, Shawn guessing it had been only moments after he'd left. But the returned photo, though framed as were the others, had a matte-surround several times those of the larger images.

As Shawn approached, he saw why.

The photo of Tommy Chen was the same as the Hawkeye-size print Lily Yue had shown him: Tommy leaning against the tree, hat at rake, Lily smiling up as if it were the biggest moment of her life. Protected by glass, it nonetheless had the patina of age…as if it had lain in the back of a drawer or between the pages of a book on an upper shelf. Waiting for its due, its owner to return and reclaim it.

He started going through the altar's drawers and niches: single twenty-five-dollar gaming chip in one, ladies' leather-band wrist-watch hooked through the loop of a man's watch in another, both times set at four o'clock, Shawn pegging it from his notes as the time *Constance* went down. Added to the glazed jars, the square-holed Chinese coins, the artifacts he'd seen before, were a number he had not: dimes and quarters circa 1940; ivory-inset pocketknife and matching fountain pen, both with initials *TJC;* folding nail file and clipper on a chain. A derringer.

It was as if Tommy Chen were about to walk in, fresh from the shower and ready for a night at the tables, scoop all into his pockets, be on his way with a wink and a finger pop. And there was something else: the incense he'd detected in Lily's office.

As if someone were trying to keep it from dissipating.

Shawn swung open the final drawer, spotted something in a corner, a tiny delicate coil. He drew it out, examined it: a silver anklet three-fingers large, no more. The tiny name strip just enough for the initials engraved there: *CLC.*

Son of a bitch...

"How dare you enter this house. How dare you be in this room."

He'd not heard the door behind him open; now it slammed shut. Denim shift, Keds, silver breastpin, hair around the edges still damp: Catherine Mulvhill straight up, eyes flashing. One fist clenched, the other holding a chrome-plated revolver.

He held out the penknife and anklet. He said, "I know who these belong to."

No reaction he could perceive. Then, "Breaking and entering will be of far greater interest to the sheriff. Whom I have called and you have perhaps five minutes to avoid if you leave now."

"No you haven't, you're too interested in what I know. See, I'm even beginning to think like you."

"What you know about what, Mr. Rainey? A few mementos I hold dear?"

Starting gate: Ski to Die. "They're down there, aren't they? In that goddamned ship. That's the why, isn't it?"

She said nothing as he strode to the model.

"Which leads us to the where," he said. "My guess would be the ballast tanks." Tapping the glass. "Anyplace else, they might bob up and point fingers at someone. Now you *tell* me I'm wrong."

"Get out of my house."

"The way it is, I don't even need everything straight. I just need the media clamoring for a dive to clear up my allegations, dovetailed into the facts. That old devil public opinion again, remarkable how things melt under it. Political support, for instance. And I doubt you want me leaving just yet because if I do, it is surely over."

She raised the gun. "On second thought, it is a very deep lake. Better than you have gone down in it."

Keep going. "That what you used on Frank Love when he turned into a liability?"

"Mr. Rainey, your theories are beginning to bore me. I fired Frank Love."

"That's one way to do it."

"Are you planning to listen or just spout nonsense?"

"Lord, if only I were that good."

"Frank Love was terminated for disobeying me," she said. "For what he did at the museum. Ask him."

"How convenient for you that he's not around."

She slipped the gun into a pocket "No wonder you come to these conclusions. Frank was arrested in a low-end Sacramento hotel, drunk and nearly comatose – the news had it earlier. The woman who drove him there was only slightly better. She said he'd been like that for five days."

"Doubly convenient."

"Mr. Rainey, why are you here? Do you think love or what comes of it makes one less than human? Once, perhaps, it did, which only indicates you're sure of nothing. Otherwise you'd be spewing it out to ruin me. So why?"

Shawn felt it slipping, her regaining the momentum despite his fury over Joe Don and the rest. And, as quickly, *the hell*: momentum, winning edge, winning period – all of it.

"I'm not here to ruin you," he said. "I'm here to make a deal."

Her surprise was short-lived. "A deal for what?"

"Not in here. It's all I can do to keep from drowning."

They sat at the iron table: water lapping, bird sounds, thunderheads roiling up behind from Carson Valley, the breeze cool.

"We'll have an early fall," Catherine Mulvhill said. "The grass had frost this morning. I had to wear my coat to feed the geese."

The chair's scrolling hit his back wrong, wrought-iron ivy leaves that poked him. He waited.

"Back to business: nothing to anyone ever. The truth as you see it and think I know it in exchange for my help in getting back your children. That's the deal."

"I'll even throw in Frank Love," Shawn said, leaning forward.

"Which means what?"

"Alibi him, say he was working me over when Joe Don was being murdered. The time frame works, and I have the bruises."

She regarded him. "Why would you do that?"

"Simple. He didn't kill Joe Don."

"If he didn't, who did?"

"Not you and not him." Shifting again in the chair.

A moment passed. "What about you and *Constance*? This endless digging for dirt?"

"It stops here. The project for me, Katie and whatever else for you. Suing Joe Don's estate over the bank fire, if you had that in mind."

"In other words, every card in my hand."

"And mine – remember?"

"Which, aside from your theatrics, I've yet to see."

Through the chutes, one-tenth up. "Fair enough. Before your father puts you in private school, you and Tommy Chen get involved. If anything, private school gives you *more* freedom to see him. Late spring, 1940, you turn up pregnant in a physical and the old man finds out, yanks you back home, virtual house arrest. Still, Tommy finds a way to get the anklet to you, get word he wants to marry you, get you out of there, with the chip as a token of what he's managed to save. Playing so far?"

"I'm still in my chair."

Amazing, he thought, *not a flinch.*

"Now it gets compressed. Your father finds out and hits the roof. No Chinaman, especially one related to Ling Chen, is getting his daughter that way. Worse than married, away from him. He sees a way to cut his losses – Landon Mulvhill, who maybe had eyes for you from his perch on daddy's shoulder. What doesn't hurt is the larcenous streak he's already demonstrated, cooking the books and helping drive down old man Chen. Pregnant as you are, daddy promises him *you* and he jumps at it. In exchange, of course, for certain favors."

He paused to let it sink in.

She was staring out at the lake, so he went on.

"Looking no farther than *Peregrine* and the other ship, they come up with a plan. Buy back *Constance,* sink her under the guise of compassion for the floating derelict she's become. Meantime, stage Tommy's disappearance as an accident."

No reaction, the stare unbroken.

"Don't hesitate if I'm wrong."

"It's all wrong," she said. "All of it."

Which meant right. Into the moguls, ahead by two. "You have your baby – early, I'm guessing, while daddy's off somewhere. You call Nana Chen to midwife, which seals her fate and May's as well because she knows about it. Lily's, too, if they can find her."

"I think that is enough, Mr. Rainey."

Straightaway tuck, no tomorrow. "But part of Landon's deal is no half-Chinese babies, thank you, no off looks at the men's clubs. So he does what daddy signs off on, he–"

"I said that was enough." The gun again in her hand.

"He puts the baby aboard with Tommy."

"Damn you, I don't care who your father is, I can still fire this thing."

"The way you fired it when you found out what Landon had done?" *Gambling curiosity still outweighed trigger-pull.* "Or did Landon just stop being able to look in mirrors and do himself before the old man turned on him the way he turned on everyone."

"They're your theories. What do you think?"

Final pump and finish. "I think you did no more than I'd have done. I think you sent him to hell. I think you knew your father was dying or Landon would have had company."

"If that's the case, aren't you taking quite a chance?"

"You tell me."

She shuddered a breath, regarded the gun, set it down. "My

father was a monster. He drowned my mother so he could tomcat around on her money, which at that point was the only thing he hadn't squandered. He totally corrupted Landon, you could see it happening. Believe it or not, at one time I even liked Landon. My father took care of that." Eyes back on the lake, a spot beyond the point. "At least I was able to watch him die slowly."

A runabout with a man and woman in old-time yachting caps roared around the point and past. They waved, their thirties-style pennant waved, but Catherine Mulvhill did not.

"We'd named her Constance Lily Chen, for once in this house a product of love. She and Tommy were the reasons I could get up in the morning, if you've ever known that."

Shawn ran past it. "So you went into seclusion."

"Call it what it was, a three-year nervous breakdown. In the bedroom that had been mine with the windows walled so I couldn't spoil his parties."

"The room we just left."

"The room where he told me about Tommy. To teach me a lesson, is the way he put it. For two days they beat him before putting him in the ballast. But he was alive, my father said. He'd wanted it that way."

Shawn was about to tell her about Burl Ruttan, but backed off, asking instead, "Who cared for you during that time?"

"Our doctor, an alcoholic in my father's pocket, and the people he hired. Dead, I'm sure, even if you could find them."

"It's not them I'm looking for, Mrs. Mulvhill."

"And if I say no more?"

"Then we both miss our chance at redemption."

She said nothing but made no move to leave, so he went on.

"When your father died, you got well enough to go back to

Wisconsin – forty-three to forty-seven – which didn't square with the newspaper accounts. I assume that was to cover the breakdown?"

She drew a cigarillo from her bag, lit it. "I made myself a promise. Keep on as I was, or get hard like him and spend my life trying to make up for the things he did. That was my choice. The first step was to learn, rebuild his base in my image, make it everything he'd failed at. Not a day goes by I don't look up at his portrait and remind him."

"Yet you kept Landon's name."

"Mulvhill was convenient, or else it would have been unthinkable. I was able to secure credit. After a while, it served the same purpose as the conversations with my father, a reminder of why I was doing it, whatever it was."

Shawn pulled out the cracked frame with Nate and Elizabeth, handed it to her. "You're not the only one big on reminders."

She took a while with them. Then, "The boy looks like pictures of you your father showed me, the girl's a love. And did you really think I didn't know the reasons you were back?"

"I won't ask how. And I know why."

"Do you? That if I go down, the good goes with it? That all along I've provided for the Chens?"

"Everything but your acknowledgement of what your father did to them."

Catherine Mulvhill blew smoke upward. "And twenty-four hours later the lawyers would have it all. That's justice?"

"Who gets it when you die?"

"Half to the Chens, half to the charities I support."

"A nice thought, but Lily may not live that long. Although she looks as if she'll outlive us both."

She sat bolt upright. "Lily died in Southern California. She was struck by a car. How dare you?"

"Check your resources, then drop in at the old Chen store. A door at the back marked PRIVATE."

"Mr. Rainey, if this is a game, you will not play another. That is a promise." She flicked ash off the cigarillo.

"Ask her and see what she says about games. She's a widow, her married name is Yue." Spelling it for her. "There's no mystery about it, either. She was afraid."

"Afraid of whom? Of me?"

"Not at first. Of your father at first."

The fire smoked out. "My Lord. Does it never end?"

Shawn pulled out a sheet of paper, watched as she unfolded it. "And this is…?"

"Information you need for Nate and Elizabeth, names and how to contact them, details, timelines. Everything I could think of, including my own actions. Things I'm responsible for."

She read it and looked up. "People lie when it suits them, even me. How do I know I can trust you to keep your word if I keep mine?"

"Apples and where they fall," he said. "Whatever I've done, I come from good stock."

"As far as that goes."

Wind shook the aspens and the birch grouping, stippled the lake, lapped small waves onto the rocks. Shawn thought about what it might take to seal the deal, the cards he had left.

The one card.

He played it: he and Cort.

39

FROM THE TIME THEY CAST OFF, *the day has a bone in its teeth. According to his brother, that is the magic — taking it all.*

"Damn," *he says as Shawn settles at the mainsail and jib sheets, Cort already at the helm.* "Why ski if not for the rush? Why do anything?"

Shawn thinks, answers, "Because you can?"

The smile. "Good thing you have me. You may have started because you can, but you ski like you do to win. Watch your boom there." *And, after the tack,* "No stories out here, bro. Just us." *Sun lighting up his grin, his blue eyes, the heavy bracelet he has fashioned from a Rocket 88 piston and buffed up. Foil for the stainless chronometer on his other wrist.*

"You feel that?" *Shawn looking off to port after another tack.* "Wind's picking up."

"Oh yeah." *Veering for the chop.* "Blackbird flies, son. Watch her."

Over the burst of a wave that gasp-patterns him with ice water, Shawn says, "I think I'd rather get there."

Cort: "You live once and guess when? Speaking of which, how you doing? Seems like we never see each other anymore."

The comment is loaded, he knows, a casually placed trip mine. Shawn hesitates, decides absolution is worth the risk, and plunges.

"Cort, listen. About Robin…"

"Hey, win some, lose some. Ancient history. Besides, you deserve her more than I do. Man your jib."

Shawn does. With their speed and the effort it takes to stay abreast of booms, lines, and sails in such a blow, South Shore and the reason for the trip comes up in no time, Cort telling Shawn to wait at the Camp Richardson dock while he picks up what he came for.

Shawn is admiring the girls trying to keep their beach towels from fluttering up, gold sand out of their Coppertone, when Cort trots back carrying a blue nylon duffle. Feeling to Shawn about twenty pounds as Cort hands it down and drops aboard.

"Go," Cort says. "Move it."

Catching the sharpness, Shawn glances inside the bag, sees a package bound in braided nylon line. He looks at his brother.

"I said move it!"

"Why the rush?" Shawn says, something different about Cort's eyes as well. "They just ran up the small-craft advisory."

"Do it. One captain aboard, and you're looking at him."

"Aye-aye. Bro."

A mile outside Richardson, they run into it, or vice versa: chop, gusts, water over the rail when they heel, across the bow when they trough. The sky darkening along its eastern edge, Shawn spotting flashes inside the front.

"You see that lightning?" he shouts.

"So?" Cort shouting back. "We can always put in at Emerald Bay. Don't be such a wart."

Suddenly the picture clears, a lens regaining focus: "Cort, you take a hit back there or something?"

Off-kilter grin. "Why, you want one?"

"Just us, remember? No bullshit."

"Sorry I can't oblige you right now." Nodding at the starboard locker where he'd stowed the bag and the package. "Don't want water getting in there and turning it to cinderblock, right?"

"You're asking me?" Shawn says. "What is it?"

"Primo stuff, kid. Coke enough to snow the whole lake. And in the process, make your enterprising bro-ski rich."

Shawn feels black crows rising inside him, a weird tilting. "Are you out of your mind?"

No holdback, no bullshit.

What brothers are to each other, or should be.

"For the first time, the exact opposite," Cort comes back. "You have any idea what it's like living in a shadow smaller than yours? Younger than yours?"

Stunned, Shawn can only say, "I don't know what you're talking about, but if it's me—"

"Shut the fuck up and listen. You ever look at Pop, dragging his ass to work and back at night? That the way you want to end up?" Pause while a wave slams them. "Hell, you know how long I've been dealing grass out of that station?"

Somehow Shawn finds the words: "You imagine Pop hearing that now?"

"Going to tell him, are you? See how it flies when I deny it?" The grin spreading like dawn. "Like they'd believe it, the dues I've paid."

Shivering as much from this as from cold, Shawn says, "Turn us around. We're going back and shove it up this guy's ass, whoever he is."

Cort whoops: too high, too wound.

"Why sure, Billy Kidd. Behind you all the way. Into the valley of death."

"That's enough, Cort. Where's the two-way?"

"Reach out and touch someone, huh? While you're at it explain what you're doing aboard a runner with a street block worth six mil."

"The two-way...?"

"There, under the. towel. Think I'd watch my head though."

Too late Shawn feels it coming: the unbalancing as Cort wrenches the helm, the boom crack against his skull. He doesn't know how long he's been out, but when he comes around, they've passed the entrance to Emerald Bay. He sees the clouds that by now have reached the lake's western edge, no other boats, hears the wind's howl.

"Welcome back," Cort shouts. "Sorry about the radio, but it didn't float. And don't look at me like that. All those heroes of yours on the ski circuit do it, why you think there's a market in clean urine? There's a sideline for you. Find a niche and fill it."

"Cort, look at the sky. There's a pier at Rubicon. Put in there."

"And miss what I live for? Not on you're life. Foul weather gear, all hands."

Cort's pupils are as dark as the clouds. He is standing to flip open the port locker that holds the slickers, the helm balanced in one hand, when Shawn makes a lunge for the starboard. In a flash that lid is up, the package free of the duffle and in his hand.

"Now, Cort, or over it goes," he says. "Dead serious. Head in."

Cort shakes his head, almost sadly. "Bound to disappoint me, aren't you? You know how much for both of us is tied up in that thing?"

"You'll see it once that crap wears off."

Shrug. "Well, hell, can't beat an inside straight. You win. Watch your head again, though." And in that instant he makes his own lunge for the package, the lashing catching in his bracelet as Shawn falls back against the hatch.

"Sorry, kid. The best laid plans."

Looking up, Shawn sees what is about to happen. "Boom!" he yells,
Cort still grinning as it sweeps him over the side. At their speed, the
splash is gone, fading white on slate.

"Cooorrrt...!"

He tries for the helm and his brother's hand, which has somehow
managed to grip the rail, locking onto Cort's wrist as the boom slews
above his ducked head. "Reach up your other hand."

Cort's face rises from the wake. "Can't," he gasps. "Too fast."

Through the froth, Shawn makes out the package weighting
Cort's bracelet like a drogue. "Hang on," he says. "I'll try to stall us
into the wind."

But when Shawn grabs for the helm, it has wedged out of reach;
they are heeling with Cort's bulk, gaining speed and taking on water.
Trying to stay under the boom and unable to snag the helm, inches
from swamping, Shawn can gain no leverage.

Lean over too far past ballast and the whole boat goes.

"Can you raise a leg over?" Lash of rain making him blink.

"Don't think so..."

He sees Cort try, but no go, the weight and their speed.

Plus a new enemy: cold.

He sees Cort form the words: Freezing. Hurry.

"I'm going to lash you to the rail. Just hang on."

But he knows it is useless. Cort's fingers are white, their grip past
his palm and slipping toward the pads, the first joints. By the time
Shawn finds a line, there will be nothing at the rail. All he can do is
grasp Cort's wrist with both hands, slick as they are, his own fingers
almost beyond feeling.

Cort reads it.

"Let me go, Shawn. Maybe I can–" The rest is drowned out. Then
Cort's face, oddly peaceful, the eyes now clear, lips mouthing: "One

captain…let me go…order."

"Cort, you hang on or I'm going to kick your butt, I don't care how big you are. And I never meant to take Robin, and I love you, you're my brother. You hear me, goddamnit?"

Shawn feels the boom just miss him, feels the impact of another thudding wave, then the rail is leaving the water as Cort twists in his hands and is gone.

Silence.

Sounds gradually coming back. Catherine Mulvhill saying, "And you said nothing to anyone? Your father and mother?"

Shawn shook his head. "It would have killed them. They wouldn't have known that son. For that matter, neither did I. But someone did."

"I'm not following you."

"The silent partner protecting him, and I don't mean the one at Richardson. I mean someone with the cover and clout to pull it off, the money to finance the initial buys. Rogue shakedowns or drugs missing from evidence rooms would be my guess. Both, maybe."

Pause. "You're saying it was a policeman?"

"One I've talked to enough to know. Clean now."

"Meaning you don't want it brought to light."

"As you said before, enough."

"So I did," she said. "What did your mother believe?"

"Cort was her firstborn. She died thinking I was envious of him, or could have prevented it, or worse. Cain and Abel worse. That's how well I shielded her from it."

"Liam?"

Shawn watched sailboats on a parallel reach, one that reminded him of *Blackbird* pulling ahead. "He doesn't say much."

"Sometimes it makes a difference coming from someone else. That is, if you want me to tell him."

"I'll think it over. He cared for you once, you know that – when it had died for him at home."

"He also had children at home."

"Such as we were," he said.

She focused on the lake. "Don't wait too long."

A squirrel ran a jay off a pinecone, the jay squawking in protest. Wind stirred the tops of the cedars.

"Then I guess we have a deal," she said.

He nodded, watched the light dapple the beach, the flag-stones, the glass table with the gun on it. "A deal."

"Mr. Rainey, I'm finding it chill out here. You'll contact your friend Dahl about returning the donations, what's left of them?"

"He's anything but my friend."

"Then you'll be hearing from me," she said, extending a brief cold hand. "Feel free to leave by the front door."

"Thanks. I'll take the path."

"Now, what told me you'd say that?"

For a while after she'd left, he sat looking at the spot where *Constance* had gone down, was down there still, trying to imagine what it had been like that night, the ballast tank as it filled. The blackness Catherine Mulvhill had endured as well, hers for sixty years.

He rose stiffly and left.

40

SHAWN TURNED UP THE HILL, went slowly past Joe Don's place. There were no cars in front, just the foundation, chimney sticking up amid the char, singed trees and trampled plants, burn debris and crime-scene tape, water leaking down along the fringe. He flipped a U and retraced a route made familiar in his teens.

The modest ranch-style house looked visibly fatigued, as did Robin's mother when she answered his knock. "Hello, Shawn," she said. "It's good to see you again. We've been following you on television."

"Sorry to just show up like this, Mrs. Vasquez. I'm looking for Robin. Is she in?"

"Robin's out back. I'll get her." Pause. "Before I do, would you mind if I asked you a question?"

"Of course not," he said. "And it's good seeing you, too."

She inhaled deeply, let it out as if it were smoke. "What happened to it all? You and Robin, now Joe Don? What happened?"

"I'd be the last one to ask, Mrs. Vasquez. I suppose what happens to everything."

"It makes you wonder, doesn't it?"

"Yes, ma'am, it does."

"I'm here, Mom," Robin said from behind her: jeans, white Adidas, Lakers tee with the sleeves rolled up. "Would you get Conner a Diet Coke for me? He's driving me nuts." When her mother had left after a look at Shawn, "Didn't think I'd be seeing you for a while."

"No? Take a walk with me."

As though not hearing him, she said, "Conner's being a pain, at least the little one's at day camp. They wouldn't take Conner this year, too roughhouse or something. Personally, I think it's a–"

"You don't want this on your doorstep, Robin."

She looked at him for clues. "All right. Mom...?" Turning to shout inside. "Going for a walk, back in a few."

They walked to an undeveloped area between houses, took the path through a wooded expanse of pine and cedar, chokecherry, mountain alder. Aside from a dog barking, it was as if no other houses existed. She glanced at him, stopped at a cut-off stump by a dry streambed.

"Remember what we used to do in here, Shawn?"

"Kids, Robin," he answered.

"Whatever you may be now, I'm not that much different. In case you were wondering."

"I'm not. I talked to Arn," he said. "They found the gun."

"They *what?* How could they have—" Realizing then what it meant.

"You *bastard*," she said.

"Where is it really, Robin? In the woods? In your mom's yard? The lake?"

She said nothing, wrapped her arms around her as if cold.

He said, "You know, it would have worked except for Joe Don's playing a game one night when I was over. Scared the shit out of me with it."

Silence. Then, "What game?"

"A drunken staged suicide he regretted the next day. Pure Joe-D. Point is, I'd have sworn to it if they'd found the gun. Case closed. But that wouldn't have worked because insurance companies don't pay off suicides. Murder though, they have to — unless it's the beneficiary. They don't care a lot for that."

"I have no idea what you're talking about."

"Fair enough. That's all I came about." Turning to go.

"Wait. What are you going to do?"

The way the light struck her, he saw her at fifteen again, her eyes sweet dark *molé*. "What do you think I'm going to do?"

"I think we're more alike than not, Shawn. I think you know that. I think we could still make it and you know that, too. With the money–"

"For which you walked up to him and blew his head off." Coming closer, enough to want her all over again, turn back time and fuck everything else. "Payback time."

"Easy enough said. Hell, look at me." Raising her shirt to show him bruises at which he flinched, some turning colors, others that hadn't. Lowering it, then. "And this is nothing."

"You could have left him. You said as much."

"And gone where and had what? That was talk, Shawn. What the IRS doesn't take next year, the bank will."

"So you shot him and got what you wanted."

Her right hand went to her wedding set; oblivious to it, she said, "You'll still have to prove it."

"That's the second time somebody's said that to me today. You think it might be a trend?"

"Fuck you, Shawn. What is next?"

He took a moment framing it, trying to keep his eyes off her.

"Depends on how clever you are. See, it won't come from me, I'm already Frank Love's alibi. So it's up to you. That's what I meant by pure Joe Don. He'd just laugh it off, say it was the breaks, that maybe it was best for his kids to get the insurance money. Maybe even the least he could do to square some things."

"You have no idea who you're dealing with. But then you never have."

"Goodbye, Robin. Do right by them or all bets are off. That you *can* bank on."

"And you can go to hell. You think some jury would convict me? Up here? In your dreams." As if she said it enough she might actually believe it.

Shawn left her there and walked out into the sunlight, no look back.

It was nine when Shawn finished giving his statement to one of Catherine Mulvhill's attorneys representing Frank Love. Already she'd called his cell phone to say she'd talked with Theda Sandstrom on the adjusted timeline, run through it in person and with Frank through the attorney.

The attorney's name was Grace Vanderbyl: signatures in triplicate, Polaroids of his bruises, both sheriff's detectives handling the case on hand to hear it again and ask their own questions. And though it obviously derailed their hopes for quick closure, they took it in stride because he also told them of Joe Don's suicide game. He could see the light come back to their faces at that, though without the gun it would be a tossup, Robin's insurance claim put off, yet likely holding up.

But that was Robin's roll of the dice.

Back at the house, the Giants playing somebody-or-other, Shawn ran through it in his mind: Lily Yue, Catherine Mulvhill, Robin – gray areas three, not to mention the grayest, himself, the deal he'd cut with the Loch Monster. Which, of course, could lead nowhere, stall and dodge and lawyer-speak, the appearance of living up to her part. Still, with a little luck, Nate and Elizabeth were closer than they knew. Despite the hour, he had a sudden urge to call them and tried, got the machine.

"Quick call," Liam Rainey said when he'd returned and sat down.

"Probably in bed," Shawn told him. "I'll try morning."

"You okay?"

"Running around all day." Then, "Listen…Pop?"

Barry Bonds homered, scoring two ahead of him, the Giants going up a run. Shawn rewrapped his take-out and put it in the fridge.

"More like it," his father said. "You were saying something?"

"Time enough tomorrow, Pop. Sleep well."

"Long as they don't blow it." Then, "By the way, that girl of yours? She left a message on the machine saying tomorrow's fine if you got in late. And something about the past I won't use the phrase she did. Nothing your mother ever said about anything."

"I imagine not."

"Pay attention to her, Shawn. Words to the wise."

"Thanks, Pop. I love you."

He didn't wait for an answer; the look he got was reward enough.

Shawn slept until eight, Liam long since intermittent grinder whine coming from the garage. He showered, tried reaching Nate and Elizabeth, this time adding a message. He'd hung up and was composing a note that he was out of it, he'd found nothing and it was over, the money had to go back and Terry had to honor their agreement, when he logged on and saw Terry had messaged him.

Both barrels. Full-fucking-circle.

Shawn-boy,

No idea when you'll get this. You might even have phoned the house and found us gone. Well, there you go. Sorry to leave you hold-ing the bag, but you know how it works. Somebody has to take the fall. Not that I'm not grateful. I figure you padded the house a good ten mil before the bitch reared up. Not a bad payday, whatever it might have been.

Why now, you ask? Writing on the wall. That and the feds sniffing around. But it was that way from the start, you just couldn't see it. Live and learn, right? Exactly what I said when my client pulled out and I was going to have to give back what was left. In other words, when I first thought of you. So cheer up. Maybe the peasants won't drown you in the lake when they catch you.

Love, Terry (And Loren)

P.S. Brazil's light on extradition, so don't waste your time. Uncle Sam won't. And the guy following you who tossed your room? Just Bob Lamont checking on the investment. He put that tape in your car to get your Irish up. No need looking for him either. You know Tahoe...

Terry

Shawn was half in shock, the other half wondering what to do, that this thing had cost Joe Don his fucking *life,* when the door opened and his father poked his head in.

"Shawn?"

He was conscious that the whine had ceased.

"Kind of busy right now, Pop."

"That deputy, used to call himself a friend of Cort's?"

"Arn Tennell," Shawn said. "What about him?"

"He's in the drive, three cars with him. Says he has a warrant. For you to back out the door, hands on your head, or they're coming in."

41

S HAWN GAVE HIS STATEMENT AND SIGNED IT, the key turned
on him. The nature of the charges – grand theft, fraud, conspiracy to commit – had bought him a cell by himself,
though the noise level was intense: shouts, curses, lewd jokes,
commands, rattles, metal-on-metal clang, hard soles heavy on
concrete. There was a bunk and a toilet, a stainless steel mirror
he avoided, a pillow and a blanket.

On the plus side, he had Elizabeth and Nate in their frame,
Arn interceding to let him keep it. Now he lay on his back looking at the ceiling, scanning for tip-offs to the setup – aside from
those inherent in Terry's general nature – and realized he'd
known it all along, that it was a brass ring he'd had no choice but
try to grab.

All for nothing.

A deputy appeared, spoke through the bars.

"Rainey? Lawyer named Vanderbyl, says she's your attorney.
You wish to see her?"

"Why not?" he said.

She was in one of the attorney rooms. Designer jeans, white top under a navy blazer with a crest on the pocket, hair chopped off at the neck, half-glasses on a cord. She cleared her throat.

"Grace Vanderbyl, if you didn't remember. Catherine Mulvhill has retained my services on your behalf. Is that agreeable to you?"

"Beats how things were going," he said. "Please thank her for me."

"We're pressing for bail so we can get you out, but it may be tomorrow or later. This is largely the FBI's doing."

"I have nothing to put up for bail."

"Let's wait and see where it's set. We've already submitted the Dahl e-mail to the court and the feds. Together with Catherine Mulvhill's statement, we believe them sufficient for dismissal, but that is not a guarantee. Is this clear?"

A word stuck. "Her statement regarding what?"

"In particular, your verbal commitment to contact Mr. Dahl to have the money returned to donors," she said. "Evidence of good faith and intent, we feel. Correct so far?"

"You could say that."

"Yes or no, Mr. Rainey."

"Yes."

"I also have a message from your father." Straight-faced. "He said the Giants are on TV tonight and to get your butt home."

Shawn heard him say it, had to smile.

She donned her glasses, ruffled through the papers she'd brought. "Is there anything else you wish to tell me, other than that which is included in your statement? That you had no conscious part in the fraud or theft, the conspiracy to commit them?"

"No. Nothing."

"Any truth that Mr. Dahl was in fact your partner and left

you, as he said, holding the bag?"

"At no time was money my incentive, and I know better than to partner with Terry Dahl. Trust me on that."

She almost smiled. "I neither trust nor distrust, Mr. Rainey, I do my job. What about the reference Mr. Dahl makes to Mr. Lamont?"

"Lamont threatened me on a tape, his work by Terry's admission. It's in the Cherokee's glove box, if nobody's found it yet. Lamont also followed me and searched my cabin to see if I was freelancing. He was always in the loop, passing things on, which means he was in deep. And whatever cut Terry promised him, Lamont won't be seeing any of it. Bottom line is, I wouldn't put anything past Terry."

"I'll locate the tape. Would you care to venture an opinion on Mr. Lamont's whereabouts?"

"Eight to one on the lake," Shawn said. "A bullet in the ear and a length of chain, a pro hit. Terry was never one for loose ends. Let alone sharing the take."

"Maybe you should count yourself lucky."

"I'm lucky, all right. Just ask me."

She pushed a button beside her elbow. "Try to concentrate on anything that might help. Needless to say, that includes no statements or interviews." Standing until the guard came for him.

In passing, she said, "Mrs. Mulvhill said you were a ski champion with a tendency for self-sabotage. Care to respond?"

"That was on my good days."

"Goodbye, Mr. Rainey, I'll be in touch."

Shawn was heading back to his cell when the deputy said another woman had been waiting for him in the visiting area.

"Your girl?" he asked as they approached the Plexiglas dividers.

"I hope so," Shawn said.

"Lucky you." Taking up a position by the door.

She told him she'd barely made it, couldn't work, had to see him, wanted to know what she could do, anything. She wore a gray blouse over white pants, held one hand against his on the Plexiglas, the other on the receiver. Nothing, he told her, people were on it. Just look the way she did right now.

"Shawn, about yesterday, the grief I gave you about not giving up. I felt like hell after you left."

Fixing on her, the way she swept back her hair, the dusting of sun freckles on her arms and nose, he said, "It's all right. I did, too. How are things outside?"

"A lot of talk, none of it good. People feeling betrayed."

"I would, too. No lynch mobs, though?"

"Don't even joke." Then, "I got a call. You'll never guess who."

"I might surprise you."

"For sure she surprised me. We talked about Gatesville and Alice, then she asked me to give you a message." Katie unfolded a piece of notepaper from her bag, read from it: "Some things you write off. It's time to let go. Do you know what she meant?"

He nodded.

She looked at him, waited, gave it up. "Then I won't ask you any more unless you tell me. Just come home."

"I will. I love you." Wanting to hold her, tell her all it meant, able to do neither. "If I have to break it down, I will."

She attempted a smile he couldn't match.

Then the deputy was at his shoulder and the visit was over.

42

SHAWN SLEPT BADLY, all of it running like a worn loop in a cheap tape player. Much of it was centered on how little he could do from in there, what was being done outside, not being done, was building up. Deputies had him fed and in a van by seven AM, the air warming as they descended Interstate 80 through belts of fir and granite, red earth and black oaks, scrub pine and brown grass, to valley heat. By nine it was closing in on ninety and they were in the Sacramento FBI office meeting with two San Francisco agents who'd met them halfway.

Splitting time and mileage with the lake sheriffs, Shawn figured.

The questions started then – everything picked over or rehashed, both agents trying to poke holes in his statement: on and on through vending-machine ham-and-cheese sandwiches, weak coffee. By three, the agents' sleeves were rolled back down and he was back in the van. Digger pines were showing when the escort deputy turned in his seat behind the wire mesh as if he'd had a thought.

"Hey, Rainey," he said. "You really think you could beat this guy Dahl at his own game?"

"It occurred to me."

"One born every minute, huh?"

"Got that right."

They passed over concrete-joint bumps, asphalt stretches, the scenery reversing. At length the deputy said, "Reason I asked is, I got an aunt who actually gave money to it. Told me to tell you she couldn't afford it, but that she did it anyway."

"Please tell her I'm sorry."

"Ain't it always the way."

"She still might get it back," Shawn said at length. "What's her name?"

"Aunt Martha. Bancroft. But you want to hear the best part? She said she'd do it again, hope was worth that much to her." Dual laughs from up front. "Go figure."

Shawn tried coming back with something that went nowhere, swallowed up by the road.

Next morning he was told Grace Vanderbyl, was waiting for him. She was in a suit this time, on her way to court, judges obviously better arbiters of dress than jail personnel. Without preamble, she said, "Mr. Rainey, I have news. The FBI is willing to deal. They'll drop the charges if you'll agree to testify against Terry Dahl. Then again, we can always hold out for unconditional."

The thought spun, a top set loose. "Hold it a second," he said. "They've caught him?"

"I meant when and if they do."

The top ground down, bumping off things until it fell over and lay on its side.

"Where do I sign?"

"Good. I was going to recommend it. The papers are in my case."

He signed, she left, came back, and he was out by two that afternoon, reality bent enough after four days in jail for it to feel truly odd. He called Katie's number on Vanderbyl's phone, the lawyer waiting as he did, but as he'd assumed, Katie was at work. He left no message, would drop in on her later. Vanderbyl then led him outside to where a black limo with smoked windows waited under a tree. She said she'd rented it for a client, opened the door for him, went off to have a cigarette with the driver.

Shawn got in to a whiff of cigarillo.

"You survived," Catherine Mulvhill said as his eyes adjusted.

"Due largely to you. Did your attorney relay my thanks?"

"Grace did, and whatever you're going to say, I didn't even have to put up bail." She drew in smoke, exhaled. "My people have located Terry Dahl. It's what I came to tell you."

The top spun again, hummed this time, the way they did when you really worked the plunger. "I'm impressed," he said. "Where?"

"Rio, as you said, a hotel there. It wasn't that hard. He's not doing much to hide."

Shawn tempered his boil with a cold thought: not much longer, if what he had in mind worked, his knowledge of the man. "He doesn't think he has to."

"Which gives us the advantage, should we wish to exploit it."

"Thanks, I have one more card to play. I'd appreciate an address, though, in case it's a trey."

She handed him an unmarked white envelope.

"The hotel name and address is inside, and this meeting never happened," she said. "And I went to see Lily."

Shawn waited.

"We're too old for tears, so we talked – about how fast it's gone and the ones who took it with them. How we've changed and stayed the same."

"And…?"

"And it's a start. A good one, I think."

"All anyone can ask."

She'd leaned forward, was about to signal the driver, when she paused. "I've yet to ask you. Will you be staying on at the lake?"

"That depends on the climate."

"Then I'd say we're in a definite cooling trend. Tomorrow's paper should bear me out. Front page."

"I'll look for it."

"You might also recognize some things at the museum. Old photos and memorabilia, a certain ship model."

"Taking your own advice."

There was the hint of a smile. "Give my best to your father. Perhaps the three of you could come to the house. She's bright, your friend."

"I'll pass it on."

"Theda is expecting me."

He hesitated; then, "You think there might a whiff of redemption in this? Once we got going?"

"That's important to you, isn't it?"

"Don't tell me it's not to you, because I know better."

"At the risk of sounding like a broken record, don't wait if you're going to tell him what happened out there. Time, remember?"

"I remember."

He watched the Loch Monster drive away, thinking *Tell me how I'd forget.*

Grace Vanderbyl dropped him home.

He found his father gone, a note saying he'd left to fix a riding mower, back late afternoon in case he was released. Shawn cleaned up, used the quiet to open the laptop and compose a message to Terry Dahl's e-mail address, banking that Terry hadn't gotten around to changing it, that he had enough right now to worry about.

For once, the words came easy.

Terry,

Charges dropped, I'm out. Think I'll let you guess if I know where you are, but C.M.'s been more than helpful. I believe I'd sweat the two of us, if I were you. Not to mention the feds, who it turns out want you more than I do.

One thing that's not a guess: no rules, your choice. Right now the only thing keeping you from me is this one-time offer: Put Nate and Elizabeth on a flight for Reno and you're home free. Face it, they were just bargaining chips, no loss to you or Loren, your new marimba life.

Forty-eight hours from the time of this message. That's it, no mañana. After that you can't run fast or far enough, even if you were alone.

Shawn

He included his and Liam's phone numbers, collect anytime, night or day, crossed his fingers, and pressed SEND.

Catherine Mulvhill's open letter was in the paper next morning.

She was glad that *Constance* would remain a monument, convinced Shawn was unaware of the deception – that though his views were in opposition to hers, she knew him to be a person of character who had suffered also by it. He was rereading her words when Arn called: the office, right now, more questions regarding Frank Love.

Shawn went. And though they went at him, in the end they

waived Love's bail and released him. The investigation was posted as ongoing.

He was having lunch with his father when the phone rang.

"Figured you'd be old news by now," Liam Rainey grumped.
"Let the machine pick up?"

"I'll get it," Shawn told him. "Rainey…"

He listened, nodded, couldn't speak, handed over the receiver.

"Me?" his father said. "Who is it?"

"It's your grandson," he composed himself enough to say.
"He's in Reno at the airport. With Elizabeth. He wants to know if
you want to go fishing and watch the game later."

Liam took the call, smiled for once. Shawn listened to his
father talk lake trout and morning hotspots where they were
thick as fry, batting averages and earned run averages and
homers, Nate no more than an hour distant, *an hour.* Then he
went into his room and lost it.

They took Liam's pickup.

Driving North Lake, trying to keep to the speed limit, Shawn
saw the thunderheads rising again from the hundred-plus Carson
side. Not that it mattered. At this moment the clouds were beautiful, big and sunlit. They promised twilight rain, rushed fat
drops to make the fish bite, to make the air smell of damp woods
and sprinkled dust, to wash things clean.

And, of course, there was the lake, always the lake.

When the time was right, he'd tell his father about Cort. That
is, maybe he would. Or maybe the dead were better left in peace,
thoughts for later. For now, at least, the light was clear and warm
on the mountains, the shadows were going the other way for
once, and it all felt like home.

Epilogue

School opened the week after Labor Day, so they still had some days, camping at Fallen Leaf Lake amid turning aspens and pine trees whose fissured bark, to the kids' delight, smelled of vanilla. They hiked Desolation and the rim trail, squished roasted marshmallows and pieces of Hershey bar between graham crackers. Shawn promised to teach them to ski when the first real storm came through.

Catherine Mulvhill invited them to Stonehouse for Thanksgiving, Lily Yue as well. They ate everything in sight, walked the grounds while the kids tossed snowballs from the shade patches. On the way back, Liam revealed he'd been invited back. Nothing more was said.

Shawn and Katie married in April, despite a wind off the lake that shook the flowers and rearranged hair. He'd begun researching the history of the Chen family for a book he thought might work, when they got word that Loren had been apprehended at SFO by a customs agent who decided her disheveled appearance warranted a run though the computer.

Shawn took the kids to visit, but she declined to see them, illness her excuse. She also testified that with the bribed officials and the failed ventures, Terry Dahl had run through most of the money and had taken up with a Spanish divorcee he thought had some.

Talk of *Constance* had faded by the time Catherine Mulvhill again was news. She'd dismissed Millicent early, was thought to have set out for her usual lake spot. Next morning Millicent discovered her towel, bag, and lighter still on the table.

A search effort was mounted, but she was never found.

Shawn and Liam and Katie attended the Stonehouse memorial, no service her request. A number of people paid tribute, Shawn among them: the skier her support helped make him, the respect he felt for her. Arn nodded from an aisle row, acknowledgment of sorts. Then it was over and Liam and the kids were headed back, Katie waiting for him in the car.

He started her way, instead walked to the lake.

He offered a prayer that Catherine Mulvhill had at last found her family. Wind and waves took it. For valediction he picked up a handful of birch leaves from the stand of three she'd planted overlooking Echo Bay, leaves that when he let them fall shone like gold pieces on the water.

Echo Bay was printed by Capra Press in March 2004.

Fifty copies have been numbered and signed by Richard Barre
and authors George Pelecanos, Laura Lippman,
and Steve Hamilton.

Twenty-six copies in slipcases were also
lettered and signed by all.

About Capra Press

Capra Press was founded in 1969 by the late Noel Young. Among its authors have been Henry Miller, Ross Macdonald, Margaret Millar, Edward Abbey, Anais Nin, Raymond Carver, Ray Bradbury, and Lawrence Durrell. It is in this tradition that we present the new Capra Press: literary and mystery fiction, lifestyle and city books. Contact us. We welcome your comments.

815 De La Vina Street, Santa Barbara, CA 93101
805-892-2722; www.caprapress.com